BREAKING SILENCE

LINDA CASTILLO

THORNDIKE
WINDSOR
PARAGON

This Large Print edition is published by Thorndike Press, Waterville, Maine USA and by AudioGo Ltd, Bath, England.

Copyright © 2011 by Linda Castillo.

Thorndike Press, a part of Gale, Cengage Learning.

The moral right of the author has been asserted.

Thorndike Press® Large Print Mystery.

The text of this Large Print edition is unabridged.

Other aspects of the book may vary from the original edition.

Set in 16 pt. Plantin.

LIBRARY OF CONGRESS CATALOGING-IN-PUBLICATION DATA

Castillo, Linda.
     Breaking silence / by Linda Castillo.
        p. cm. — (Thorndike Press large print mystery)
     ISBN-13: 978-1-4104-3809-6 (hardcover)
     ISBN-10: 1-4104-3809-0 (hardcover)
     1. Women police chiefs—Ohio—Fiction. 2.
Amish—Ohio—Fiction. 3. Amish—Crimes against—Fiction. 4.
Amish Country (Ohio)—Fiction. 5. Large type books. I. Title.
PS3603.A8758B74 2011b
813'.6—dc22   2011012371

BRITISH LIBRARY CATALOGUING-IN-PUBLICATION DATA AVAILABLE

Published in the U.S. in 2011 by arrangement with St. Martin's Press, LLC.

Published in the U.K. in 2011 by arrangement with Pan Macmillan Ltd.

U.K. Hardcover: 978 1 445 85862 3 (Windsor Large Print)

U.K. Softcover: 978 1 445 85863 0 (Paragon Large Print)

Printed and bound in Great Britain by the MPG Books Group
1 2 3 4 5 6 7 15 14 13 12 11

This book is dedicated to my family:
my husband, Ernest, my real-life hero;
and Debbie and Jack Sargent for
all the good times. I love you all.

ACKNOWLEDGMENTS

The creative process is a long and sometimes arduous journey. As with every book, I have many people to thank, either for their expertise or moral support along the way. First, I wish to thank my agent, Nancy Yost, because she is brilliant and she always gets it. I thank my editor, Charles Spiccr, whose editorial genius is just the tip of the iceberg. In the U.K., many thanks to my editor, Trisha Jackson, and her assistant, Thalia Suzuma, for her terrific editorial direction and enthusiasm for the books (not to mention the lovely vase of flowers on release day)! As always, my heartfelt gratitude also goes out to all of the top-notch publishing professionals at St. Martin's Press in New York: Matthew Shear, Sally Richardson, Andy Martin, Matthew Baldacci, Sarah Melnyk, Bob Podrasky, Kerry Nordling, and Allison Caplin. No doubt there are many more talented people I failed to mention, but please know I am thankful for your expertise, support, and enthusiasm. I'd also like to extend a big thank-you to my childhood friend Colleen Jessup, for welcoming me into her home during my many trips to Ohio, and for that fantastic ride on her Tennessee Walker, Sonny. Finally, I would be remiss if I didn't mention my fabulous, dedicated, and talented critique group: Jennifer Archer, Anita Howard, Marcy McKay, and April Redmon. Thank you, ladies. You make it fun, and you always make it better.

These be
Three silent things:
The falling snow . . . the hour
Before the dawn . . . the mouth of one
Just dead.
— "Triad," by Adelaide Crapsey

PROLOGUE

The dogs were going to be a problem.

He'd driven by the place twice in the last week, headlights off, windows down, looking, listening. Planning. He'd heard them barking from their pens. Fuckin' beagles. He could see the tops of the chainlink kennels from the road. At least a half dozen of them. The old lady had a whole herd of flea-bitten, barking mutts. But then, that's what dirty old bitches did. Collected dirty animals. Lived like a pig herself. If she thought dogs would keep them from doing what needed to be done, she had something else coming.

Something else.

The wind had come up in the last hour, hard enough to rattle the tree branches. The cold wasn't a hardship; the wind would help cover any noise. With a little luck, they might even get some rain or snow. Messy with the mud, but messy was good when you didn't want to get caught.

He'd killed the headlights a mile back. Lowered the window as he rolled past the place one last time. No lights in the house. Dogs were quiet. The moon was a fuzzy globe behind thickening clouds, but then the dark was a plus for the task ahead. He knew what to do, knew the layout of the place, didn't mind working blind.

Glancing at his passenger, he nodded. "Time to rock and roll."

He parked the truck on a dirt turnaround a hundred yards from the mouth of the gravel lane. He'd duct-taped the dome light, so there was no telltale glow when he opened the door. Then they were out of the truck. Gray-white breaths puffing out. Winter silence all around. The click of tree branches in the wind. The hoot of an owl down by the creek. The cornfield had been cut, and the fallen stalks whispered like disobedient children.

Standing at the passenger door, he quickly toed off his boots, shoved his feet into knee-high muck boots. Going to need them tonight, and not just for the mud.

The leather sheath came next. He strapped it around his hips like a gun belt. On the backseat, the blade of the bowie knife gleamed like blue ice. It was German-made — the best on the market — with a thick six-inch blade and an epoxy-coated leather handle. He liked the handle a lot. The texture kept your hand from slipping when the blade got slick. The guard was small, so he couldn't do a lot of jabbing. But the piece was heavy enough to slash and do some serious damage. He'd gotten a free sharpening stone when he'd ordered it four years ago. Damn good knife.

A thrill ran the length of him when he picked it up. It was a comfortable weapon in his hand. Deadly and beautiful. A piece of art to a connoisseur like him. Dropping it into the leather sheath, he silently closed the door.

Then they were across the bar ditch and walking through the cornfield, toward the wire fence on the south side of the property. Nylon hissed against nylon as they walked, but their muck boots were nearly soundless on the cold, wet ground. Twenty yards from the livestock pens, he heard the animals milling about. They reached the fence.

As they ducked between the bars of a steel-pipe gate, a dozen or more sheep began to dart around. With the exception of pigs, most slaughter animals were stupid. But sheep were especially dense. Mindless herd animals. Reminded him of his human counterparts. Stupid. Trusting. Diluted. Letting themselves be led to slaughter. Not him. He knew what was going on, and he was tired of having it shoved down his throat. Time to make a stand. Do something about it.

They stood in the pen, ten feet apart. His eyes had adjusted to the near blackness. The sheep were moving in circles, trying to blend in with the rest of the herd, avoid the threat. There was no safety in numbers tonight.

He could see his partner on the other side of the pen, picking out an animal, lunging at it. A hard rush of a dozen hooves. The glint of a blade. He heard the strangled scream of the condemned animal. Saw the black spurt of blood on the muddy ground. The old bitch was in for a surprise come morning.

The leather handle was rough and comforting against his palm. He spotted a fat old ewe in the corner. That made him think of the old lady. Dirty old bitch. Human pollution. He leapt, grabbed the ewe around the neck, locked it against him by bending his elbow around its throat. The animal bleated, tried to run, kicked out with its hooves. Cursing, he grasped wool in his fist, jammed the stinking, lumpy body against his chest. A single slash. Wet heat on his hand. Slick on the leather handle. The sound of the death gurgle, like wet gravel in his ears. The animal's body twitched, then went limp.

A righteous kill.

He dropped the dead sheep. He could hear the dogs barking now. No lights yet, but it wouldn't be long. Time for one more.

He looked around, saw another ewe standing in the corner, looking dazed. He rushed her. The animal tried to dart past him. He brought the knife down hard. Sank in deep. Heard the steel snap of the blade hitting bone. The animal went down.

Not thinking now, just acting, getting the job done. He grabbed the sheep's ears. Yanked its head back. Slashed hard. The spurt of blood looked black in the darkness. Hot against his hand. On his clothes. Never liked that part of it. . . .

"Lights," his partner whispered. "Gotta go."

He turned, saw the yellow glow through the trees. The dogs were going nuts in their kennels. "Fuckin' dogs."

Already moving fast. Not speaking. Ducking between the bars of the gate. Mud sucking at his boots. And then he was running full out. Arms pumping. Breaths billowing white. Adrenaline running hot.

They reached the truck, wrenched doors open, clambered in.

"How many you get?" he asked.

"Two." The passenger yanked off his cap. Still breathing hard. "How 'bout you?"

"Two." Thinking about it, he smiled. "Dirty old Amish bitch."

CHAPTER 1

The rain started at midnight. The wind began a short time later, yanking the last of the leaves from the maple and sycamore trees and sending them skittering along Main Street like dry, frightened crustaceans. With the temperature dropping five degrees an hour and a cold front barreling in from the north, it would be snowing by morning.

"Fuckin' weather." Roland "Pickles" Shumaker folded his seventy-four-year-old frame into the Crown Vic cruiser and slammed the door just a little too hard. He'd known better than to let himself get sucked into an all-nighter. It wasn't like he was getting any younger, after all. But his counterpart — that frickin' Skidmore — had called in sick, and the chief asked Pickles to fill in. At the time, cruising around Painters Mill at four o'clock in the morning had sounded like a fine idea. Now he wondered what the hell he'd been thinking.

It hadn't always been that way. Back in the day, the night shift had been his salvation. The troublemakers came out after dark, like vampires looking for blood. For fifty years, Pickles had cruised these not-so-mean streets, hoping with all of his cop's heart that some dipshit would put his toe over the line so Pickles could see some anxiously awaited action.

Lately, however, Pickles could barely make it through an eight-hour shift without some physical ailment reminding him he was no longer twenty-four years old. If it wasn't his back, it was his neck or his damn legs. Christ, it was a bitch getting old.

When he looked in the mirror, some wrinkled old man with a stupid expression on his face stared back. Every single time, Pickles stared at that stranger and thought, *How the hell did that happen?* He didn't have the slightest idea. The one thing he did subscribe to was the notion that Father Time was a sneaky bastard.

Pickles had just pulled onto Dogleg Road when his radio crackled to life. "You there, Pickles?"

The night dispatcher, Mona Kurtz, was a lively young woman with wild red ringlets, a wardrobe that was probably a nightmare for the chief, and a personality as vivacious as a juiced-up coke freak. To top it off, the girl wanted to be a cop. He'd never seen a cop wear black tights and high heels. Well, unless some female was working undercover, anyway. Pickles didn't think she was cut out for it. Maybe because she was too young, just a little bit wild, and her head wasn't quite settled on her shoulders. He had his opinion about female cops, too, but since it wasn't a popular view, he kept his mouth shut.

Of course, he'd never had a problem working for the chief. At first, he'd had his doubts — a female and formerly Amish to boot — but over the last three years, Kate Burkholder had proven herself pretty damn capable. His respect for her went a long way toward changing his mind about the female role in law enforcement.

He picked up his mike. "Don't know where the hell else I'd be," he muttered.

"Skid's going to owe you big-time after this."

"You got that right. Sumbitch is probably out boozing it up."

For the last two nights, he and Mona had fallen to using the radio for small talk, mainly to break up the monotony of small-town police work. Tonight, however, she was reticent, and Pickles figured she had something on her mind. Knowing it never took her long to get to the point, he waited.

"I talked to the chief," she said after a moment.

Pickles grimaced. He felt bad for her, because there was no way the chief was going promote her to full-time officer. "What'd she say?"

"She's going to think about it."

"That's something."

"I don't think she likes me."

"Aw, she likes you just fine."

"I've been stuck on dispatch for three years now."

"It's good experience."

"I think she's going to bring someone in from outside the department."

Pickles thought so, too, but he didn't say it. You never knew when a woman was going to go off on a tangent. The night was going to be long enough without having his dispatcher pissed off at him, too. "Hang in there, kid. She'll come around."

Relief skittered through him when he heard beeping on the other end of the line.

"I got a 911," she said, and disconnected.

Heaving a sigh of relief, Pickles racked the mike and hoped the call kept her busy for a while — and didn't include him. He used to believe that as he got older, women would become less of a mystery. Just went to show you how wrong a man could be. Women were even more of an enigma now than when he was young. Hell, he didn't even get his wife 90 percent of the time, and he'd been married to Clarice for going on thirty years.

Rain mixed with snow splattered against the windshield, so he turned the wipers up a notch. His right leg was asleep. He wanted a cigarette. His ass hurt from sitting.

"I'm too old for this crap," he growled.

He'd just turned onto Township Road 3 when Mona's voice cracked over the mike. "Pickles, I've got a possible ten-eleven at the Humerick place on Folkerth."

He snatched up the mike. "What kind of animal trouble?"

"Old lady Humerick says something killed a bunch of her sheep. Says she's got guts all over the place."

"You gotta be shitting me."

"She thinks it might be some kind of animal."

"Bigfoot more than likely." Muttering, Pickles made a U-turn and headed toward Folkerth. "What's the address out there?"

Mona rattled off a number that told him

the Humerick place wasn't too far from Miller's Pond and the greenbelt that ran parallel with Painters Creek.

"I'm ten-seventy-six," he said, indicating he was en route, and he hit the emergency lights.

The Humerick farm was lit up like a football stadium when Pickles arrived a few minutes later. A mix of snow and rain sparked beneath a giant floodlight mounted on the barn facade. A widow for going on twenty years, June Humerick was the size of a linebacker and just as mean. She claimed to Amish, but she neither looked nor acted the part. A decade earlier, she'd thumbed her nose at the bishop and had electricity run to her farm. She drove an old Dodge pickup, dipped tobacco when it suited her, and cursed like a sailor when she was pissed. The Amish church district no longer claimed her as one of its own. The widow Humerick didn't seem to mind.

She stood next to her old Dodge, wearing a flannel nightgown, knee-high muck boots, and a camo parka. She clutched her late husband's double-barrel shotgun in one hand and a flashlight in the other. "I'm over here!" she bellowed.

Leaving the cruiser running and the headlights pointing toward the shadowy livestock pens on the backside of the barn, Pickles grabbed his Maglite and heaved his small frame from the car. "Evening, June," he said as he started toward her.

She didn't bother with a greeting, instead pointing toward the pens ten yards away. "Evenin' hell. Somethin' killed four of my sheep. Cut 'em to bits."

He followed her point. "Lambs?"

"These was full-grown ewes."

"You see or hear anything?"

"I heard 'em screamin'. Dogs were barkin' loud enough to wake the dead. By the time I got out there, those sheep was dead. I got guts ever'where."

"Could be coyotes," Pickles conjectured. "I hear they're making a comeback in this part of Ohio."

"I ain't never seen a coyote do anythin' like this." The widow looked at him as if he were dense. "I know who done it, and if you had half a brain, so would you."

"I haven't even seen the dead sheep yet, so how the hell could I know who done it?" he replied, indignant.

"Because this ain't the first time somethin' like this has happened."

"You talking about them hate crimes against the Amish?"

"That's exactly what I'm talkin' about."

"Killing a bunch of sheep is kind of a roundabout way to go about it, don't you think?"

"The hell it is. Some folks just plain don't like us, Pickles. Us Amish been prosecuted for damn near a hundred years."

"Persecuted," he said, correcting her.

The widow glared at him. "So what are you goin' to do about it?"

Pickles was all too aware of the recent rash of crimes against the Amish. Most of the infractions were minor: a bashed-in mailbox, a broken window, eggs thrown at a buggy. In the past, the Painters Mill PD as well as the Holmes County Sheriff's Office had considered such crimes harmless mischief. But in the last couple of months, the crimes had taken an ominous turn. Two weeks ago, someone had forced a buggy off the road, injuring a pregnant Amish woman. The chief and the Holmes County sheriff were working on getting a task force set up. The problem was, the Amish victims had unanimously refused to press charges, citing an all-too-familiar phrase: "God will take care of us."

"Well, June, we ain't been able to get anyone to file charges," he said.

"Gawdamn pacifists," she huffed. "I'll do it."

"Before we lynch anyone, why don't we take a look at them sheep and make sure it wasn't dogs or something." Pickles sighed, thinking about his new Lucchese cowboy boots and the mud he would soon be introducing them to.

June's nightgown swished around her legs as she took him over the gravel drive, toward the deep shadows of the pens. The steel gate groaned when she opened it. Pickles could smell the sheep now, that earthy mutton stench mixed with mud, compost, and manure. She had a couple dozen head, and they all chose that moment to bleat. He could hear them stirring around. Mud and sheep shit sucked at his boots as he and June traversed the pen. The skittish animals scattered as they passed.

"Heck of a night to be out," Pickles said, wishing he were home in his warm, dry bed. He shone the flashlight beam along the perimeter of the pen. Midway to the wood-rail fence, he stumbled over something and nearly went down. Cursing, he shone the beam on the ground, only to realize he'd stumbled over the severed head of a sheep.

"Holy shit," he said. "Where did that come from?"

"That'd be Bess." June Humerick lowered her voice. "Poor old girl."

The ewe's head lay in a pool of muck and blood. The mouth was partially open, revealing a row of tiny white teeth. A pink tongue hung out like a deflated balloon. Pickles shifted the beam to study the throat area. He didn't know how that head had been severed from the carcass, but it didn't look like the work of some scrawny coyote. The flesh was cleanly cut. Red tissue and the pink bone of the spine jutted from the base.

"Don't think a coyote did this." Pickles stared, aware that the hairs on his neck were standing up like porcupine quills. "Looks more like a knife."

"I coulda told you that." She ran her beam along the periphery of the pen. "If I'da gotten out here faster, I'da plugged that sumbitch's ass with lead."

Stepping back from the severed head, Pickles swept the beam to a second carcass. He'd never been squeamish about blood, but a quivery wave of unease washed over his stomach when he saw pink entrails ripped from a belly that had been sliced open from end to end.

"What the fuck?" he said.

Taking his language in stride because she'd been known to use the same word herself on occasion, the widow Humerick

26

walked to him and shone her light on the dead sheep. "This is just senseless."

"If it wasn't raining, we might have got some tracks." Pickles swept his beam left and right. "You sure you didn't see any lights out here?"

"I didn't see nothin'."

Pickles leveled his flashlight beam on the carcass. "Could be them devil worshipers down south."

The big woman crossed to him, jabbed her thumb at the decapitated carcass. "They didn't take nothin' for sacrifice."

He could tell by the widow's expression that she wasn't buying into the devil-worshiper theory. He wasn't going to stand out here in the rain and snow and debate it. "Well, I'll drive around back behind them woods and then get a report filed."

She shot him an incredulous look. "What if they come back? What if they're out in them woods waitin' for you to leave so they can come hack up the rest of my sheep?"

"There ain't no one here to arrest."

"You could search the woods."

"Too dark to be tromping around those woods, especially in this weather."

"That's just a crock of horseshit, Pickles."

He sighed; twenty years ago, he'd have been chomping at the bit to get into those dark woods and snag him a couple of Amish-haters. The hunt would be on. Tonight, with his knees aching and a chill that went all the way to his bones, he was more than happy to wait until daylight and pass the buck to the next shift.

"I'll talk to the chief first thing in the morning, get the ball rolling on that task force." He started toward the gate that would take him back to the driveway and his nice warm cruiser. "You might lock them sheep in the shedrow the rest of the night."

June held her ground. "Gonna take more than that rickety old shed to keep out whatever lunatics done this."

"Have a nice evening." Pickles was midway to his cruiser when his radio cracked to life. "What now?" he growled.

"Pickles, I got a ten-fifty-two out at the Slabaugh farm. David Troyer just called, said they got three people down in the manure pit."

"Shit." Pickles fumbled for his lapel mike. Back in the day, a cop had a radio in his cruiser. If he chose to ignore a call, he could. Now, you carried the damn thing around like some weird body part, one end clipped to your belt, one end stuck in your ear, and a microphone pinned to your chest like some damn medal. "You call EMS?"

"They're en route. Thought you might want to get out there."

Pickles heaved another sigh; he'd just about had all the mud and shit he could handle for one night. But he knew a manure pit could be a dangerous place. There were all sorts of nasty gases that would do you in faster than a gas chamber if you weren't careful. "What's the twenty on that?"

"Three six four Township Road Two."

Pickles knew the area. It was a dirt track south of town that would be hell to traverse without a four-wheel-drive vehicle. Figuring this was the end of his Lucchese boots, he cursed. "You might want to call the chief."

"Roger that."

"I'm ten-seventy-six," he said, and forced his old legs into a run.

CHAPTER 2

Insomnia is an insidious thing: a silent and invisible malady that robs the afflicted not only of sleep but also peace of mind, sometimes for months on end. It dulls the intellect, demoralizes the spirit, and eventually leaves the affected open to a host of ailments, both physical and emotional.

I've never been a good sleeper, but in the last couple of months my occasional sleeplessness has degenerated into chronic insomnia. Sometimes, as I lie awake in bed watching the shadows dance on the window, I wonder how long a person can go without sleep and not suffer repercussions. I wonder how and when that ax will fall on me.

I'm staring at the glowing red numbers on my alarm clock when the phone on my night table jangles. I'm so surprised by the sudden blast, I jump, then quickly reassure myself it's Tomasetti calling to check on me. He's a friend, lover, and fellow insomniac, the latter being one of many things we have in common.

A quick glance at the display tells me the call isn't from John, but the station. Considering the fact that I'm the chief of police and it's 5:00 A.M., this doesn't bode well for whatever news awaits me on the other end of the line. Still, I'm relieved to be called away from the dark cave of my own mind.

"Chief Burkholder, it's Mona. Sorry to wake you."

"No problem. What's up?"

"Got a 911 from Bishop Troyer. One of the Slabaugh boys says he's got three people down in the manure pit out at the farm."

Alarm rattles through me. Born and raised Amish, I'm well aware of the dangers of a poorly managed manure pit. Methane gas. Ammonia. Drowning. The Slabaughs are Amish and run a hog operation just out of town. I can tell by the smell when I drive by their place that they don't utilize good manure management. "You call EMS?"

"They're on the way. So is Pickles."

"Victims still alive?"

"Far as I know."

"Call the hospital. Let them know we have multiple vics en route." I'm already out of bed, flipping on the light, fumbling around

31

in the closet for my clothes. "I'll be there in ten minutes."

The Slabaugh farm is located on a dirt road a few miles out of town. Rain mixed with snow is coming down in earnest when I make the turn onto Township Road 2, so I jam my Explorer into four-wheel drive and hit the gas. Less than a hundred yards in, I find a Painters Mill PD cruiser stuck in the mud. I pull up beside it and stop.

The driver's side door swings open and Pickles, my most senior officer, slogs toward me through ankle-deep mud. Opening the passenger door, he climbs into my Explorer, bringing a few pounds of sludge with him. "County ought to pave that damn road," he grumbles as he slides in.

"EMTs make it?" I ask.

"Ain't seen 'em."

"This road is the only way in." The Explorer fishtails when I hit the gas, then the big tires grab, slinging mud into the wheel wells, and we bump toward the Slabaugh farm half a mile ahead. I'm well aware that the human brain can survive only about four minutes without oxygen before suffering permanent damage, so I drive too fast, narrowly avoiding the bar ditch a couple of times.

I'm afraid of what we'll find when we get there. Depending on how bad the ventilation is, gases emanating from a manure pit can be lethal. That's not to mention the ever-present risk of drowning. Two years ago, a pig farmer by the name of Bud Lathy died when he went to the barn early one morning. It was cold, so the night before Bud had closed all the doors and windows. Without proper ventilation, the gases built up inside all night, suffocating several pigs. When he went out to feed them the next morning, he fell unconscious within minutes and died of asphyxiation.

"Look out!"

My headlights wash over the figure of a small boy just in time to avoid hitting him. Adrenaline sweeps through me like an electrical shock. I stomp the brake and cut the wheel hard. The truck slides, missing the boy by inches, and comes to rest crossways in the road. "Shit."

Pickles and I throw open our doors and slosh through mud toward the boy. He's standing in the center of the road, looking lost and terrified. Despite the cold, he's not wearing a coat. I can tell by his flat-brimmed hat and suspenders that he's Amish. "Are you okay?" I ask him.

He's about twelve years old, crying hysterically, and soaked to the skin. "We need help! *Mamm* and *Datt . . ."* He points toward the long gravel lane behind him. "They fell in the pit!"

I don't wait for more information. Grasping a skinny arm, I usher him to the Explorer and muscle him into the backseat. Pickles and I slide in simultaneously, then I floor the gas and we start down the gravel lane.

I look at the boy in the rearview mirror. "Are they awake?"

"No!" he sobs. "They're sleeping! Hurry!"

A quarter mile in, the lane opens to a wide gravel area. The white clapboard house is to my right. The hog barn is straight ahead. I don't slow down until I'm within a few feet of the barn, then I brake hard. The wheels lock, cutting ruts in the winter-dead grass. Gears grind as I ram the shifter into park. I fling open the door. My boots hit the ground before the SUV comes to a complete stop. Grabbing my Maglite, I rush around to the rear of the vehicle, throw open the hatch, and snatch up a twenty-foot section of rope. A mix of rain and snow slashes at my face as I sprint toward the barn.

I shove the door open with both hands. "Police!" I shout. The ammonia and rotten-egg stench of wet manure staggers me, but I don't stop. I see lantern light ahead and rush toward it. Somewhere to my right, I hear a young girl keening. A teenage boy and a younger boy stand just beyond the wood rails of a large pen, looking down. Shoving open the gate to the pen, I cross to them. "Where are they?"

They point, but I already know. The concrete floor is slightly angled so that the urine and feces from the pens drain into the six-foot square hole. The steel grate cover has been removed. I spot the snow shovel and hose on the ground a few feet away and realize someone had been cleaning the pens. I shine my flashlight into the hole. Six feet down, three people lie motionless in a pool of oozing black muck.

"How long have they been down there?" I snap.

The eldest male looks to be about seventeen years old. His terrified eyes find mine. "I don't know. Ten minutes." He says the words through chattering teeth. His face is the color of paste. He wears trousers with suspenders. The knees are wet with muck.

I shove my finger at him. "Open every door and window in this barn right now. Do you understand? Get some air in here."

"*Ja.*" Nodding, he sets off at a run.

I shine my light into the hole again. There

are two male victims and one female. I can tell by their clothing that they're Amish. The two men are facedown. *Too late for them,* I think. The woman is faceup. Still alive, maybe. "We're coming down to get you!" I shout. "Can you hear me?"

None of the victims stirs.

"Hang on!" I hear movement behind me and turn, to see Pickles and the young boy approach. "Where the hell is that ambulance?" I snap.

Shaking his head, Pickles hits his mike.

I point at the boy. "Help your brothers open all the doors and windows. We need fresh air in here. If you can't get the windows open, break them. Go! Now!"

Nodding through his tears, he turns and runs.

Cursing, I glance down at the rope in my hands. The last thing I want to do is go into that pit; I've heard of more than one would-be rescuer unwittingly becoming a victim himself. But there's no way I can stand by and do nothing while a mother of four slowly asphyxiates.

That thought pounds my brain like fists. I look around for something with which to anchor the rope. Ten feet away, I spot the support beam. It's a huge six-by-six-inch length of hundred-year-old oak sunk in concrete. I wrap the rope around the beam, yank it tight. I'm in the process of looping the other end around my hips when Pickles walks up to me. "You're not going down there, are you?" he asks.

Ignoring the question, I walk to the pit and sit, my legs dangling over the side. "I need you to spot me."

Pickles looks alarmed. "Chief, with all due respect . . ."

"Get your gloves. Lower me down."

He looks at me as if he's just been told he'll be facing execution by firing squad. "You go into that pit without a respirator, and you'll be joining the other three."

"You got a better idea?" I snap.

"No, damn it." He doesn't make a move toward the rope. "Maybe we could loop the rope around them, drag them out one at a time."

"Goddamn it, Pickles. She's dying." I scoot closer to the edge.

He grabs my arm. "Kate, you ain't got no choice but to wait for the fire department."

I shake off his hand a little too roughly. But I know he's right. It would be worse than foolhardy for me to go down there. Some might even call it stupid. But I'm not always good at doing the smart thing, especially if someone's life is at stake. Or if there are kids involved. Urgency and indecision pummel me. I think of the children growing up without their parents and I want to scream with the injustice of it. In the last months, I've seen too many bad things happen to too many good people.

"Let's bring them up," I say after a moment.

Looking relieved, Pickles loosens the rope from around the beam, feeds me the slack. I get to my feet and step out of the loop. Standing at the edge of the pit, I widen the loop and toss it into the hole. Vaguely, I'm aware of the distant blare of a siren, but I don't pause. All I can think is that every second could mean the difference between life and death.

I guide the looped end of the rope toward the female victim. She's faceup, which tells me she probably hasn't drowned. If she hasn't succumbed to the gases, there's still a chance. . . .

She's closest to the near wall, almost directly below me, which means she'll be relatively easy to capture with the rope. Planting my feet solidly at the edge of the pit, I lean forward and extend my arm, trying to position the loop around the upper part of her body. A stiff cable would have been more suitable, but I don't have one handy and I don't want to waste time going back to my vehicle, so I've no choice but to work with what I've got.

After several tries, I'm able to drag the loop over the victim's arm. I jiggle the rope, work it up her arm all the way to her shoulder, then over her head, and draw it tight. It won't be a comfortable ride up, but I figure a few rope burns are a lot better than being dead.

"I've got her!" I shout. "Pull!"

Pickles glances around, spots the eldest boy a few feet away, and whistles to get his attention. "Give us a hand!"

The boy rushes over, grabs the rope, wrapping it several times around his bare fist. Hope is wild in his eyes. "Okay!"

In tandem, we begin to pull. The slack goes out of the rope. The woman's arm lifts out of the muck when the rope goes taut. Even though there are three of us, pulling 120 pounds out of thick muck is no easy task. Grunts and growls sound behind me as Pickles and the boy strain. Boots slide and scrape against wet concrete. I use my weight, leaning hard against the rope. I didn't think to put on my gloves, and the rope cuts painfully into my palms, but I put every ounce of strength I possess into the task.

With painful slowness, the woman's limp body inches out of the muck — first her head and shoulders, her torso and hips, and finally her legs and feet. I dig in with my boots, heaving against the rope. I'm too far from the pit now to see the victim, but I can hear her body scraping up the wall as we pull her upward.

When I see her arm and the top of her head at the rim, I glance back at Pickles. "Keep the rope taut."

His face is red with exertion, but he gives me a nod. I slide my hand along the rope until I reach the victim. Putting my hands beneath her shoulders, I give Pickles a nod. "Pull!"

I guide the victim onto the concrete. The first thing I notice is that her skin is cold to the touch. Her clothes are soaked with muck. Her lips are blue. I see tea-colored water in her mouth, so I drop to my knees and roll her onto her side. Voices and the shuffle of shoes sound behind me. I jolt when someone places a hand on my back. I look up, to see a uniformed firefighter and young EMT looking down at me. Both men carry resuscitation bags in their hands.

"We'll take it from here," the EMT says.

I look down at the victim. Filmy eyes stare back at me, and in that instant I know she's gone. The realization makes me want to slam my fist against the concrete. In the smoggy haze of my thoughts, I'm aware of the teenage boy coming up beside me, looking down at his mother. I hear the girl crying nearby. Another child falls to his knees, screaming for his *mamm*. That's when it hits me that these kids are alone.

The next thing I know, someone — the firefighter — puts his hands beneath my arms and pulls me to my feet. I'm in the way, I realize. I feel shaky and cold, and I wonder if it's the gases from the pit that have rendered me useless or if it's the effects of my own impotent emotions.

The EMT kneels next to the woman, placing the mask over her face. I hear the whoosh of air as he compresses the bag, forcing oxygen into her lungs. A few feet away, two respirator-clad firefighters lower rescue equipment into the pit.

I look down at my hands. They're slick with a rancid mix of water, blood, manure, and mud. It's sticky on my skin, gritty between my fingers. I see rope burns on the insides of my knuckles and realize the blood is mine, but I don't feel the sting. At the moment, I don't even smell the manure. All I can do is stand there and watch the paramedics work frantically to resuscitate the motionless woman.

A few feet away, the four Amish children huddle, their eyes filled with hope that the *Englischers* and all their high-tech rescue equipment will save their *mamm* and *datt*. I see faith on their young faces, and my heart breaks, because I know faith often goes unrewarded.

"You look like you could use some air."

I turn, to see Officer Rupert "Glock" Maddox standing a few feet away, looking at me as if I'm a dog that's just been hit by a car — a badly injured dog that might bite if touched. I have no idea how he got here so quickly; he doesn't come on duty until 8:00 A.M. It doesn't matter; I'm just glad he's here.

"She's gone," I say.

"You did your best."

"Tell those kids that."

Grimacing, he crosses to me. "Let's get some air."

Glock isn't a touchy-feely kind of guy. I've worked with him for two and a half years now, and I can count on two fingers the number of intimate conversations we've had. It surprises me when he takes my arm.

"Goddamn it," I mutter.

"Yeah." It's all he says, but it's enough. He gets it. He gets me. It's enough.

He ushers me through the main part of the barn. It's not until I step outside that I realize I'm woozy. Though the barn doors and windows have been thrown open wide, there's not much of a cross breeze, and the air inside is polluted with an unpleasant mix of ammonia and stink. Not to mention all those nasty gases. I've been inside only for ten minutes or so, but I can already feel the effects. A headache taps at my forehead from inside my skull.

For a full minute, I do nothing but stand in the rain and snow and breathe in the clean, cold air. It feels good, like cool water on heated skin. After a minute or so, I look at Glock. "I'm okay."

"I know you are." Sighing, he shoots a glance in the direction of the barn. "Tough scene."

I think of the kids, and a lead weight of dread drops into my stomach. "Worst is yet to come."

"You want me to give you a hand with their statements?"

"I'd appreciate that."

"We going to do it here?"

I look around. We're standing twenty feet from the barn. Around us, emergency workers — paramedics and firefighters — move in and out of the big door. The strobe lights of a fire truck and two ambulances from Pomerene Hospital glare off the facade. To my right, the pretty white farmhouse looks cold and empty. The windows are dark, as if some internal light has been permanently extinguished.

"We'll do it in the house. The kids'll be more comfortable there. They'll need to eat something." I know it seems mundane, but even in the face of death, people need to eat. "I'll call Bishop Troyer to be here with them."

If Glock is surprised by my response, he doesn't show it. I don't have a maternal bone in my body, but I'm feeling protective of these kids. All children are innocent, but Amish youngsters possess a certain kind of innocence. They have further to fall when that innocence is shattered. I was fourteen years old when fate introduced me to tragedy. I know what it feels like to be abruptly plunged into a world that is so far removed from the only one you've ever known.

I glance toward the barn and see Pickles and the four kids standing outside the big door. Firefighters and EMTs pass by them without notice. The last thing I want to do is question them about the horrors they witnessed, but as is the case with most of the curveballs life throws at us with indiscriminate glee, I don't have a choice.

CHAPTER 3

Ten minutes later, I'm standing in the big Amish kitchen with Glock and Pickles. The four children sit at the heavy wood table, their pale faces lit by the flickering kerosene lamp. The house is warm inside and smells of hot lard and lamp oil.

I take a few minutes to light a second lantern on the counter next to the sink. A lifetime ago, the dim lighting wouldn't have bothered me. Up until I was in my late teens, it was all I'd ever known. This morning, the lack of fluorescent bulbs makes me feel half-blind.

An old-fashioned kerosene stove next to the sink is still hot from earlier this morning. On its top, a cast-iron skillet filled with scrapple, an Amish breakfast staple, sits in a bed of cooling, thickening lard. On the table, the remnants of a breakfast left unfinished sits cold. I see a basket of bread and a small bowl filled with apple butter. A pitcher of milk, fresh, probably. Seven plates. Seven glasses. Three cups for coffee.

I move the cast-iron skillet onto a hot burner to warm it; then I go to the table. I feel Glock's and Pickles' eyes on me as I pour milk into four glasses. It's a strange role for me, but I'm compelled to play it. I place a slice of bread in front of each child. Bread that I know was baked by their mother just a day or two before. A mother who will never make breakfast for her children again.

The kids are probably too upset to eat, but I serve the warmed scrapple anyway. When I run out of things to do, I sit down at the table and fold my hands in front of me. "I'm sorry about what happened to your parents," I begin.

The youngest child, a boy I guess to be about ten years old, looks at me. "Is *Mamm* coming?" he asks.

"I'm sorry, but your *mamm* and *datt* passed away." Because I'm not sure if he understands the expression, I add, "They're with God now."

"But I saw you save her. I *saw* you."

"I couldn't save her. I'm sorry."

The boy looks down at his plate and begins to cry. "I want my *mamm*."

"I know you do, honey." Reaching across

the table, I pat his hand. It's small and soft and cold beneath mine. Feeling helpless and inept, I turn my attention to the eldest boy. He stares back at me. I see defiance in his eyes, and I wonder if he's trying to defy death or maybe deny his own grief. "What are your names?" I ask.

"I'm Salome." The girl sitting across from me is in her mid-teens, with mouse brown hair and a pale complexion mottled pink from crying. Her eyes are forest green and skitter away from mine when I look at her. She's the only one who has picked up her fork and sampled the scrapple.

I give her a nod, then I turn my attention to the boy sitting next to her.

"I'm Samuel," he says.

"How old are you, Samuel?" I ask.

"Twelve."

I give him a smile I hope looks real, then I look at the youngest child, who's sitting two chairs over from me. He's a blond-haired boy with blunt-cut bangs and a sprinkling of freckles across a turned-up nose. "How about you?"

"I'm Ike and I'm ten." The words are barely out when he lowers his face into his pudgy hands and bursts into tears. "I want my *mamm.*"

I feel like crying, too, but of course I can't.

That kind of emotion is as contagious as any virus, and I can't afford to allow it into my psyche. Instead, I touch Ike's shoulder and then look across the table at the eldest boy. "What's your name?"

"Moses, but they call me Mose."

He's a tall, thin boy with greasy blond hair and patches of bright pink acne on both cheeks. But any hint of teenaged homeliness ends there. His eyes are crystalline blue beneath blunt-cut bangs. I see the unmistakable glint of intelligence in those eyes, and I know he's smart enough to realize that all of their lives are about to change in a very profound way.

"How old are you, Mose?"

"I am a man." His voice cracks, belying the words, and he sits up a little straighter. "I'm seventeen."

"My name's Kate. I'm the chief of police, and I need to ask you some questions about what happened." No one says anything. No one looks at me. "What are your parents' names?"

After a moment, Mose raises his eyes to mine. "*Datt* is Solomon, but they call him Solly. *Mamm*'s name is Rachael."

"And the other man?"

"Our uncle, Abel."

"Last name Slabaugh?"

"*Ja.* He's visiting from Lancaster County."

I feel ancient as I look from young face to young face. Innocent kids whose lives, until now, have been untouched and undamaged by the ravages life can sometimes inflict. My gaze stops on Mose and I say, "I need for you to tell me what happened this morning."

His eyes go to the plate of untouched food in front of him and for a moment he looks as if he's going to throw up. He takes a full minute to gather himself, then speaks to me without looking up. "*Datt* and Uncle Abel were feeding the hogs and cleaning the pens. *Mamm* and the rest of us were in the house. She sent Samuel out to fetch *Datt* so we could say our before-meal prayer and eat breakfast." He closes his eyes briefly. "Samuel came back screaming."

I turn my attention to Samuel. "What happened?" I ask gently.

The boy looks down at his plate. From where I sit, I can see that his hands are dirty and scabbed, with short, bitten nails. Typical boy hands. Amish hands that work and play in equal measure. "*Datt* and Uncle Abel were in the pit. I didn't know what to do."

"Were they awake?"

Samuel looks at Mose. Mose gives him a nod, which seems to bolster the boy. Samuel meets my gaze, then his face screws up. "*Ja. Datt* couldn't speak. But Uncle Abel . . . he yelled for me to get help."

"What did you do?"

"I ran to the house to get *Mamm.*"

I nod, trying not to imagine the horror of that. I look at Mose. "Then what happened?"

"We ran to the barn to help them," he replies.

"Who ran to the barn?"

"All of us. *Mamm.* My brothers and sister."

"How did your *mamm* get into the pit?"

Little Ike rubs his eyes with small, dirty fists. "She tried to save *Datt.*"

Mose cuts in. "She lay down on the concrete, right in all that muck, and tried to get *Datt* to take her hand. She was screaming for him to wake up, but he wouldn't. She tried to save Uncle Abel, but he fell asleep, too. *Mamm* started to cry. She was too close to the edge and fell into the pit."

In the back of my mind, I wonder if she succumbed to the gases emanating from the manure and fell unconscious. "What did you do when your *mamm* fell in?"

"We were scared. It was like a bad dream. Too bad to really be happening." Mose lifts a shoulder and lets it drop. "I knew the air was bad, so we opened the door. We yelled

51

at *Mamm,* tried to wake her up, but she wouldn't. The children were crying." He looks at his younger brother. "That's when I decided to bridle the horse and sent Samuel to Bishop Troyer's house for help. The bishop has a telephone."

"What did you do after Samuel left?"

"I kept trying to get *Mamm* and *Datt* and Uncle Abel out of the pit. I tried to use the hose, you know, as a rope."

I recall seeing the hose lying on the concrete, and I nod. "Were any of them conscious at that point?"

Salome cuts in, tears streaming down her cheeks. "They wouldn't wake up. We yelled and yelled, but we couldn't get them to wake up."

"Why wouldn't they wake up?" Ike whines.

I glance over at the boy. Generally speaking, I've found Amish children to be slightly more stoic than their English counterparts. But kids are kids, regardless of culture. Most are unequipped to handle this kind of situation. Some grief is simply too heavy a load for such a young heart to bear. "It's the gases that made them sleepy," I say.

"I want my *mamm!*" Ike cries. "I want her back. Why couldn't she just wake up? Why couldn't you save her?"

The accusation in his voice hits me like a slap. I know it's only the grief talking. Still, I can't deny there is a part of me that feels guilty for not being able to save them.

Salome gets up from her place and goes to the boy. The sight of her setting her slender hands on his bony, shaking shoulders, and pressing her face against his cheek is so heart-wrenching that I have to look away. "Shush now, Ike," she coos. "*Mamm* and *Datt* are with God now. Remember that when your heart hurts for them."

The back door creaks open. I turn in my chair, to see my youngest officer, T. J. Banks, peek his head in. "Coroner is here, Chief."

I'd hoped Bishop Troyer would arrive before I had to leave the children to deal with the coroner. The bishop's farm is only a couple of miles away, but he's getting on in years and it takes time to harness and hitch a horse and cover that much distance. I look at T. J. "Can you stay with the kids until Bishop Troyer gets here?"

"Uh . . . sure." He eyes the four youngsters with trepidation as he sidles into the kitchen.

I motion for Glock and Pickles to follow me and we head toward the barn. I'm midway there when I spot the coroner, Dr. Ludwig Coblentz, sliding out of his Escalade. Large medical bag in hand, he waits for me to approach.

"I was hoping your dispatcher had somehow gotten the call wrong," he says when I reach him. "I can tell by the look on your face that's not the case."

"I wish it was." I motion toward the house. "There are four kids inside who will never see their parents again."

"Kind of thing that makes you question just how benevolent God is sometimes, doesn't it?"

"Makes me question a lot of things." Like why I'm still a cop when the last two cases I've worked have taken such a heavy toll. Don't get me wrong; I love what I do. I'm an idealist at heart, and I love the idea of making a difference. But it seldom works out that way, and it's not the first time I've questioned if I'm cut out for the job.

We pass by two firefighters when we enter the barn. The rotten-egg and ammonia stench has dwindled, but it's still strong enough to make my eyes water. Twenty-five feet away, in a concrete-floored pen, a young paramedic stands near the three bodies, scribbling furiously on a clipboard. He looks up when we approach and greets us with a tight smile. "We figured you'd want to do a quick field exam before we bag and transport," he says to the coroner.

"Thank you." Doc Coblentz goes directly to the nearest body, that of Rachael Slabaugh, and kneels. Pickles, Glock, and I stop several feet away to let the doctor do his work. I haven't smoked for a couple of months now, but it's moments like this when I want a cigarette most.

"Hell of a way to go," Pickles mumbles.

"Ain't that the truth." Glock shakes his head. "Death by shit."

The older man nods in solemn agreement. "It's almost worse when it's an accident. No one to blame."

"No one to shoot." Glock offers a grim smile. "Makes it even more senseless."

Nodding in agreement, Pickles looks at me. "Seems pretty cut-and-dried, don't it, Chief?"

I nod. "Kids' statements are consistent with an accident." I watch Doc Coblentz move from body to body. Using the stethoscope, he checks for vitals. Because the cause of death is evidently accidental, he forgoes the kind of thorough preliminary field exam a murder would warrant, such as ascertaining body temperature to help pinpoint the time of death. I know he'll take a core liver temp for his final report once he gets the bodies to the hospital morgue. Because the deaths were unattended, he's required by law to perform autopsies, which will tell us the cause and manner of death. In this case, the cause is either asphyxiation or drowning; the manner is accidental.

I force my gaze to the nearest victim. Rachael Slabaugh was in her mid-thirties. An Amish mother of four. She'd once been pretty, but in death her face has a blue-white cast that lends her a ghostly countenance. Her left eyelid has come open halfway, and the cloudy white of her eyeball is stained with a coffee-colored film. Her mouth hangs open. Glancing inside, I see the dark mass of a tongue and teeth colored brown from muck. She wears a green dress, an organdy *kapp,* and an apron that had once been white. The dress is twisted at an uncomfortable-looking angle, and I have to resist the urge to go to her to straighten it.

Her husband lies next to her. I estimate Solomon Slabaugh to be about forty years old. He wears dark trousers with a blue work shirt and suspenders. His full beard is clotted with solids from the pit. At some point during the retrieval of his body, the insulated jacket came off one of his shoulders. No one bothered to right it, so his left arm is twisted and slightly beneath him.

I guess Abel Slabaugh to be the younger of the two brothers. His lack of a beard tells me he is unmarried. He wears brown trousers with suspenders, a blue work shirt, and insulated coveralls. I'm sure he'd been wearing work boots as well, but they are nowhere to be seen. I imagine them sliding off his feet as he was pulled from the pit.

The three bodies are a horrific sight to behold as they shimmer wetly beneath the glare of the emergency work lights set up by the fire department volunteers. A lot of stomachs couldn't handle it, but you get used to things in my line of work. My thoughts drift to the four orphans, and I wonder if they have relatives to take them in. If they don't, I know there are dozens of Amish families in the church district that would be more than happy to open their homes and hearts. I'm obligated to contact Children Services, but I know this is one of many instances where the Amish will go above and beyond the call of duty.

"Chief Burkholder."

Doc Coblentz's voice pulls me from my thoughts. I start toward him as he stands and snaps off a pair of latex gloves. "It's a damn shame."

I stop a few feet away from him. Neither of us looks at the bodies. "You'll autopsy all three victims?"

He nods, grimaces. "My schedule's pretty

57

clear, so I should be able to start this afternoon."

I want to say, "Good," but this is so far from good, I can't manage the word. For a moment, the only sound comes from the rumble of the generator, the buzz of work lights, and the occasional grunt from the hogs in a nearby pen.

"Do they have next of kin?" the doctor asks.

"I'll check with Bishop Troyer. Notify them as soon as possible."

"I don't envy you that part of your job."

Notifying next of kin is undoubtedly one of the most difficult aspects of being chief. But I've always thought cutting into a dead body would be worse. This morning, I'm not so sure. "Will you fax your reports over when they're finished?"

He gives me a nod, then motions for the two paramedics standing by to bag the bodies for transport.

Having grown up Amish, I have mixed feelings about the lifestyle. Like most things in life, there was some good and some bad, with a whole lot of in-between thrown in. Leaving was the right decision for me, the only one I could have made at the time. But it wasn't done without some regret. One of

58

the things I loved most about being Amish was the sense of community, of belonging, of being part of something bigger than myself. I loved the way my Amish brethren pulled together in the face of tragedy. It didn't happen that way when disaster struck my family, but looking back, I realize now that we were an anomaly.

By the time I leave the barn, the Amish have begun to arrive in force. Men wearing work clothes and insulated coats congregate near the barn. I know they're here to feed the livestock, clean the pens, and keep the farm up and running. The women will busy themselves with household chores — laundry, cooking, and caring for the children. In the coming days, the Slabaugh house will be overflowing with the help of a community that is as generous as it is selfless.

I spot the bishop's buggy parked near the back door as I head toward the house. A boy not much older than the youngest Slabaugh child tends the old horse. Two additional buggies I don't recognize are parked behind the bishop's. Beyond, the windows of the house are illuminated by yellow lantern light.

I enter to the aromas of kerosene, wood smoke, and cinnamon. T.J. stands near the back door, looking out of place and uncomfortable. His relief is palpable when he spots me. "Bishop Troyer arrived, Chief."

I give him a nod. To my left, two plump Amish women wearing traditional garb — homemade dresses with white aprons, their hair tucked into organdy *kapps* — stand shoulder-to-shoulder at the kitchen counter. One of the women rolls out a round of lard and flour pastry crust. The other slices apples into a large plastic bowl. I'm not surprised to see that they're making pies. If food were a cure-all, the Amish would be the healthiest culture in the world.

Moving into the next room, I see Bishop Troyer and a silver-haired woman sitting in straight-backed chairs someone dragged in from the kitchen. All four Slabaugh children sit side by side on a sofa, lined up like sad little ducks. One of the cushions has a hole in it. I see a closely matched piece of fabric has come loose, and I know at some point Rachael Slabaugh had tried to patch it. It was probably one of a thousand things on her list of chores. A chore she will never get the chance to complete.

"Katie." The bishop stands and extends his hand to me.

"Thank you for coming." I take his hand and we shake. "I'd like to speak to you if you have a few minutes."

"Of course."

The bishop looks over his shoulder at the woman. She gives a minute nod, telling him without words that she'll remain with the children.

I'm keenly aware of the children's eyes on us. They're wondering about their fates, I realize. Where will they live? Who will take them in? Will they be kept together or will they be separated, the family shattered once again? Little Ike still looks at me as if I might be able to conjure forth his dead *mamm.* I know it's self-defeating, but I feel guilty because I can't.

The house is getting crowded, so I motion toward the front door and we step onto the porch. For the span of several heartbeats, the only sound comes from the tinkle of sleet against the roof.

I break the silence. "Do the Slabaughs have relatives?" It's so cold, my breath billows when I speak.

"There is a brother." The bishop looks out across the darkened field. "We will take care of those children."

I wait for more information on the brother, but he doesn't offer it. "What's his name?"

"Adam."

"Does he live around here?"

"Millersburg, I believe."

I stare at his profile, wondering why he's so reluctant to offer information about Adam Slabaugh. "I need to notify next of kin."

The bishop turns his attention back to me. "What of the children, Katie?"

"Children Services will probably place them with relatives. Or the brother."

The bishop shakes his head so hard, his jowls jiggle. "Not Adam."

"Why not?"

"He is not Amish. Solly would not have wanted his children raised by a man who has been excommunicated."

The reason behind his earlier reluctance suddenly becomes crystal clear. "Is there any other family?"

"No."

"Bishop, with all due respect —"

He cuts me off. "These children were raised Amish. An Amish family would feel blessed to take them in and raise them as their own."

"This isn't a matter of Amish versus English."

The bishop gives me a sage look. "Yes, it is."

It's an old argument, one that's taken on a painful new twist this morning because four young lives hang in the balance. "The decision isn't mine to make," I tell him. "Nor is it yours. I'll have to involve Children Services."

For the first time, the bishop looks alarmed. "No, Katie. Do not do that. Your English government does not care about the Amish way. They do not care about the broken hearts of those children."

I've known Bishop Troyer since I was a child. He was tough on me when I was an unrepentant teenager and made the decision to leave the plain life behind. We've had many disagreements over the years. But my respect for him is high. I'm old enough now to know he's a decent man with a good heart and a fair mind. None of those things changes my responsibilities.

"Can you see to it that someone stays with the children until we get this settled?" Under any other circumstances, I wouldn't ask. In fact, I would have already notified Children Services and asked for a social worker to assist with placement in temporary foster homes. But because these children are Amish, I know they will be safe and loved in the hands of their brethren.

The old bishop nods and says, *"Mer sot em sei Eegne net verlosse; Gott verlosst die Seine nicht,"* which means "One should not abandon one's own; God does not abandon his own."

I've heard the old adage before. Because I know life isn't always that kind — even if you're Amish — I don't respond. "I've got to tell Adam about his brothers and his sister-in-law." I turn to leave, but he reaches out and snags my arm.

"These children have lost enough," he says. "Do not take them away from everything they know. Do not take their faith from them. *Solly would have wanted them raised Amish.*"

I leave with those words ringing in my ears.

CHAPTER 4

There are few things I've done in my life
that are more difficult than telling someone
they've lost a loved one. It's a helpless,
hopeless feeling to break that kind of news
and not be able to do anything as the bottom drops out of that person's world. In my
nine years of law-enforcement experience,
I've seen grief in all its insidious forms.
Though I'm merely the messenger, I've
been cursed, screamed at, threatened, spit
on, and struck. Cops aspire to believe
they're not affected by such things. But it
takes a toll. That's one of many reasons I've
never put the burden of notification on my
officers. Still, I don't ever go alone. This
morning, I've got Glock with me.

Adam Slabaugh lives on a well-kept farm
on a quiet township road between Millersburg and Painters Mill. The old house is
white, with a green tin roof, green shutters,
and a wraparound porch that's sheltered by

a hulking spruce. The place sits on a hill, overlooking acres and acres of plowed fields. I park the Explorer in the gravel area between the barn and the house and shut down the engine.

For the span of several heartbeats, Glock and I sit there, watching snow gather on the windshield.

"Hell of a way to start someone's day," he says.

"Hell of a way to start our day."

"Is this guy going to take the kids?"

I tell him about my conversation with Bishop Troyer. "Might be some problems there."

"Tough situation for the kids," he says.

"And everyone else involved."

Neither of us wants to walk up to that house and knock on the door. Of course, we don't have a choice. I reach for the door handle first. We're midway to the house when the back door opens. A Border collie and a fat yellow Labrador bound out, tails wagging, tongues lolling. Behind them, a man shrugs into an insulated coat and closes the door behind him. He's a tall, thin man who doesn't look Amish. No beard. No hat or suspenders. But he possesses the kind eye I've come to associate with the culture.

"Good morning." He's still buttoning his coat when he reaches us. "Is something wrong?"

Glock and I start toward him. "Adam Slabaugh?" I ask.

He has light blue eyes, which remind me of a summer sky, and a face that has seen a lot of years of Ohio's sometimes extreme elements. He takes in our uniform parkas, and his eyes go wary. I see his shoulders stiffen in a brace, and I know at some point he's done this before. "Yes?"

I show him my badge and identify myself. "There's been an accident. I'm afraid I've got some bad news."

"Accident?" His gaze flicks to Glock and then back to me. "What happened? Did someone get hurt?"

"I'm afraid so." I motion toward the house. "Would you like to go inside and sit down, so we can talk?"

"Must be bad if you want me to sit down." He looks down at his boots, blows out a breath, as if preparing himself for the blow. "Who is it?"

"Are Solomon and Abel Slabaugh your brothers?"

"Yes." He blinks rapidly. "What happened to them?"

"Your brothers and sister-in-law were

67

killed this morning at their farm."

"Aw, God." He takes a step back. "Killed? All three of them? Are you sure?" He looks at Glock, as if expecting him to contradict me.

"We're sure," I say. "I'm very sorry."

He makes a choking sound, takes another step back, as if to distance himself from us and the news we bear. "How in God's name did it happen?"

"We believe it was methane gas asphyxiation from the manure pit."

"My God." Tugging off a glove, he bows his head, scrapes a trembling hand over his face. "I told Solly to keep that old barn ventilated. He never listened to —" He stops speaking mid-sentence and raises his gaze to mine. "The children?"

"They're fine," I say. "Unhurt. Physically anyway."

He closes his eyes briefly, as if thanking God for sparing them, and I know that even though he's no longer Amish, he's still a religious man. "How did it happen?" he asks.

I tell him what I learned from the kids' statements. "Apparently, Rachael was trying to rescue her husband and brother-in-law. I suspect she succumbed to the gases, blacked out, and fell into the pit. The kids tried, but they couldn't get them out."

"Poor, poor children. Where are they now?"

"They're still at the house. Bishop Troyer is there with them."

Adam's face darkens. "Then you know I've been excommunicated."

"The bishop told me."

"I bet he gave you an earful." His laugh is bitter. "What else did he tell you?"

Knowing the value of silence, I say nothing.

"They're my nephews and niece, Chief Burkholder. They should be with family. With me."

I can't dispute the statement. From all appearances, he's a decent, hardworking farmer. More importantly, he's a blood relative. Their *only* blood relative. The house and property are neat and well kept. I'll run a criminal check on him, but I'm betting he doesn't have any convictions. There's no reason why he shouldn't assume custody of his niece and his nephews. I don't mention the bishop's assertion that the children should be raised Amish. But I can tell from Adam's reaction that he's already keenly aware of this.

"Were you and the kids close?" I ask.

"Up until four years ago, I was a big part

69

of their lives." Adam looks away for a moment, then raises defiant eyes to mine. "As you can see, I'm no longer Amish."

"Do you mind if I ask why?"

"Lust, of course." He gives me a wry smile. "I fell in love with an English woman." The smile turns bitter. "We married, which is against the *Ordnung,* so I was put under the *bann.* I was unrepentant, refused to confess my so-called sins, so I was eventually excommunicated." He shrugs. "Solly cut me out of the children's lives."

"I'm sorry," I say.

"It was a bad time."

"So you were estranged from the family," I say.

"Yes." His sigh is tired and heavy. "Maybe this is God's way of bringing those children back to me. Maybe it's His way of punishing those with small minds."

The statement takes me aback. It seems odd at a time like this — when he's just been informed of his brothers' deaths. Anyone who's ever lived any length of time knows God doesn't even the score and that sometimes that bitch Fate gets her way, right and wrong be damned.

"Are you married?" I ask.

"My wife died. I'm a widower."

I look down at the dogs, letting that bit of information settle in my brain. For a moment, the only sound comes from the caw of a crow perched on the fence.

"I would like to see the children," Adam says after a lengthy pause.

I know the Amish will not keep this man from seeing his niece and his nephews. But he will not be welcomed by them. He's an outsider now, an interloper. As a cop, I know the Amish have no right to keep Adam Slabaugh from his own blood.

"Are there any other relatives?" I ask. "Aunts? Uncles? Grandparents?"

He gives me a sage look. "You mean Amish relatives?"

"I'm asking you if the children have any other living relatives," I reply firmly.

"Rachael's mother, their grandmother, passed away just two months ago. She was old and frail. I am the only family they have left."

I nod, understanding all too well, and knowing everyone involved is destined for heartache. "Are you going to pursue legal custody?"

"Of course. Why shouldn't I? Those children need to be with family. I'm their uncle." He blinks, his eyes watery. "I love them."

I don't expect any trouble from the Amish, but I know from experience that when kids are involved, emotions many times supersede civility. I offer the best piece of advice I can. "If you plan to pursue custody, you might want to get yourself a lawyer."

"Do you think I'll need one?"

"A lawyer will be able to help you navigate through the legal end of it. That'll make things easier for you. Probably best to do things by the book in this case." I reach into my pocket and hand him my card. "Let me know if you have any problems."

Back in the Explorer, I put the vehicle in gear and head down the long gravel lane. Glock breaks the silence with the same question that's echoing inside my head. "You think there's going to be a custody issue?"

"I don't think the Amish will fight him. Not legally anyway. They're not big on the whole litigation thing. But that's not to say there won't be problems. People do crazy things when it comes to protecting their kids."

Glock nods, and I know he's thinking about his own child, a little boy not yet a year old. "Maybe Solomon had a will. Maybe he specified provisions for the kids."

"Most Amish don't use a legal will and

testament. Everything's almost always passed down to the children. Property goes to the eldest male child."

"Simpler that way, I guess," he says.

"No one ever expects to die young."

We're two blocks from the police station when my cell phone erupts. I'm surprised to see Doc Coblentz's name appear on the display.

"Hey Doc," I say, giving him only half of my attention.

"I was about to begin the autopsy on Solly Slabaugh when I found an irregularity I think you'll want to see."

"What kind of irregularity?"

"During my preliminary examination, I found evidence of blunt-force trauma to his head."

The words yank my full attention to the call. A small part of my brain hopes I misunderstood. *What?*

"Solly Slabaugh sustained a substantial blow to the head before his death."

For a moment, I'm speechless. Then my brain kicks back into gear. "Is it possible it happened in the fall? The sides of that pit are concrete."

"Judging from the location of the laceration, I don't believe that's the case."

Shock is like a battering ram against my

73

brain. A hundred questions fly and scatter inside my head as the repercussions start to sink in. "Are you saying this wasn't an accident?"

"I won't know the cause or manner of death until I complete the autopsy, so I don't want to jump to conclusions at this juncture. But this is very suspicious, Kate. I thought you might want to see for yourself."

A glance at the clock on the dash tells me it's already past noon. "I'll be there in a few minutes."

My mind is still reeling when I clip my cell phone to my belt.

"That didn't sound good," Glock comments.

I relay to him my conversation with the coroner.

He looks as shocked as I feel. "Shit."

"Are you up to a trip to the morgue?"

He grimaces. "I don't think we have a choice."

With a population of about 5,500, Painters Mill is too small to have its own morgue per se. As Mayor Auggie Brock is so fond of saying in town council meetings, "We don't have enough dead people." Up until three years ago, autopsies were farmed out to either Lucas or Stark counties. Now, however, when there's an unattended death or suspected foul play, Holmes and Coshocton counties have the option of utilizing the morgue facilities at Pomerene Hospital in Millersburg, which now receives funding from both counties.

It takes Glock and me ten minutes to make the drive from Painters Mill to Millersburg. The earlier snow has turned to a cold, driving rain. Fog hovers like smoke in the low-lying fields, creeks, and wooded areas. With the temperature hovering at just above the freezing mark, I suspect driving conditions will deteriorate rapidly once the sun goes down.

Pomerene Hospital is a fifty-five-bed facility located on the north side of town. I park illegally outside the Emergency Services portico. Neither Glock nor I have an umbrella, so we flip up the hoods of our coats and make a run for the double glass doors. Once inside, we pass by the information booth, where a young African-American man in Scooby-Doo scrubs waves us through. I'm still shaking rain from my coat when we step into the elevator that will take us to the basement.

"What's up with all this fuckin' rain?" Glock comments as the car descends. "I thought it was supposed to snow in December."

"Mother Nature likes to keep us on our toes, I guess."

"That bitch is on crack."

That elicits a smile from both of us, but I know we're only working up to our next task. In the back of my mind, I'm already wondering how much animosity existed between Adam and Solly Slabaugh. I wonder if there was enough of it to drive the forsaken uncle to commit murder.

The elevator doors swish open and we step into a hushed gray-tiled hall that reminds me of some deserted underground nuclear facility. We pass a yellow-and-black biohazard sign and go through dual swinging doors mounted with a plaque that reads: MORGUE: AUTHORIZED PERSONNEL ONLY. A middle-aged woman in a navy dress looks up from her desk when I enter. "Hi, Chief."

"Hey, Carmen." The fact that I'm on a first-name basis with the coroner's administrative assistant tells me I've been spending too much time here. "This is Officer Maddox."

We cross to her desk. Smiling, Glock extends his hand. "Call me Glock."

"I'm not going to argue with a man who goes by that nickname." She chuckles.

"How're the roads out there? Guy on the radio says we might be in for some freezing rain."

"Good for now. Might get a little tricky later." I glance toward the swinging doors, already dreading what comes next. "Doc in there?"

"Go right in. He's expecting you."

"Thanks."

We go through another set of swinging doors. The medicinal smells of formalin and alcohol and the darker stench of death envelops us like cold, clammy hands as we traverse the hall. The autopsy suite is straight ahead. I can already feel the tension climbing up my shoulders. Glock is silent, but I know he feels it, too. All of us are born with an inherent aversion to death. No matter how many times I make this pilgrimage, it never gets any easier.

To my right is a small alcove where the doc stores supplies, including biohazard protection. To my left, I see Doc Coblentz's glassed-in office. The miniblinds and door are open, and I can see him sitting at his desk. An old John Lennon Christmas song oozes from a neat little sound system on his credenza.

He looks up when we enter and gives us a somber shake of his head. "I'll bet you

77

thought you were going to be able to sit this one out."

I look toward the autopsy suite. "Are you sure about the head trauma?"

He offers a grim nod. "I'm certain. Of course, I can't rule on the manner or cause of death until I complete the autopsy. But Solomon Slabaugh definitely sustained a substantial blow to the head shortly before his death."

"Are you sure it happened *before* he died?"

"Even though the wound site was compromised with contaminants from the muck, there was some bleeding visible. The victim's heart was beating. I'm certain."

"How substantial?"

"There was enough force to break the skin."

"That's a lot of force," Glock comments.

Rising, the doc motions toward the alcove, where the biohazard gear is stowed neatly on the shelf. "Suit up, and I'll show you."

Glock and I enter the alcove and hang our coats on hooks mounted on the wall. Anxious to see the head trauma for myself, I quickly don shoe covers, a sea-foam green gown that ties at the back, a hair cap, a disposable mask, and latex gloves. The doc is waiting for us when we emerge.

Our paper gowns crackle as we traverse the hall. The doc pushes open one of two swinging doors and we enter the autopsy room. The temperature is so cold, I almost expect to see my breath, or maybe the cold emanates from someplace inside me.

The thing that always surprises me most when I come here is the smell. Even with a state-of-the-art ventilation system and a constant temperature of sixty-one degrees, the stink of decaying flesh is ever present. I've been here more times than I care to count, and no matter how short my stay, I invariably feel the need for a long soapy shower afterward. Not for the first time, I wonder how this veteran pediatrician deals with it day in and day out.

Stark fluorescent light rains down on gleaming stainless-steel counters. To my right, a dozen or more white plastic buckets are stacked on a portable stainless cart. I see trays filled with unfathomable medical instruments, two deep sinks with tall, arcing faucets. A scale that looks as if it belongs in the produce department of the grocery hangs above the counter to my left. Ahead, three draped bodies lie atop guttered aluminum gurneys.

Doc Coblentz crosses to the nearest gurney and pulls down the sheet. Solomon

Slabaugh's face and shoulders loom into view. His skin is gray. Blue lips are stretched taut over yellow teeth. His left eyelid has come up, revealing a filmy eyeball that's rolled back, exposing the white of his eye. Though the bodies have been rinsed, the stench of manure mingles with the darker, sweeter stink of death, and I get a quivery sensation in my stomach.

"The bodies have been photographed and the clothing sealed in bags," the doctor begins.

"We'll want all the clothing and personal effects sent to the BCI lab," I tell him.

"I figured you would. I'll have everything couriered immediately." The doctor tugs the sheet down a few more inches and smoothes the fold. "Because of the manure contamination, I had to rinse the bodies before my preliminary external examination."

"So we may have lost hair or fiber," I venture.

"I'm sorry, Kate, but I had no way of knowing at that point that we might have been looking at foul play." Doc Coblentz looks at me over the tops of his glasses. "It wasn't until after I'd rinsed the bodies that I noticed the contusion." He moves to the head of the victim, turns it to one side so that the back of the head is visible from where we stand. Solomon Slabaugh's hair is still wet and sticks to his scalp like a greasy cap.

"How can you tell there was bleeding, since his body was immersed in liquid manure?" I ask.

"There was a good bit of blood that coagulated and matted in the hair at the back of his head. He was facedown, so that area was not completely immersed. The amount of bleeding indicates the contusion occurred before death. But it was initially difficult to detect." Using his fingers, Doc Coblentz separates the hair. "See here?"

I see a white scalp and the red-black fissure of an open wound.

"There's bruising here." Using a cotton-tipped swab, he indicates the scalp surrounding the wound. "Some of the purpling could have occurred postmortem. But there's enough bleeding and bruising present for me to safely say the trauma occurred while he was still alive."

"Any idea what might have made that sort of wound?" Glock asks.

I glance at Glock, to find him staring down at the corpse with the rapt attention of a kid working on some fascinating science project. He's one of those people who can remove himself from the emotional aspect of almost any situation. He keeps his cool, doesn't get angry or outraged. That's one of many traits that makes him such a good cop. I wish I could do the same. On the other hand, maybe my passion for the job is the instrument that drives me forward when it would be so much easier to quit.

"A blunt object, more than likely," the doc answers. "Probably quite heavy, or at least wielded with some force. Something sharp would have opened the flesh even more. The edges of the wound would be more cleanly cut. There would be less bruising. Less swelling." He crosses to a light box on the wall next to an overhead cabinet. "I suspected there might be some fracturing, so I took the liberty of taking an X-ray." Moving to the counter, he picks up a film and takes it to the wall-mounted illuminator. He flips on the light, then shoves the film beneath the ledge.

A monochrome image of Solomon Slabaugh's skull materializes. Taking a pen from his lab coat, the coroner indicates the upper-rear section of the skull. "You can see here that there's a break in the outline of the parietal vault. See this small crescent?"

Glock and I move closer. I find myself squinting. Though the image is slightly blurred, I can make out the minute indentation in the curvature of the skull. "A fracture?" I ask.

He smiles, as if I'm an astute pupil who's pleased him with the correct answer to a difficult question. "It's a fracture of the right parietal bone. There's also an acute extradural hematoma. The convexity here displaced the brain matter, producing the small crescent."

I stare at the image. "Is it possible this could have happened a while back? Maybe he fell or was in some kind of accident and didn't realize he had a fracture?"

The doc shakes his head. "This injury would likely have caused a concussion. There would have been pain. Confusion. Nausea. Possibly even unconsciousness. Of course, I'll know more once I open the cranium and examine the brain. But I'm ninety-nine percent certain this injury occurred very shortly before his death."

"Are we talking minutes? Hours?"

He shrugs. "I can't say for certain. My best guess would be a matter of minutes."

"Is it what killed him?" Glock asks.

"I can't rule on COD until I complete the autopsy."

The three of us stare down at the body. Above us, the buzz of the fluorescent lights seems inordinately loud. "Is it possible he struck the back of his head on the concrete wall of the pit when he fell in?"

"At first glance, I surmised the same scenario." The doctor gives me a look that tells me there's a gotcha moment on the way. "Then I discovered this." Lowering the sheet, he lifts the dead man's right hand.

The skin is gray and mottled. The fingers are clawlike; several fingernails are broken to the quick, as if he'd tried to claw his way out of the pit. Disturbing images scratch at my brain, but I quickly bank them. Then I notice the small red-black mouth of a cut on one of the fingers and I feel myself go still inside.

"Those three fingers are broken," the doc says. "At first, I thought perhaps it had happened during the fall."

"That seems like a logical train of thought," Glock says.

"Until I looked at the X-rays." The doc picks up another film and takes it to the X-ray illuminator. He removes the first film, jams the second one into place.

I stare at the film. Even with my proletarian eye, I see clearly that three of the four finger bones are broken at the same general point.

Glock asks the obvious question. "So what

caused the fractures?"

The doctor picks up the dead man's hand. "The index, middle, and ring fingers are fractured," he says. "The breaks are clean, with little or no chipping. As you can see, the flesh of the index finger has been incised, as well." The doc looks at me over the tops of his bifocals. "I would say this man was hanging onto the side of the pit and someone struck his fingers with a relatively sharp object."

"Causing him to fall to his death," Glock says.

"That would be my guess," Doc Coblentz replies.

A horrific sight flashes in my mind's eye. A man fighting to save himself from certain death. Someone else making damn sure he didn't succeed.

I look at Glock, and I know we're both wondering the same thing. "Would a boot or shoe have done it?" I ask.

"This type of injury would require a relatively sharp object or, at the very least, something heavy."

"Murder straight up," Glock says.

"Is it possible he was hanging on to the side of the pit until the weight of his body broke his fingers?" I ask.

"That's a good question, Kate, but the

answer is no. That kind of stress would not cause this type of fracture. It certainly wouldn't have opened the flesh. Had this man been hanging on to the side of the pit with his fingers for any length of time, the metacarpophalangeal joint might have eventually dislocated, causing him to lose his grip. As you can see, the joints are intact."

I nod, but my mind is reeling. I can't fathom someone killing an Amish father in such a cold-blooded manner. "Did you find anything unusual with the other two victims?"

"Not during the prelim exam."

"How soon can you finish the autopsies?" I ask.

"I'll need at least a couple of hours per body."

I nod, but I'm deeply troubled by these new developments. "In that case, we'll get out of your hair. Thanks for the heads-up." I start toward the door.

I hear Glock behind me as I leave the autopsy suite. In the alcove, I yank off my gown and gear and toss everything into the biohazard receptacle. I hear Glock doing the same, but I don't look at him. I don't want him to see the emotions banging around inside me: outrage, anger, a keen

86

sense of injustice. Contrary to popular belief, those kinds of emotions are not a cop's best friend, particularly if you're female and trying to maintain some semblance of credibility. But when I think about the four orphaned children, the emotions swamp me all over again.

It's still raining when we leave through the Emergency Services exit. Neither of us bothers with a hood this time. In the face of such a brutal act of murder, petty discomforts seem enormously inconsequential.

By the time I yank open the door of the Explorer and slide inside, I've gotten myself under control.

"Pretty damn cold-blooded," Glock comments as he slides in beside me.

"We need to talk to those kids." I shove the key into the ignition.

"You think they saw something?"

"Or someone."

"If that's the case, why didn't they mention it?"

"Maybe we didn't ask the right questions." I think back to my interview with them and shake my head. "I didn't ask them specifically if they'd seen anyone else at the scene."

"Still, you'd think they'd have mentioned it."

"True. But they had an awful lot to deal with. They'd just lost their parents and uncle. They were upset and not thinking clearly."

"Or scared," he adds.

Considering all the implications of that, I shove the Explorer into gear and start down the lane toward the road. "Only one way to find out."

CHAPTER 5

John Tomasetti unpacked the last moving box, set the framed commendation on his desk, and looked around at his new digs. The office was bigger than most — big enough to piss off some of the more senior agents. A window looked out over the new-ish business park dotted with winter-dead Bradford pear trees. The rosewood desk had a matching credenza with a hutch. There was a comfortable leather chair with adjust-able lumbar support. Not bad for a guy who, a year ago, had been on his way out the door.

John had tried to be optimistic about the move from the Bureau of Criminal Identifi-cation and Investigation headquarters in Columbus to the smaller field office in Richfield, near Cleveland. This was another chance for a fresh start, replete with a new office, new work environment, new supervi-sor. All of those things were nice perks. But the truth of the matter was, none of them had impacted his decision to make the move. The real reason was solely jurisdictional — so he could continue working Coshocton and Holmes counties. He didn't have a particular fondness for either county. What he did have a fondness for was a certain chief of police.

The truth of the matter was, he hadn't wanted to go back to Cuyahoga County. Hadn't wanted to go anywhere near Cleveland. Too many memories there. Too many mistakes. Too much of everything, and all of it was bad. Yet here he was. . . .

Three years had passed since his wife and two children were murdered. They'd been tough years — the kind that could break a man if he let it. John had skated close to that dark edge a couple of times, done a lot of things he wasn't proud of. He'd spent a year addicted to prescription drugs — anti-anxiety medications, painkillers, sleeping pills. If the doctors had prescribed them, John had obliged by taking them with the glee of a suicidal junkie. Somehow, he'd always managed to wake up the next morning.

And then there was the small matter of the retribution he'd doled out a few months after the murders. Everyone knew he'd done it — his fellow cops, the Cuyahoga County district attorney, his friends. But cops make the best criminals, and when the grand jury came back after five hours of deliberation, they'd handed down a no bill, and John Tomasetti had walked away a free man.

He'd come a long way since those dark days. He'd left Cleveland, left the Cleveland Division of Police, and landed a position as special agent with the great state of Ohio in Columbus. He'd cut out the pills and most of the booze. He was down to seeing the company shrink just one evening per week now. Tomasetti was on the road to recovery, with the fragile hope of, if not happiness, at least a normal life. He figured it was the best a man like him could shoot for.

He'd just opened his laptop to check e-mail when a tap on the door drew his attention. He looked up, to see Deputy Superintendent Lawrence Bates step into his office. "I like what you've done with the place."

Since he hadn't done shit except haul in boxes and clutter things up, Tomasetti smiled. "I have a knack."

Bates slid into a chair, leaned forward, and set his elbows on his knees. He was a tall, lanky man of about fifty who smoked like a chimney, drank like a fish, and somehow still managed to run six miles a day. He was married, with two college-age kids and a couple of Labrador retrievers. He'd come over to BCI from the FBI office in Dallas, Texas, six years ago. Rumor had it that he'd had an affair with his administrative assistant. Things had gotten ugly when his wife found out, and she'd given him an ultimatum. Larry had chosen his marriage over the bimbo and made the move to Cleveland. He looked like a man who'd been paying for his transgressions ever since.

"I understand you've spent some time in Holmes and Coshocton counties in the last year," Bates says.

John thought of Kate and smiled. "I'm familiar with the area."

Eleven months ago, he and Kate had worked a serial murder case in Painters Mill. It was a brutal case. They'd spent some intense days together, butted heads a few times, and somehow forged a friendship that had, so far, withstood the test of time. Looking back, Tomasetti realized that the Slaughterhouse Killer case and, more specifically, his relationship with Kate, had probably saved not only his career but his life.

"You have a pretty good working relationship with the local law-enforcement agencies down there?" Bates asked.

"I do."

"This came in this morning." Bates handed him a blue sheet of paper, which John recognized as a Request for Assistance form. "I spoke with Sheriff Rasmussen down in Millersburg. He tells me there's been a string of hate crimes in the area in the last six months."

"Hate crimes?" John knew from experience most were against minorities: African-Americans, Hispanics, Jews, and gay men. "Against who?"

"The Amish."

"That's a twist." But John knew hate for the sake of hate had no boundaries. Vaguely, he recalled that Kate had told him about several incidents. "Doesn't that fall under the FBI's jurisdiction?"

"Hate crimes are against the law whether it's on a state or federal level. Since we got the call, we show up." Bates continued: "Rasmussen tells me there've been half a dozen incidents. Started out with a few bashed mailboxes. The usual kind of thing you see in small towns. Then a couple of weeks ago, someone ran a buggy off the road. A pregnant Amish woman was injured, lost her baby."

Tomasetti picked up the RFA form and

skimmed the particulars. "Any of the vics press charges?"

"Not a one."

"So even if we catch the perpetrators, we basically have nothing."

"We have you."

"Because I have such a charismatic and persuasive personality?"

Bates chuckled. "Because you know Chief Burkholder."

John wondered if someone had it written down in some file that he and Kate were sleeping together.

"I understand she was born Amish," Bates said, clarifying.

"That's what I've heard."

"I thought she might be able to persuade some of these Amish to come forward, press charges, and testify, if we get that far."

"If anyone can do it, Kate can. She's . . . determined."

A picture of Kate materialized in his mind — not the cop, but the woman. She was girl-next-door pretty, with big brown eyes and a sprinkling of freckles over her nose. She kept her brown hair cut a tad too short — when she bothered having it cut at all. She wasn't beautiful in the classic sense, but she was attractive as hell. And she appealed to Tomasetti on a level that went a lot deeper than the flesh.

Working with her again would be no hardship. He and Kate worked well together. Better than well, if he wanted to be honest. It had been over two months since he'd seen her, and he'd been looking for an excuse to drive down to Painters Mill. Last time he was there, they'd closed a difficult murder case. An Amish family gunned down in their home. The case had taken a heavy toll on Kate. He'd been wanting to check up on her.

Leaning back in his chair, John looked around the room. "When do I leave?"

Bates glanced at his watch. "How about five minutes ago?"

The sky hovers low and ominous when I turn into the long gravel lane of the Slabaugh farm. The rain has stopped, but I know there's more coming, probably in the form of freezing rain. It's late afternoon, but the temperature has already begun a precipitous drop. To make matters worse, the storm clouds that have been building to the west most of the afternoon are creeping this way. Welcome to northeastern Ohio in December.

Bishop Troyer's buggy is still parked in the gravel near the back door of the house.

Two additional buggies are parked near the barn, and I know friends and neighbors of the Slabaugh family are taking care of the livestock, mucking and feeding and doing what needs to be done to keep the farm and up and running until decisions can be made. I know I'll find the women inside with the children, comforting them with food, prayer, and reassuring words.

None of that makes what I have to do next any easier. The barn is now a crime scene, off-limits to everyone until it's been processed and any evidence removed. More than likely, the pigs will have to be loaded onto a stock trailer and hauled away. Another disruption to four lives that have already been devastated.

"Scene is probably going to be pretty trampled," Glock says.

"I'll call Tomasetti and request a CSU." I look at the barn, aware of gossamer snowflakes melting on the windshield. "We need to get it taped off. Talk to someone about getting the pigs hauled away."

"What are we going to do about the kids?"

Thinking about the four children inside, I sigh. I can't put off calling for a social worker much longer.

"I hate to see them uprooted or separated." I kill the engine and punch off the lights. "But I'm going to have to contact Children Services."

"Can't the Amish take care of them until Slabaugh is cleared?"

I nod. "If he's cleared."

"He a suspect?"

The thought makes me feel slightly nauseous. "Let's just say he's a person of interest."

"Got it."

I give him a look as I reach for the door. "Let's get the barn taped off."

At the rear of the Explorer, I open the hatch and pull out my crime-scene kit. There's not much to it — just a box of disposable gloves, several pair of shoe covers, yellow crime-scene tape, a sketch pad and notebook, evidence bags, a dozen tiny cone evidence markers, a couple of inexpensive field-test kits — for cocaine and crystal meth — and a digital camera.

"Going to be a tough scene to process," Glock comments.

He's right. The place has literally been trampled — by the fire department volunteers, the police and paramedics, whoever has been caring for the livestock. "We're not going to find much."

"Whatever we do find is contaminated."

"Won't do us much good if this ever goes

97

to court."

The big door still stands open, someone's attempt to air the place out. The smells of hogs, hay, barn dust, and manure greet us like an offensive old adversary when we walk inside. The barn is filled with deep shadows. Looking around, I spot a lantern hanging from a rafter, pull it down, and light the wick.

Setting my crime-scene kit on the wood windowsill, I open it and hand disposable gloves and shoe covers, the crime-scene tape, and adhesive tape to Glock. "Let's get it taped off."

"A little late for shoe covers and gloves."

"Gotta treat it like a crime scene from here on out." I look around. "Keep your eyes open for anything that might have been used as a weapon."

"Will do."

Quickly, we don the protective gear. While he strings crime-scene tape, I cross to the livestock pens and look around. Someone put the hogs outside, but I can hear them grunting and slopping around in the mud beyond the door. The concrete is slick with muck, both liquid and solids. The smell is overpowering. It strikes me that the pit will need to be emptied, all of its contents gone through. Some lucky BCI agent isn't going to have a very good couple of days.

I lift the gate latch. The steel groans when I push it open and enter the pen. A hundred or more cloven hoofprints mar the thick sheet of mud. I see human footwear marks with a dozen different treads, and I curse myself for not having been more careful. Looking at the destroyed crime scene, I tell myself there was no way any of us could have known. Still, some caution might have given us a better chance of finding something useful in terms of evidence.

Vaguely, I'm aware of Glock stringing tape a few yards away, the wind hissing through the open door behind him, sleet tapping like delicate fingernails against the glass panes. I grew up on an Amish farm. Being here brings back a lot of memories of my own childhood. We raised cattle for beef, but we also had horses, chickens, and several goats. We farmed corn, soybeans, and wheat. Our barn was much like this one: old, but built to last. The manure pit was smaller, but the concept was the same. I was a tomboy and spent many hours exploring the barn with my brother, Jacob. *Datt* always left the grate over the pit. I made my sister, Sarah, cry once when I told her there were monsters living in the muck. I never thought of it as an instrument of murder.

I walk the perimeter of the pen. I'm not sure what I'm looking for. Something that seems out of place. You never know when something that initially appears mundane will become a piece of evidence. Spotting a pair of leather work gloves on the window-sill, I remove the camera from my pocket and snap four shots from different angles. I do the same with a two-pound coffee can someone probably used to measure feed. I snap two more photos of a big pocketknife that was probably used to cut hay twine. Next, I take a dozen shots of the manure pit from different angles. This is the first step in documenting the scene. Once the CSU arrives, every movable object will be bagged and sent to the lab for examination.

Lowering the camera, I spot a snow shovel leaning against the far wall. The blade is caked with dried muck and I realize it was probably being used to shovel solids into the pit. I think of Solomon Slabaugh's head wound and realize a shovel would make a pretty good weapon. Stepping back, I snap half a dozen photos. I put the camera in my pocket and squat next to the shovel to examine the blade. A quiver goes through me when I see hair on the back of the scoop. "Shit."

"Do you mean that literally or figuratively?"

I nearly start at the sound of Glock's voice. Rising, I glance over at him and motion toward the shovel. "There's hair on the blade. Looks human."

"Murder weapon?"

"Maybe." I bend for a closer look at the hair. "Definitely not from a pig."

He approaches and squats next to me. "Same color as Solomon Slabaugh's."

I'm tempted to put some of the hair in an evidence bag for safekeeping, then decide to let the CSU handle it — mostly for chain-of-evidence reasons. Straightening, I sigh, thinking of the children. As much as I hate the idea of subjecting them to another interview, they're my best bet at getting my hands on some solid information. "I've got some garbage bags in my kit. Bag the shovel. See what else you can find and mark it."

"You got it."

Rising, I start toward the gate that will take me out of the pen. "I'm going to talk to the kids."

"You want me to go with you?"

Snapping off my gloves, I toss them into a trash can, then stop and turn to him. If we weren't dealing with Amish kids, I might take him up on the offer. But I don't want to overwhelm or intimidate them. "The fewer non-Amish people present, the more likely they'll be to open up."

"Gotcha."

"You want the bad news?"

"Lay it on me."

"I'm going to need you to stay here and keep the scene secure until the CSU arrives."

"No problem." He pats the coat pocket where he keeps his cell phone. "Just give a call if you need anything."

"Thanks, Glock."

I go through the door and into the cold. A strong west wind buffets me as I head up the sidewalk toward the house, and I huddle deeper into my coat, wishing I'd put on a few more layers. At the back door, I knock and wait. A moment later, a tall, thin Amish woman I've never met answers. She's wearing a blue print dress with a black apron, the requisite *kapp,* opaque hose, and well-worn black shoes. I show her my badge. "I need to speak with the children."

She doesn't look happy to see me, even less happy with my request. I'm relieved when she opens the door and ushers me inside. *"Sitz dich anne."* Sit down.

The smells of coffee and cinnamon titillate my olfactory nerves as I step inside.

Heat from the kerosene stove warms my face. A second woman stands at the kitchen sink, washing dishes. She turns as I sit at the table, nods a greeting, then returns her attention to her task. Being here in this Amish kitchen brings back memories. Growing up, I spent countless hours sitting at a big table just like this one while my *mamm* fussed at the stove, and I feel an uncharacteristic jab of melancholy for things lost. Not because I want to be Amish, but because I know that once pieces of your past slip away, those pieces are gone forever, and there's no going back.

I think of my brother, Jacob, and my sister, Sarah, and for an instant I miss them so much, my chest aches. As children, we'd been close. Now they're strangers; it's been weeks since I've seen either of them. I have two nephews I barely know and a brand-new niece I've never met, mostly due to my own evasion. I don't know why I avoid them the way I do. To say it's complicated would be an understatement. As I sit at the table with the smells of an Amish house all around, I wonder if they're part of my lost past, or if they're part of a future I simply haven't been able to reach for yet.

"I'm Ellen."

I'm pulled from my thoughts to see the

thin woman who'd answered the door eyeing me suspiciously as she dries her hands on a towel. "Would you like coffee and pie?" she asks.

I wonder if she'd be offering these if she knew I'd once been Amish and that I'd been excommunicated for going on fourteen years now. "Coffee would be nice. Thank you."

She pours from an ancient-looking enamel pot and carries the cup to me. "The younger children are in their room, sleeping," she says. "They have had a very trying day."

I pick up the cup and sip. "What about Mose?"

"Wait." She disappears into the living room. A moment later, Bishop Troyer appears. He's a short man with bowed legs, a round belly, and thick gray hair that's blunt-cut above heavy brows. A salt-and-pepper beard hangs from his chin, reaching nearly to the waistband of his trousers. He's looked much the same since I was a child: old, but never seeming to age further.

He doesn't look happy to see me. "Chief Burkholder."

"I need to speak with the children," I say without preamble. "It's important."

He sighs as he crosses to the table and takes the chair across from me. "Katie, the children are grieving. They have been through much already this day."

"Solomon Slabaugh may have been murdered."

"Murdered?" The bishop recoils as if I'd splashed hot coffee in his face. "Solly? But I thought he fell into the pit. How can that be murder?"

I tell him about the head trauma. "I need to talk to the kids, Bishop Troyer. Right now."

The old man looks uncertain as he rises, as if he doesn't know what to make of this new information I've just thrown at him. "The three youngsters are in their rooms, sleeping. Mose is outside in the workshop with the men."

"Gather the younger kids for me." I take a reluctant last sip of coffee, then rise. "I'll speak to Mose first."

The bishop bows his head slightly, then disappears into the living room.

Leaving my coffee and the warmth of the kitchen, I go back outside. The wind penetrates my parka as I make my way down the sidewalk. Midway to the barn, I turn left toward a newish steel building, noticing for the first time the dull glow of lantern light in the windows. The sky is even darker now, the gray clouds to the west approach-

105

ing like some vast army. There's no snow yet, but I can smell it — that cold, thick scent that tells me we're about to get dumped on.

I open the steel door of the workshop and find a single lantern burning atop a workbench. The air smells of kerosene and freshly sawed wood. Two Amish men sporting insulated coveralls and full beards stand in the circle of golden light, talking to Mose. The three males eye me with unconcealed suspicion as I approach.

"Hello," I say, but my focus is on Mose. Even in the poor lighting, he looks pale and troubled and unbearably sad.

Looking away, he mumbles something I don't quite hear.

I nod a greeting at the two men. I've met them both at some point, but I don't recall their names. "Bishop Troyer said I'd find you here," I say to Mose. "I need to ask you a few questions about what happened this morning."

The boy glances at the other two men, as if hoping they'll intervene and send me packing. Of course, neither man does. Looking at Mose, I realize that the reality of everything he and his siblings face in the coming days and weeks and months is starting to hit home. He's apprehensive, sad, maybe a little scared.

"I know this is a tough time for you and your sister and brothers," I begin, trying to put him at ease. "But I need to go over some things with you that we didn't cover this morning."

He shoves his hands into his pockets. "Okay."

I want to speak with him away from the men. Not because I don't trust them, but because I know the Amish are as bad about spreading gossip as the English.

The workshop isn't large. Looking around, I see a dozen or so unfinished cabinet doors stacked neatly against the wall, and it strikes me that Solomon Slabaugh was also a cabinetmaker.

"Did your *datt* make these cabinets?" I ask.

Mose ventures closer to me, eyeing the cabinets. *"Ja."*

"He was very good."

"He liked to work with his hands."

"Did you help him?"

"I made the one on the left. It's red oak."

"It's nice. I like the wood grain." I walk to a half dozen intricately made Victorian-style birdhouses. "He make these, too?"

The boy glances uncertainly at the men, then follows me. *"Ja.* The mailboxes, too."

"They're really lovely."

We're standing about ten feet from the men now. It's the farthest away I can get him without being too obvious about getting him alone. "Are you doing okay?" I ask, lifting the roof of a birdhouse and peeking inside.

Shoving his hands into his pockets, he mumbles something that sounds like *yeah.*

"You feel up to answering a few questions?"

He fixes his gaze on me and I see him resign himself to dealing with me, dealing with whatever reason I'm here. "What is this about?" he asks.

"Did your *datt* and uncle Adam get along okay?" I say the words easily, but I'm watching Mose carefully now — his eyes, his body language, his hands.

He looks confused by the question for a moment, then shrugs. "They used to."

"What about recently?"

He shakes his head. "*Datt* wouldn't let Uncle Adam come over to see us."

"Why not?"

"Because he doesn't keep the faith."

"Did they ever argue?"

"Once or twice."

"What about?"

Mose doesn't want to answer; I see it in

his eyes. Amish roots run deep. Though his uncle has been excommunicated, Mose still wants to protect him. But the boy was raised Amish and taught from an early age to respect and obey his elders. "Us kids."

"Did Adam ever get angry?"

A lengthy pause ensues, then a reluctant "Sometimes."

"Did he ever threaten your *mamm* or *datt?*"

"No," he snaps.

"When's the last time you saw him?"

"I don't know. A long time, I think."

I move on to my next question. "What about your uncle Abel? Did he get along with your *datt?*"

"Sure. They got along. They were brothers. They loved each other."

"Did they ever argue?"

"Not that I know of."

"Any recent disagreements?"

"No." His brows go together. "Why are you asking me these things?"

I don't want to unjustly accuse the dead. But I know the possibility exists that the two brothers had some kind of confrontation before Rachael and the kids got to the barn. Abel could have struck Solomon with the shovel. They could have struggled and fallen to their deaths. Or maybe Abel pushed

Solomon into the pit, realized what he'd done, and then attempted a rescue, only to succumb to the methane gas and become a victim himself. It's a long shot, but I've been a cop long enough to know it's an avenue that needs exploring.

Ignoring Mose's question, I move to the next. "What about your *mamm* and *datt?* Were they having any kind of disagreement?"

He tosses me an indignant glare. "No."

"Did they argue?"

"*Mamm* and *Datt* never argued."

The Amish are a patriarchal society. Even so, at some point in their marriage, husbands and wives have disagreements. Generally speaking, Amish women have a strong voice when it comes to decision making, but males have the final say. "You sure about that? No disagreements at all?"

Shaking his head, he turns away and starts toward the two men. I snag his coat sleeve and stop him. In my peripheral vision, I see the two Amish men shift restlessly and exchange glances. "Did you see anyone else in or near the barn this morning?" I ask.

"I told you before. I din see no one."

The two Amish men are within earshot and stare at us with rapt attention. Turning my back to them, I pull my notebook from my coat. "Mose, I need for you to start at the beginning and tell me everything you remember, okay?"

He takes me through the same turn of events as he did this morning. "After Samuel came in screaming, *Mamm* and the rest of us ran to the barn. We were scared, because we knew something bad had happened. The first thing I noticed was that the barn door was open. I remember thinking *Datt* wouldn't leave the door open, because it was cold and he was always trying to keep the barn warm so the water wouldn't freeze."

Frustrated by the lack of new information, I sigh. "Is there anything else?"

His brows go together again, as if I've posed some complex math equation. "I don't think so." He looks at me, his brows knitting. "Do you think someone killed my *datt?*"

"I don't know," I say honestly. "But I promise you I'm going to find out."

Salome is fifteen years old and beautiful in the way that young girls are. She has huge eyes the color of a forest at dusk and a complexion the beauty industry has been trying to emulate for decades and never quite managed. Wearing a sky blue dress with a white apron and *kapp,* she sits at the kitchen table, looking as broken as a baby dove that's fallen from its nest.

Next to her, young Ike spoons hot cocoa into his mouth. Samuel stares down at his empty cup, one elbow on the table, resting his chin on his palm.

"I know you guys have had a rough day," I begin, "but I need to ask you some more questions about what happened this morning."

Ike looks up from his cocoa, the spoon sticking out of his mouth. "Did the English doctor bring back my *mamm?*" he asks around the spoon.

I'm not a big fan of kids in general. But this little guy is cute and sweet and moves me in a way I'm not accustomed to. Maybe it's because he's Amish, or maybe because the grief I see in his eyes is so damn pure. So *real.* The urge to go around the table and put my arms around his skinny shoulders is strong, but I don't. I'm afraid if I do, I'll feel something I can't afford to feel. "No, honey, he didn't. I'm sorry."

Taking the spoon from his mouth, he lowers his head and begins to cry.

Sitting next to him, Salome sets her hand on his shoulder. She's got pretty hands. They're soft and dimpled at the knuckles, like baby hands. I give them a moment, then move on to the purpose of my visit. "I wanted to go over a few things about this morning."

Salome raises her head. Her eyes find mine, and for an instant I'm taken aback by her natural beauty. "Things like what?"

I know how easy it is to plant thoughts in a young mind, so I phrase my questions carefully. Without prompting her, I need to know, in her own words, every detail of what happened this morning. "I want you to think back to this morning again for me. I want you to tell me everything that happened. Everything you saw or heard. Details, even if you think it's not important."

Salome pats her brother's back as if she were burping a baby, then folds her hands and stares down at them. The wash of pain over her features is so profound, I feel the same emotions knocking at the door to my own psyche.

Looking at her, I find myself thinking of my own life when I was her age. Until the age of fourteen, I was a typical Amish girl — happy, innocent, chock-full of a young girl's hopes and dreams. I had all of those things stripped away in the summer of my fourteenth year, when a man by the name of Daniel Lapp introduced me to violence.

By the time I was fifteen, Salome's age, I was well on my way to eternal damnation — drinking, smoking, making out with guys I barely knew. I even did some shoplifting at the local drugstore — cigarettes, nail polish, makeup; things I didn't need but couldn't seem to live without. I got into a lot of trouble in my fifteenth year, and most of the time I didn't get caught.

The contrasts between me and this girl are stark. Looking back, I don't think I was ever as innocent. As I stand here and wait for her to recount a scene no child should ever have to endure, I feel guilty because I know I'm at least partly responsible for the death of her innocence. I don't let that keep me from asking the questions that need to be asked.

"We were just sitting around the table, waiting for our scrapple," she tells me. "We were hungry, waiting for Samuel to come in with *Datt* and Uncle Abel so we could say our before-meal prayer and eat." She picks at a nail with intense concentration. "Then all of a sudden, Samuel came in, screaming. At first, I thought he was playacting, like he does sometimes. But *Mamm* got scared. She grabbed him and asked him what was wrong, and I knew something terrible had happened."

"What happened next?" I ask, pressing her.

"We ran outside. I remember seeing that the barn door was open. *Datt* never left it open. He scolded us when we did. There was lantern light inside. We ran to the barn."

"Why do you think the barn door was open?"

"I don't know."

"Did you see anyone else?"

She shakes her head. "It was just us kids. And *Mamm*."

"Was anything out of place?" I ask.

"Not that I recall."

"Did you see any vehicles? Or buggies?"

"No, but I wasn't really looking or paying attention. We were just so scared." She looks at me as if she's somehow failed me, then shakes her head. "I'm sorry."

"It's okay." I smile to reassure her. "You did good."

I can tell by the way her eyes slide away from mine that she doesn't believe me. She may be only fifteen years old, but she knows these are not idle questions.

I query Ike and Samuel, but aside from the barn door being left open, neither boy remembers seeing anything out of place. In the backwaters of my mind, I find myself thinking of Adam Slabaugh, the estranged uncle, and I can't help but wonder if he wanted a relationship with his niece and his nephews badly enough to kill for it.

I spend the next ten minutes going through every detail of the morning again, step by terrible step. But the kids are unable to offer anything new. I'm in the process of tucking my notebook into my pocket when another line of questioning occurs to me. "Did your *datt* ever hire anyone to help him around the farm?"

Salome nods. "Once or twice. He preferred to do the work himself, but sometimes it was too much for him and he would hire someone, when he had money to pay or goods to trade."

"Who did he hire?"

"I don't know their names." She lifts her shoulders. "Men or boys in need of work."

"Were they Amish or English?"

"Amish, mostly. Except one time he hired an *Englischer*."

I look at the boys. "Do any of you remember the names of the people your *datt* hired?"

Two heads shake in unison.

I move on to my next question. "Did your parents keep money in the house?" It wouldn't be the first time some day laborer decided stealing money was easier than working for it and turned on his employer.

The two boys defer to their older sister. "*Datt* kept some paper bills in a canning jar in the basement," she says.

I rise. "Can you show me?"

"Sure. I know exactly where it is." She gets to her feet. "You think one of the workers came back to steal the money?"

"I think it's worth checking."

I feel the Amish women's eyes burning into my back as Salome takes me to the mudroom. They don't trust me; they want me to leave the children alone. I wish I could, but at the moment, these kids are my best source of information.

The mudroom is a large, drafty room with half a dozen windows and a plywood floor. A defunct potbellied stove squats in the corner, its door hanging open like a slack mouth. Behind it, an ancient hunting rifle with a glossy wood stock leans against the wall.

"It's always cold in the mudroom," Salome says with a shiver.

In the dim winter light creeping in from the windows, I see that her hair is very shiny. I'm so close, I can smell the clean scent of it, see the soft perfection of her skin. Lifting a lantern from the sill next to the door, she lights the wick. "It's dark in the cellar. Watch your step."

The door creaks when she opens it. The odors of damp earth and rotting wood fill my nostrils as we descend the steps. Cold and darkness embrace me like strong, icy hands. Holding the lantern in front of her, Salome leads me into the bowels of the house. The basement is divided into several rooms with low ceilings, which make me feel slightly claustrophobic.

"I heard the women talking," she says as we enter the next room. "They said you used to be Amish. Is that true?"

I walk beside her, hoping I don't trip over some unseen object. "A long time ago," I reply.

I see curiosity in her eyes, the same kind of curiosity I felt when I was her age. The only difference is that hers is innocent; mine was not.

"Did you do something wrong?" she asks.

"I did a lot of things wrong."

"Like what?"

I don't have a canned answer ready for a question that's so far-reaching, especially for an innocent. "It's complicated," I say, hedging.

She appears to struggle with her next question, but in the end curiosity wins. "I heard you disobeyed the *Ordnung* and that

118

Bishop Troyer put you under the *bann*."

"I wasn't baptized," I tell her. "I decided to leave."

"What did you do?"

"I made a lot of mistakes."

"Oh." She considers that for a moment. "Bishop Troyer is mean sometimes."

"He's a good bishop."

She bites her lip, thinking. "Didn't you miss your *mamm* and *datt?* Your sisters and brothers?"

I still miss them, a whisper inside me replies, but I don't give it voice. "I missed them a lot."

"If you missed them, why didn't you confess your sins and stay? How could you leave them?"

How could I, indeed? It's a question I've asked myself a thousand times over the years. My answer is always the same: "I didn't have a choice."

Her eyes flick to mine. In their depths I see the burn of curiosity. I can tell she wants to ask me about my transition from Amish to English. But Salome is too well mannered to pry any more deeply than she already has.

"I think about what it would be like sometimes," she says after a moment.

"The grass isn't always greener on the

other side of the fence."

Tossing me a sideways look, she laughs. "That's a funny way to put it."

Because I don't want to encourage her one way or another, I say nothing.

Our feet are silent on the damp earthen floor as she takes me to a wall of shelving filled with dusty canning jars. Each is meticulously labeled: PEARS, APPLES, BEETS, GREEN BEANS, SAUSAGE, RHUBARB. I watch as she moves aside a jar and pulls one from the back. Unscrewing the lid, she peeks inside. "Oh no!"

"What is it?"

Eyes wide and searching, she shoves the open mason jar at me so I can look inside. "*Datt's* money. It's gone. Someone took it!"

I mentally kick myself for having let her pick up the jar. "Set it down, Salome. I'm going to take the jar and have it processed for prints." Even in the dim light, I can see recent smudges in the dust. Fingerprints, maybe. Damn. Damn. Damn.

She looks distressed as she places the jar back on the shelf. "Who would do such a thing? How did they get down here in the cellar without us seeing them?"

"I don't know." I think about that a moment. "Do you know how much money was in there?"

She shakes her head. "I wouldn't even know it was here if I hadn't seen *Datt* drop in some money when I was getting sausage for *Mamm*."

"When's the last time you saw it?"

She traps her lower lip with her teeth. "I don't know. I never pay attention."

I pull a pair of latex gloves from my coat pocket, slip them on. I don't have an evidence bag with me, but I pick up the jar anyway, decide to carry it out to the Explorer to bag it.

Salome turns wide eyes on me. "Whoever stole the money," she begins. "Did they kill my *mamm* and *datt* and Uncle Abel, too?"

I look down at her, shocked that her mind had already made the leap. She stares back at me, her expression as guileless as a child's. The lantern casts pin lights in her eyes. "I don't know, honey, but I'm going to find out."

She blinks back tears, and for an instant her grief turns to anger. "I don't understand why this had to happen. If someone needed money, *Datt* would have given it to them."

"These kinds of crimes never make any sense," I tell her. But even to me, the words sound like a practiced understatement. She deserves a better answer. Because there isn't one, I sigh and motion toward the stairs.

"Come on. Let's go."

Mose is sitting at the table when we return to the kitchen. Salome takes her place at the table and puts her face in her hands. As if knowing something has changed, the younger children stare at her, wondering about the tears. They look up to her, I realize. And in that moment, I vow to do everything in my power to keep them from being separated.

I remain standing. "If any of you remember anything about the men who worked for your *datt,* let me know, okay?"

The request elicits four blank stares. After a while, Mose perks up. "The *Englischer* had a white dog. I remember because it killed one of our chickens."

"What kind of dog?"

"It was a mongrel. Small. With wiry hair."

I make a mental note to canvass the area and ask about any day laborers with white dogs. "Did your *datt* keep records? Write things down?"

Three heads shake in unison. Samuel pipes up with a solution. "Do you want us to look for his papers?" When I look at him, he smiles. He's anxious to help, the kind of child who likes to please. He stares at me with the most innocent blue eyes I've ever seen. He's got a smudge of dirt on his cheek, freckles on his nose. His lashes are still wet from an earlier cry. Before realizing I'm going to touch him, I lean forward and run my fingers through his mussed hair. "Thank you, Samuel, but I'll have one of my officers do it," I say.

My heart turns over in my chest when he smiles. The emotions running through me are so powerful, I take a step back, closer to the door. "You guys did good," I say after a moment. "Thanks for all your help."

One of the Amish women approaches the table with a dishcloth in her hand, gives me a firm look, and then addresses the children. "Supper's ready," she says softly. "Go wash your hands."

Knowing that's my cue to leave — or escape, I'm not sure which — I turn and start for the door. I may not be able to bring back these kids' parents, but the one thing I can do is find the son of a bitch who killed them.

CHAPTER 6

I'm still thinking about the children when I climb into the Explorer, bag the mason jar, and start down the gravel lane. Their pain is palpable, and my meeting with them has left me feeling uncharacteristically bleak. Maybe it's because I know that even if I solve the case — and I have every intention of doing so — it won't bring back their parents. No matter what I do, three lives have been lost forever. Four other young lives have been irrevocably changed. This is one of those times when justice will make for a very cold bedfellow.

A cast-iron sky spits sleet pellets against the windshield as I turn onto the township road and head toward town. I flip on the wipers and defroster, then grab my cell and dial T.J.

"Hey, Chief, what's up?"

I tell him about the day laborer and the missing cash. "I want you to recanvass the farms around the Slabaugh place. Find out if anyone remembers seeing someone. See if you can come up with a name."

"Will do."

"One of the men who worked for Slabaugh supposedly had a white dog with him. Ask about that, too. Can you give Skid a call and get him out to the Slabaugh place? I want him to look around for any kind of records Solly Slabaugh might have kept. If we can get the names of the men he hired, we might catch a break."

"Sure thing." T.J. pauses. "Where are you?"

"I'm on my way to the station." I ring off and dial the switchboard.

My daytime dispatcher, Lois, answers with a high-speed utterance: "Painters Mill PD!"

"You sound busy," I say.

"That's kind of an understatement, Chief. Phones are ringing off the dang hook. Folks asking about the Slabaughs."

I know from experience that the volume of calls will double once word gets out that we may be dealing with a triple murder. "Media catch wind of it yet?"

"Steve Ressler has called a couple of times, looking for you. *Columbus Dispatch* is sending a reporter. *Ohio Farm Journal* is going to do a piece on the dangers of methane gas. And a couple of radio stations have called."

Ressler is the publisher of Painters Mill's weekly newspaper, the *Advocate*. He's a pushy, type-A bully who has a difficult time accepting the words *no comment*. "Tell them I'll have a press release this afternoon."

"Sure thing."

"Patch me through to Pickles, will you?"

"Yup. Hang on."

A click sounds and then Pickles growls his name. That's when I remember he covered for Skid last night and probably hasn't slept for twenty-four hours. "You feel up to a little overtime?" I ask.

"I don't think it will kill me," he replies.

I'm glad to hear the humor in his voice. We're going to need all the humor we can muster in the coming days. "I need you to run Adam Slabaugh's name through LEADS for me." LEADS is the acronym for the law enforcement automated data system police departments used to check for outstanding warrants.

"That's a mighty interesting request, since this was an accident."

"Doc Coblentz is pretty sure it wasn't."

"I'll be damned." I hear computer keys clicking. "You on your way in?"

"I'm almost there."

A few minutes later, I pull into my reserved spot next to Lois's Cadillac. I push through the front door and see her at her workstation, the phone pasted to her ear. She pirouettes in her chair and shoves a handful of message slips at me. "You've got two messages from Sheriff Rasmussen. John Tomasetti called twice. And Pickles wants to talk to you."

A small thrill runs the length of me at the mention of Tomasetti, but I quickly tamp it down. I'm not accustomed to the feeling, and it unsettles me. It's been a couple of months since I last saw him. I've been thinking about calling him, but I always find a reason not to. I'm sure some shrink would tell me I have commitment issues. He would probably be right. I warned Tomasetti that a relationship with me wasn't going to be a walk in the park. He doesn't seem to mind, so things have worked out just fine so far.

I take the messages from Lois, shuffle through them, decide to call Rasmussen first. He's the interim sheriff for Holmes County, appointed last year after former sheriff Nathan Detrick tried to kill me during the Slaughterhouse Killer investigation. He's serving a life sentence in the Mansfield Correctional Institution, about eighty miles southwest of Cleveland. A good place for a man who tortured and killed over twenty women.

I've met Sheriff Rasmussen several times since he was appointed. A former sheriff's deputy from Canton, he's low-key and no-nonsense, two personality traits I greatly admire, especially when it comes to small-town politics. City and county law-enforcement agencies work together closely here in Painters Mill. The sheriff's office has a small budget and pretty much runs on a skeleton crew. We pick up the slack, taking county as well as city calls. I'm wondering what prompted two phone calls in one day as I shrug out of my coat and head toward my office.

I get Rasmussen's voice mail and leave my cell number. Without hanging up, I dial Tomasetti. I get voice mail there, too, so I leave a message. Sighing, I vaguely wonder if they're talking to each other. After checking e-mail, I snag my coat and head toward Pickles' cubicle. I catch him coming out, a cup of coffee in hand. "Anything on Slabaugh?" I can tell by his expression that he found something.

"Two years ago, Adam Slabaugh was arrested on a domestic."

"Well, that's interesting. Conviction?"

"Charges were dropped."

"Who was the complainant?"

Pickles offers a "cat that swallowed the canary" grin. "Solomon Slabaugh."

"Nice work," I say, but my mind is racing. "Want to go talk to him?"

"I'm game."

Pickles ducks back into his cubicle, sets his cup on the desk, and grabs his parka. We're on our way to the door when Lois stands up and raises her hand like a traffic cop. "Whoa!"

Pickles and I simultaneously stop and turn.

Giving us the hand signal to wait, she finishes her call and disconnects. "Chief, I just took a call from Ricky Shingle. He was out on Sampson Road and saw a buggy on fire and a runaway horse."

The first scenario that comes to mind is a spilled kerosene heater or lantern. "Anyone hurt?"

"He didn't know."

"Where on Sampson Road?"

"At the Painters Creek bridge."

"Call the fire department. Get an ambulance out there, too. We're on our way." I look at Pickles. "I think Adam Slabaugh can wait."

"Me, too, Chief. Me, too."

■ ■ ■ ■

Dusk has fallen by the time we turn onto Sampson Road. It's a little-used dirt track that runs parallel to Painters Creek, crossing over the stream twice and then snaking north through a heavily wooded area that's prone to flooding in the spring.

Only one Amish family lives out this way, so I head directly to the Kaufman farm. I've met Mark and Liza Kaufman a handful of times over the years. They're a quiet couple with three teenage children. They're of the Old Order, devout, and they tend to avoid contact with the English as much as possible.

I don't have to go far to find what I'm looking for. At the mouth of the gravel lane, the charred remains of a four-wheel buggy on its side are smoldering in the bar ditch like a pile of firewood. A plume of gray-black smoke billows into the cold air. A few yards away, several Amish people stare at my vehicle as if I'm there to cart them off to jail.

"This ought to be interesting," Pickles remarks.

"That's one word for it." Hitting the emergency lights, I park the Explorer on the shoulder and we get out.

"How in the hell would a buggy catch on fire?" Pickles grumbles as we start toward the group.

"Maybe a lantern or heater tipped over." But I don't think that's what happened. Most Amish know all too well the dangers of fire and are cautious when handling flame or any kind of accelerant.

Winter-dead trees curl over the gravel lane like curved, arthritic fingers. In the distance, I hear the sirens of the fire department. I walk around a dozen or more hoof marks that are sunk deeply into the muddy ground — the kind of mark a terrified horse might make while trying to escape danger. I find myself hoping no one was seriously injured.

"Mr. Kaufman?" I call out when I'm a few yards from the group. "Is everyone okay?"

Mark Kaufman is a stern-looking man with shrewd, intelligent eyes and an angular face, which gives him a gaunt countenance. His steel-wool beard reaches nearly to his belt. He wears a black coat, a straw hat, and black work trousers. He stares at me with unconcealed displeasure as I approach.

"Is anyone hurt?" I ask, rephrasing my question.

When Kaufman doesn't answer, I look past him and make eye contact with his wife. Liza Kaufman looks to be ten or fifteen years younger than her husband. Clad in black winter clothes, she's a petite woman with anxious eyes and quick, nervous hands. She looks away, and I sigh.

I turn my attention back to Mark. "I got a call that there was an accident."

"We do not need the English police," he states.

"I need to know if anyone was hurt," I repeat.

"No." He bows his head. "We are fine."

"Chief, I've got blood here."

I turn at the sound of Pickles's voice and see him kneeling in the grass next to the gravel lane. I cross to him and look down at the area he's indicated. Sure enough, a dinner plate-size puddle of blood shimmers bright red against the yellow winter grass.

"Horse, maybe?" he asks.

I'm no expert on horses, but I spent a quite a bit of time around them as a girl. I know if the animal was scared, it was probably moving too fast to leave a puddle of blood that size. I look at Kaufman. "If someone got hurt here, they should get themselves checked out. There's an ambulance on the way."

"We do not need anything from you," Kaufman says. "We are fine."

Shaking my head, I cross to the buggy — what's left of it. It was originally black, with four wheels and a covered top. Not cheap by any stretch of the imagination. I can see where the harness leather snapped. The right shaft is broken as well, and I imagine the panicked horse, running full out, must have fallen at some point, struggled to its feet, and then broken free.

"Looks like a total loss." Pickles whistles. "I wonder if the horse got hurt."

"Probably ran up to the barn. That's what they do when they're scared."

Pickles picks up a good-size stick, begins poking around in the pile of smoldering wood and ash.

The crunch of tires on gravel drags my attention away from the wreckage. I turn to see a young man get out of a newish Ford Ranger pickup truck. He's thin, with long hair, buckteeth, and toothpick legs. "Everyone okay?" he asks me.

"Are you the one who called 911?" I ask.

"Yes, ma'am." He crosses to me and looks down at what's left of the smoldering buggy. "Damnedest thing I ever saw in my life."

"Did you see it happen?"

"Alls I seen was this crazy horse running down the road. I almost couldn't believe my eyes when I saw that buggy. I swear to

133

Jesus, flames was shooting twenty feet in the air. There was a couple of Amish folks in the buggy. They was yelling their heads off, and I knew straight away they was in trouble."

"Did you see it catch fire?"

He shakes his head. "It was already on fire and going pretty good when I saw it."

"What's your name?"

"Ricky Shingle. I live a couple miles down the road. I was on my way to work."

"Did you see anyone else?"

"I don't know if they was part of it, but a couple of young guys in a pickup truck just about ran me off the road."

My cop's radar goes on alert. "What direction were they going?"

"Same as the buggy, and they was movin' fast. They was left of center and, I swear to Jesus, I'd be wearing their teeth in my forehead if I hadn't driven into the ditch. Crazy shits. Probably high on whatever it is them youngins get high on these days."

"Chief!"

I look over my shoulder and see Pickles holding up the stick. On its tip, I see something that looks like the broken mouth of a mason jar. "Molotov cocktail, anyone?" he says.

Only then does the implication strike me.

Never taking my eyes from the jar, I cross to Pickles for a closer look. "You sure?" I ask.

"I seen enough of 'em in my day." He hefts the stick, brings the broken jar closer. "Fill it with gas. Use a piece of fabric for a fuse. Screw on the lid." He shrugs. "Crude, but effective as hell. I betcha one of them young guys threw it into that buggy."

The images that rush through my brain are vivid and disturbing. Outrage rattles through me. I spin back to Shingle. "Did you get a look at the young guys?"

He shakes his head. "Not really. They was just a couple of guys."

"Can you give me a description? Hair? Clothes?"

"Didn't really get a good look."

Pulling my pad from my pocket, I write, "Two Caucasian males. Young." "What about the vehicle?"

"A truck. Ford, I think. Blue. Or black, maybe. Didn't really get a good look at it. I couldn't take my eyes off that damn buggy. Thought the horse was going to go right through the fence."

I hit my lapel mike, then think better of it and grab my cell. This is one of those times when I wish I had more officers. At the moment, every member of my force is tied up with the Slabaugh case. I hit the speed dial for the station. "Lois, call the sheriff's office and tell them we need extra patrols out on Sampson Road. A couple of guys tossed a Molotov cocktail into a buggy."

"Roger that, Chief."

"Tell them to be on the lookout for a dark pickup truck. Possibly a Ford with two white males inside."

"You got it."

Sighing in frustration, I hit END and cross to Pickles. "Get a statement from Shingle. I'm going to see if I can get Kaufman to talk to me."

Pickles gives me a knowing look. "Good luck with that."

We both know Kaufman isn't going to co-operate. The Amish are sectarian and strive to remain separate from the rest of the world. Having grown up Amish, it's a mind-set I understand. As a cop, the lack of co-operation frustrates me to no end.

I walk over to Kaufman. "What happened?"

"We do not want your help," he responds.

"Please, Mr. Kaufman, I need to know who did this. If you could just give me a description of the vehicle."

He stares at me, his expression as hard and unmoved as a stone statue. "This is an

136

Amish matter and will be dealt with by us."

My father cited that very same phrase a thousand times when I was growing up. Even after all these years, those words still wield the power to send gooseflesh up my arms. When you're an Amish kid, you obey your parents without question. I learned early in life that such blind trust can come back to bite you in a very big way later in life.

Shaking off thoughts of the past, I frown at Kaufman. "I'm trying to help you," I say firmly. "Please. Work with me. Help me. You can't deal with this kind of violence alone. Sooner or later, someone's going to get hurt."

"God will take care of us."

A stinging retort teeters on the tip of my tongue. But I know losing my temper won't win me any points. Trying not to gnash my teeth, I step back and walk over to Liza Kaufman. She refuses to make eye contact with me, but the two teenage boys have no problem meeting my gaze. "Can one of you tell me what happened?"

"We want no involvement in this," says a tall blond boy. I guess him to be about fourteen years old. He wears a brown wool coat that looks at least two sizes too big, and has the sharp, intelligent eyes of his father.

"You're already involved, whether you like it or not."

He tightens his lips.

"Sticking your head in the sand is only going to make things worse."

When he has nothing to say about that, I skewer the second boy with a hard look. "What about you? Do you know who did this?"

He's older. Maybe sixteen. Tall and skinny, with huge feet he hasn't yet grown into. I can tell by the way his eyes skate away from mine that he takes after his mother. Less confrontational, but no less stubborn. "I do not wish to be involved," he tells me.

"You don't have to get involved. Just tell me what you saw, and I'll leave you alone."

"Enough!"

I look over my shoulder and see the elder Kaufman glaring at me. " 'Be ye not un-equally yoked together with unbelievers!' " his voice thunders. " 'For what fellowship hath righteousness with unrighteousness? What communion hath light with darkness?' "

Those two Bible passages epitomize the Amish view of separation from the rest of the world. I heard them many times as a child. It wasn't until I was a teenager that I began to question the whole idea of separateness. By the time I was eighteen, I knew I would never fit in.

I glare back at Kaufman. *"Mer sott em sei Eegne net verlosse; Gott verlosst die Seine nicht."*

For an instant, he looks taken aback. I can't tell if it's because of the words or my use of Pennsylvania Dutch, but his uncertainty doesn't last. Bringing his hands together sharply, he motions toward the house. "I've said my piece." He looks toward his wife and sons. "There's work to be done."

I stand in the lightly falling sleet and watch the family walk away. Frustration is a knot in my chest. For the span of several minutes, Pickles and I don't speak. It's so quiet, I can hear the sleet hitting the trees and the dry leaves on the ground. The sizzle and pop of moisture against the still-hot wood of the burned-out buggy.

Pickles comes up beside me. "Chief, I hate to lay this on you, but I think I just connected a couple of dots that are starting to make a pretty ugly picture."

I start toward the Explorer, pissed, my mind still on Kaufman. "What are you talking about?"

He falls in beside me. "I took a call from the widow Humerick last night." He tells me an unsettling story about an old Amish woman whose four sheep were found slaughtered in their pens. "Them sheep wasn't killed by dogs or coyotes, Chief. Someone went into the pen and slaughtered those animals."

I've met the widow Humerick a couple of times over the last three years. She's one of the more colorful characters in Painters Mill. No family or friends. She claims to be Amish, but the church district refuses to claim her as one of its own. Of course, when she shows up for worship — albeit on a hit or miss basis — Bishop Troyer doesn't turn her away. She's got a personality like sandpaper and invariably rubs people the wrong way. She's been involved in half a dozen incidents over the years, ranging from simple assault to making terroristic threats. Every time, she's been the perpetrator, not the victim.

Regardless of her reputation, I have a sinking suspicion the dead sheep might have more to do with hate than with an old woman's prickly personality; that we may be dealing with something much more insidious than vandalism. "Used to be these kinds of crimes were harmless pranks," I say. "Bored teenagers. Drunken idiots." I sigh. "Sounds like this might be something else."

"I don't get the Amish-hating thing," Pickles says.

"Hate never makes any sense." But I've heard all the reasons behind the crimes. The Amish are stupid. They're dirty. Incestuous. Religious fanatics. The buggies hold up traffic. It's all bullshit, except for the traffic reference, anyway.

Part of the problem is that a large number of incidents go unreported. As a result, the perpetrators are rarely caught or punished. The Amish endure in silence much the same way they've endured persecution the last two hundred years.

"Someone's kicking it up a notch."

"Molotov cocktail's pretty damn serious."

"Someone could have been killed."

Killed. The word conjures a possibility my brain wants desperately to deny. For a moment, I'm so shocked by the direction my mind has gone, I can't speak. I sure as hell don't want to say it aloud. That would make the connection too real. "Shit, Pickles. You don't think . . ."

The old man's eyes widen. "The Slabaughs? I don't know, Chief."

I nod, and we go silent, our minds grinding out thoughts too ugly to voice. After a moment, I shake my head. "Triple murder would be one hell of a leap."

"Yeah."

But the thought is still echoing inside my head when I pull onto the dirt road and we head toward Adam Slabaugh's farm.

CHAPTER 7

We find Adam Slabaugh in the barn, his legs sticking out from beneath the undercarriage of a Kubota tractor. From atop a fifty-gallon drum, a radio spews static and gospel, harmonizing weirdly with the ping of sleet against the tin roof.

Adam must have heard us walk in, because he rolls out from beneath the tractor and gets to his feet. "Chief Burkholder." His eyes slide to Pickles and then back to me. "I didn't expect to see you again so soon. Is everything all right?"

I give him a level look. "Where were you last night and this morning?"

He blinks, takes a quick step back, as if trying to distance himself from something unpleasant. "Why are you asking me that?"

"I'd appreciate it if you'd just answer the question."

"I was here at the farm."

"Was there anyone with you?"

143

"No," he replies. "I live here alone." His eyes narrow. "Why are you asking me these things?"

"We learned from the coroner that your brothers and sister-in-law may have been murdered."

He staggers back, as if the words wield a physical punch. "But . . . how can that be? They fell into the pit. How can that be murder?"

I refrain from telling him about Solomon Slabaugh's head injury. You never know when someone's going to slip up and mention something he has no way of knowing — unless he was there. "One or all of them could have been shoved into the pit."

"Aw, God." He raises his hands, sets them on either side of his face, and closes his eyes, as if the horrific images are being branded into his brain. "Who would . . ." When he opens his eyes, I see realization in them, and I know he knows why we're here. "You think *I* did that?" Incredulity resonates in his voice. "You think I *killed* my own brothers? My sister-in-law? You think I'm *evil* enough to do such a thing? That I would leave my nephews and niece *orphaned?*"

"You had a beef with your brother."

"We had our differences. But I would never have hurt him. I would never have hurt any of them."

"We know about your arrest," I tell him.

"That was a long time ago."

"Two years ain't that long," Pickles puts in.

"You have no right to come to my home and accuse me of this terrible sin." His mouth flutters, as if he can't get the words out fast enough.

I sense an escalation coming. I don't know if it will come in the form of tears or violence or both, but I brace for an attack. Pickles senses it, too, because he eases his five-foot-two frame between us, daring the younger man to make a move. I stare at Slabaugh, trying to see inside his head, inside his heart, see beyond the theatrics and drama and the hard slap of grief. But when I look into his eyes, all I see are the jagged layers of shock and outrage, interspersed with flashes of sorrow so heavy that his shoulders seem to bow beneath the weight.

None of those emotions exonerates him. Experience has taught me grief doesn't equal innocence. When I was a homicide detective in Columbus, I worked a case where the killer truly mourned the loss of his victim. When the confession came, he explained how difficult it was to dismember

145

someone you loved. Looking at Slabaugh, I know it would be premature to take him off my suspect list.

"No one accused you of anything," I say.

Slabaugh takes a step toward me. "You insinuated —"

"She didn't insinuate shit." Pickles sets his hand against the other man's chest and pushes him backward. "Now back off."

Slabaugh looks down at Pickles as if he wants to strangle him. His eyes are a little wild when they find mine. "You don't know me. You don't know what's in my heart. I loved my brothers. And I love those children."

Setting my hand on the baton strapped to my belt, I sidle back a step. The last thing I want to do is get into a confrontation with this man. Guilty or innocent, if he crosses a line, I won't hesitate to take him to jail. "You need to calm down."

"I don't like your questions!" he shouts.

"I'm investigating a triple murder, Mr. Slabaugh. I'm asking questions that need to be answered. If you want us to catch who did it, you'd be wise to cooperate."

He's breathing hard. I see spittle on his lower lip. His eyes are wide and slightly out of focus. "I didn't do it. I couldn't do that. They were my brothers."

I give him a minute to regain his composure. "Did you leave the farm at any time last night or early this morning? Did you go anywhere?"

"I worked here. Feeding livestock. Mucking the pens. I worked on the tractor. I was alone the whole time."

"Did you speak with anyone on the phone?" I ask.

"No."

"Do you know of anyone who might've had a problem with your brothers or sister-in-law? Any kind of dispute or argument?"

"They were good people. Good neighbors." He shakes his head. "They were *Amish,* for God's sake. I can't see anyone wanting to hurt them."

"No money disputes? Land disputes? Anything like that?"

"Solly and I were once close, but after I was excommunicated . . ." He lets the words trail off. "He didn't exactly confide in me. But I don't believe he had any enemies. He was a decent man. Fair-minded."

Pickles jumps in with the next question. "What about his personal life? Any infidelity going on? Anything like that?"

"Solly was a good husband, faithful, and a good father. He would never betray his wife or family in that way."

"What about Rachael?" I ask. "Is it possible she was involved with someone?"

Another vigorous shake of his head. "No," he says. "She wasn't that kind of woman."

"What about drugs?" Pickles asks. "Any drug use?"

"Never."

I choose my next words carefully. "Do you mind if I ask you how your wife died, Mr. Slabaugh?"

His lips stretch into a snarl, revealing teeth that are tightly clenched. "What? Do you think I killed her, too? My God!"

"This would be a lot easier on all of us if you'd just answer my questions," I reply evenly.

"Am I a suspect?"

"We haven't ruled anyone out at this point."

He sighs heavily, as if resigning himself to some ultimate humiliation. "My wife was killed in an auto accident three years ago."

I nod, knowing there will be records I can check. "If you think of anything else that might be important, call me, day or night."

Slabaugh takes the card and stares blindly at it. Only when Pickles and I turn to leave does he raise his head and look at us. "What about the children?" he asks.

I look back at him. "They're at the farm.

Bishop Troyer and his wife are with them."

"They should be with family," he says. "With me."

"That's going to be up to Children Services."

Even from twenty feet away, I see the quiver go through his body. His fists clench at his sides. He makes a sound that's part grief, part outrage. It's the kind of sound that makes the hairs on the back of my neck stand up.

Back in the Explorer, I slide behind the wheel and start the engine. Pickles hefts himself into the passenger seat. "For a moment there, I thought he was going to knock your head off."

"That would have been a mistake on his part." I toss him a sidelong look as I turn the Explorer around. "What do you think?"

"I think he's pretty damn squirrelly." He shakes his head. "We've been cops long enough to know family dynamics play into a crime like this more often than not."

I nod in agreement. "Even if he loved his brothers, if he wanted those kids badly enough, he might've done it."

"That's some tough love."

"Let's keep him at the top of our suspect list for now." I think about everything we know about Slabaugh. "When we get back to the station, I want you to pull everything you can get on the accident that killed his wife."

Pickles gives me a look. "What are you thinking?"

"I'm not thinking anything."

He laughs. "Yeah, and I ain't fuckin' old."

One thing I've realized in the last few months is that an insomniac can get a lot done in a twenty-four hour period. While most people are sleeping, we're still hard at work. But even the sleepless eventually need sleep. At the very least, they need to turn off. I know from experience that I'm not going to sleep tonight. I've got that hum coursing like nitro in my head. An edgy, grinding energy pumping through my veins. A motor revving high and running hot.

It's nearly 11:00 P.M. when I shut down my computer and grab my parka. In the reception area, I find Mona Kurtz, my night dispatcher, at the switchboard/dispatch station, her UGG boots propped on the desk, her nose in a college text titled *Law Enforcement Through History.* She starts when she spots me. "Oh, hey, Chief." Subtly, she sets the book into an open drawer. "Calling it a night?"

She's an almost pretty twenty-something

150

with wild red hair, a wardrobe that would make Madonna blush, and the attention span of a teenager. But in the two years she's been my dispatcher, I've learned to appreciate her finer points. She's enthusiastic, with a strong work ethic and an obsessive interest in everything cop. With a little maturity and some experience, she just might make a good police officer.

"I just e-mailed you the press release," I tell her.

"I'll get it dispatched pronto."

"Everything quiet?" I ask, slipping into my parka.

"Just the usual. Skid caught that Hoskins kid speeding out by the Jackson place again, wrote him a ticket."

"Second ticket in two months."

"Kid's an accident waiting to happen." She taps her fingers on her desktop. "Oh, and Mrs. Cartwright called about an hour ago."

I nod. Mrs. Cartwright has Alzheimer's and reports a prowler at least twice a week. Anticipating the cold, I zip the parka up to my chin. "My cell's on if you need anything."

"Righto."

"You can get your book back out now."

She grins. "Roger that."

151

Snow greets me when I step onto the sidewalk, but I'm too distracted to fully appreciate its beauty. Three people were murdered in my town today. An Amish mother and father. An uncle. Here I am, nineteen hours later, and I'm no closer to knowing who did it than when I rolled out of bed this morning.

Before leaving for the day, Pickles dug out the police report for the traffic accident that killed Adam Slabaugh's late wife, Charlotte. I was shocked to learn it was DUI-related. She'd been driving at a high rate of speed with a blood-alcohol level that was twice the legal limit. She died at the scene from massive trauma. The coroner ruled her death accidental, and the Ohio State Highway Patrol concurred. There's no way her husband was involved.

The CSU from BCI arrived late in the afternoon. They'll be working through the night and into the morning gathering evidence in the barn. Glock and T.J. spent the remaining daylight hours canvassing the farms around the Slabaugh place. Unfortunately, no one remembers the day laborer Solly Slabaugh had purportedly hired.

We couldn't even manage a break on the burning buggy case. Despite the Holmes County Sheriff's Office doubling up on patrols, the dark truck was never spotted. No one saw anything. The day was a wash.

I'm not even a full day into the Slabaugh case, but already I feel battered by the dead ends I've run into, and I'm frustrated by my lack of progress. Worse, I can't shake the feeling that I'm missing something — something that's right in front of me. But for some reason, I can't get my mind around it. There's a dead space in my head I can't seem to waken.

I should go home, have some dinner, take a long, hot shower, and fall into bed for a few hours. But I know I won't sleep. The idea of spending the next several hours tossing and turning is about as appealing as a sinus infection. And so as I pull out of the station, I head west instead of east.

I'm not even sure where I'm going until I find myself on Wheatfield Road. It's a dirt track that dead ends two miles in. My sister, Sarah, and her husband live in the last house. It's been months since I last saw them. I feel guilty about that because Sarah gave birth to a little girl, my only niece, a couple of months ago. It's stupid and selfish, but I haven't been able to make myself come here. I want to believe I haven't yet met my niece because I've been too busy. That would be a somewhat acceptable excuse and a lot simpler than the truth.

A mile from their farm, I cut the head-lights and coast down the road. I park on the shoulder and shut down the engine. The kitchen window glows yellow with lantern light. The upstairs bedroom is lit as well, and I picture Sarah up there with her new baby, sitting in the old rocking chair that had once been our grandmother's, nursing. I wonder if she is the center of her universe, a place where nothing else in the world mat-ters. And I surprise myself by feeling an uncharacteristic rise of an emotion that's disturbingly close to envy.

Around me, snow floats down from a fuzzy black sky. I can see the tall yellow grass in the bar ditch sway in a light breeze. A row of blue spruce trees runs parallel with the gravel lane. I can just make out the silhouette of the barn and outbuildings beyond, and the big pine tree that grows on the east side of the house. I look at the glow-ing windows, and I feel like a fool for being parked out here with the headlights doused, like some misunderstood teenager. I know if I went inside, Sarah would be happy to see me. She would welcome me and let me hold my new niece.

But emotions can be so complicated. At the moment, I'm experiencing more than my share, and they all seem a bit too complex to be dealt with when I'm exhausted and distracted by a case. The truth of the matter is, I'm afraid to go inside. I'm afraid to reach out, to tell my sister I've missed her and that I want her in my life. Most of all, I'm afraid to hold that little baby. Maybe because there's a small part of me that feels as if I'm too tainted to hold such a precious thing as a newborn child. Maybe because it would remind me of all the things I've lost, of the things I threw away. The memories send a slice of grief through me with such force that I hear myself gasp.

I hit the window control, let the cold air wash over my face. Taking a final look at the house, I start the engine, put the Explorer in gear. And I drive away without looking back.

A few minutes later, I pull into the gravel parking lot of McNarie's Bar. I'm relieved to find only two cars in the lot. It's one of many reasons I come here. The place is low-key and quiet — in terms of clientele anyway. McNarie never asks too many questions. Though he's just a little bit shady, he keeps his ear to the grapevine and passes information on to me if he thinks it might be important. I guess you could call him a small-town version of an informant.

I stifle the little voice telling me to turn around and go home as I kill the engine and get out. Snow stings my face and blows down my collar as I traverse the lot and head for the entrance. Shoving open the heavy wood door, I step inside. The familiar smells of cigarette smoke, old wood, and spilled beer greet me like scruffy old friends. A classic Allman Brothers tune rattles from huge speakers mounted on the back wall. Two men sit on opposite sides of the bar, watching a football game on the tube. At the rear of the room, a young man with a goatee plays pool with a woman in tight blue jeans and a faux-fur coat.

I go to the last booth, where the bulb in the pendant light that dangles above the table is out. Taking off my coat, I sit facing the door. My butt has barely hit the bench when McNarie walks over to the table. He's a large man with a full beard and a dingy white hair that reminds me of a dirty polar bear. Tomasetti once said he's a dead ringer for Jerry Garcia.

"I hear them three Amish folks drowned in that pit didn't get down there all by themselves." Without looking at me, he sets a shot glass filled to the rim with Absolut and a Killian's Irish Red on the table.

"That's what the coroner says." I reach for the shot glass first and down the vodka in a single gulp. The burn rips down my throat like a fireball. Shuddering, I set the empty glass on the table.

McNarie refills it without prompting. "You know who done it?"

"Not yet." I give him my full attention. He's got small brown eyes set in a big puffy face. The white beard partially conceals a scar that bisects his right cheek and runs downward toward his chin. It looks like someone slugged him with a bottle and Mc-Narie never bothered with stitches. I ran a check on him when I first started coming here. Ten years ago, he did a year in prison for felony assault. A few years later, he did two more years on a felony weapons charge and possession of a controlled substance. He's kept his nose clean since.

He lives on an old run-down farm north of Millersburg and rides his Harley into Painters Mill nearly every day, weather permitting. He owns this place and does a good business. He's behind the bar every time I come in. I like to think this man is proof that the system works and that he's been rehabilitated. Or maybe he just decided it was easier to make a living inside the law.

"You hear anything?" I ask.

He sets a pack of Marlboro Lights and a lighter on the table. "No one's talking about it."

I think about the escalation of violence against the Amish, decide to ask him about that, too. "Did you hear about the burning buggy incident today?"

"I heard."

"Anyone bragging about it?" I smile, but it feels wan on my face. "Or have a sign taped to their back that says 'I Did It'?"

His chuckle sounds like the growl of some rogue lion. "A few days ago, a couple of young guys come in — longhaired types. Laughin' their asses off 'bout doing some shit to an Amish person."

My heartbeat trips a couple of times. "You know their names?"

"Never seen 'em before."

"You get specifics on what they did?"

He shakes his head. "Just caught snatches of what they was saying."

"Do you know what they were driving?"

Another shake. "No, but I'll keep my eye out."

I watch him walk away, wishing he hadn't left the Marlboros, because I know I'm going to smoke them.

Settling into the booth, I sip the beer and light the first cigarette. I watch the twenty-something couple play pool at the rear. They laugh and flirt, and for some reason that makes me feel old. *Go home, Kate,* that small voice of reason whispers. I silence it, down the second shot, then light another cigarette.

I watch the game and listen to the jukebox and think about the Slabaugh case. I think about family dynamics and my mind moves on to the kids. Mose, just seventeen years old and doing his best to fill his father's shoes. Salome, only fifteen and trying desperately to keep the family together. And then there's Ike and Samuel, little boys who should be out on Miller's Pond playing ice hockey and building snow forts. Instead, they're crying for their dead *mamm* and *datt* and a future that's as uncertain as the outcome of this case.

I think of Adam Slabaugh, a widower living alone, an Amish man excommunicated from his church and family, an uncle estranged from his niece and nephews. Loneliness can be a powerful force in a person's life, especially if they've lost something precious. Adam lost his wife. Is he cold-blooded enough to murder his own brothers and his

159

sister-in-law in order to gain custody of the children?

I'm midway through my second Killian's when the door swings open. I glance up absently to see two men enter with a gust of wind and a swirl of snow. Surprise ripples through me at the sight of a Holmes County Sheriff's Office parka. McNarie's is a far cry from a cop bar. It's unusual for any law enforcement to stop in, especially this time of night. Mild surprise transforms to something a hell of a lot more powerful when I recognize the second man. Long black coat, tall frame with an athletic build, dark hair shot with gray at the temples.

John Tomasetti makes eye contact with me at about the same time recognition kicks in. The jolt of his gaze runs the length of my body — an odd mix of shock and guilt and a thread of pleasure that goes all the way to my toes.

Motioning for the bartender to bring drinks, he crosses to my booth and looks down at me. "Hey, Chief."

"Don't tell me you just happened to be in the neighborhood," I manage to say.

"Something like that."

He's looking at me a little too closely with those hard, dark eyes, eyes that invariably see too much — things I don't want to

160

share. It's a struggle not to squirm beneath that gaze.

Sheriff Mike Rasmussen saunters to the booth. "Chief Burkholder."

Rising, I shake hands with him. "Sheriff."

Rasmussen slides into the bench across from me.

Tomasetti sticks out his hand. "Nice cave you've got here, Chief."

I accept the handshake. "Welcome back to Painters Mill, Agent Tomasetti."

"I take it you two know each other," Rasmussen says.

One side of Tomasetti's mouth curves, and he slides in next to me. "We do."

I've known John Tomasetti for almost a year now. We met during the Slaughterhouse Killer investigation last January. He's a good man, a good cop, and a powerful force to me and everyone around him. That case was an intense time for both of us, and somehow we ended up not only lovers, but friends. In the months since, our relationship has evolved, deepened, and I can honestly say the connection we share goes beyond anything I've ever experienced with another human being. But neither of us is very good at the relationship thing. We use our jobs as a guise to see each other, but we've been discreet; few people know we're involved.

"I tried to return your call," I say to the sheriff.

"Probably better to brief you in person anyway," Rasmussen says.

McNarie arrives at the table, sets three Killian's in front of us, then hustles away.

"What brings you to Painters Mill?" I direct the question to Tomasetti. What I really want to ask is: Why didn't you tell me you were coming?

"Sheriff Rasmussen requested our assistance." He motions toward the sheriff. "I'll defer to him to give you the details."

Leaning forward, Rasmussen sets his elbows on the table and clasps his hands in front of him. "I know you're well aware that in the last couple of months there's been an increase in crimes against the Amish, Kate."

"I am."

"I just read the report you filed on the burning buggy incident."

I look from Tomasetti to Rasmussen, wishing I hadn't done those two shots. I'm at a distinct disadvantage here. The alcohol has rendered my IQ somewhere between that of a toddler and a German shepherd. While I'm pretty sure Rasmussen hasn't noticed, I'm utterly certain Tomasetti has.

"These crimes qualify as hate crimes, Kate." Rasmussen gives Tomasetti a pointed look. "I know your department is tied up with the Slabaugh thing, so I contacted BCI."

"Isn't a hate-crimes designation usually federal?" I ask.

"Hate crimes are against the law no matter which agency does the investigating." Tomasetti shows me his teeth. "I drew the case."

"We wanted an agent who was familiar with the area," Rasmussen interjects. "Since Agent Tomasetti has worked in Painters Mill before, I thought he was the best person for the job."

I nod. "We worked the Slaughterhouse Killer case last year. A couple of months ago, we worked the Plank murder case."

"I remember," the sheriff says. "Nasty business." Rasmussen looks from me to Tomasetti and then back to me. "Agent Tomasetti and I met for dinner earlier. We were talking about the hate-crime issue, and we thought with your being formerly of the faith, you might be able to lend a hand with the Amish," Rasmussen says. "I'm batting zero because none of the victims will press charges."

"Or even report the crime," Tomasetti adds.

"You can add Kaufman to that list." I

recap my exchange with Kaufman at the scene. "He denied anything had happened and basically refused to talk to me."

"Nice." Rasmussen sighs in obvious frustration. "How the hell do these Amish assholes expect us to get these idiots off the street if they don't cooperate?" He catches himself and mutters, "No offense, Kate."

"None taken." But it makes me smile. "The Amish want to be separate from us. They want to be left alone." I shrug. "They haven't yet learned they can't do that completely when the rest of us live in such close proximity."

"It takes two to tango," Tomasetti says.

Rasmussen adds, "That makes the Amish easy pickin's if someone wants to mess with them."

"Exactly," I agree. "There are probably quite a few more crimes that have been committed, but we don't know about them because they were never reported."

"And there's not a whole lot we can do without a complainant," Rasmussen says.

"Sooner or later, someone's going to get hurt," Tomasetti adds.

I nod. "Probably sooner at the rate we're going."

"We pulled stats for Holmes and Coshocton counties," Rasmussen says. "Even though the numbers are skewed because so many of these crimes go unreported, in the last two months there's been a marked escalation." He sighs. "Because most of the incidents were mischief-type crimes, local law enforcement hadn't taken aggressive action."

I tell them about the two men McNarie mentioned earlier.

"Could be our guys," Rasmussen says.

"Or part of a concerted effort," I add. "A group."

Tomasetti nods. "Considering the escalation in such a short period of time, I'm betting on the latter. Some hate group. Loosely organized. Young Caucasian males, ages fifteen to twenty-five."

Something unpleasant scrapes at the edge of my brain. I don't want to let it in, look at it. But it's there, nagging at me like an arthritic joint: my conversation with Pickles about the Slabaugh case. "It would be a huge escalation with regard to the level of violence, but do you think it's possible the Slabaugh murders are hate-related?" I give them the particulars of the case.

"I suppose it's possible." Rasmussen's voice is slightly incredulous. "Different MO."

"Suspects?" Tomasetti asks.

I tell them about Adam Slabaugh. "He doesn't have an alibi."

"Pretty strong motive," Tomasetti says. "The kids."

Rasmussen leans back in the booth, taking it all in. "So maybe this is all one big fucked-up case."

"I don't know," I say. Both men look at me. "The Slabaugh case feels different. I think there's something else there we're not seeing."

"Like what?"

"I don't know. Something I've missed." I shrug. "Something about the family."

Both men nod, knowing that some crimes are that way. Solving them takes time, as well as persistence, perseverance, patience. You need to trust your instincts enough to follow them blind, listen to something as intangible as your gut.

"We can talk about this a little bit more tomorrow." Rasmussen slides out of the booth and tosses a few bills on the table. "It's past my bedtime." He looks at me. "Good to see you, Kate." He turns his attention to Tomasetti. "See you in the morning."

I watch Rasmussen walk away, but my attention is focused on Tomasetti. Tension creeps down the back of my neck and spreads into my shoulders.

"How are you, Kate?" His voice is deep and intimate, and I feel the rumble of it all the way to my stomach.

"I'm good." I look at him. John Tomasetti has a powerful presence. Even more so from my perspective, because my feelings for him are fervent. We're close, but sometimes I sense some unexplained chasm between us, unmapped territory, which feels vast tonight. "You could have told me you were coming."

He smiles. "You mean warned you?"

I smile back. "That, too."

"I called." He lifts a shoulder, lets it drop. "Then I got busy with Rasmussen. Didn't want to call you when I was in the car with him."

"Might have been awkward."

"Kind of like now." He softens the words with a smile.

I can't help it; I laugh. "But we're so good at awkward."

"We're good at a lot of things."

"Just not surprises."

"Even when they're nice."

Silence falls and Tomasetti lets it ride. I try going with it. I peel the label on my empty bottle. I listen to the music. Usually, silence doesn't bother me. John and I have been through a lot together; I don't need conversation to be comfortable. This is one of those times when the silence is like a tuning fork against a broken bone.

When I can stand it no longer, I ask, "How's the move going?"

"I'm all moved in. Nice digs, by the way."

"Have you found a place in Cleveland?"

He nods. "Rented a house by the lake."

"Nice."

But we're both dancing around the real subject. The fact that he's living back in the city where his family was murdered. A city where a lot of people — the cops included — suspect he went rogue and executed the men responsible. I want to ask him how he's dealing with all that, but some inner voice warns me to tread lightly, give him some space.

McNarie arrives and sets two more Killian's on the table between us. Frowning at me, Tomasetti slides the pack of cigarettes and lighter across the table toward McNarie. Smoothly, the old barkeep picks them up and drops them in his apron pocket. I give Tomasetti points for not lecturing me on all the dangers of smoking.

"Been here long?" he asks.

"About an hour."

"You look tired."

"In case you haven't noticed, I'm drunk."

"I've noticed." He sips his beer. "I guess the question is: Why?"

It's an honest question — one I should probably be asking myself. But then, Tomasetti is one of the most honest people I've ever known. He asks the hard questions, even when he knows the person he's asking probably doesn't want to answer. He also gives honest answers, even when you don't want to hear the truth. It's not easy being his friend; it's not easy caring for him. But he's got me on both counts and then some.

When I don't respond, he lets me off the hook, moves on to a topic we're both more comfortable with. "Tell me about Adam Slabaugh."

I recap everything I know about the formerly Amish man. "There was some bad blood between the brothers."

"Other suspects?"

"The kids mentioned a day laborer, but nothing's panned out. We canvassed . . ." I shrug, let the words trail.

"Uncle going to get custody of the kids?"

"Probably. Against the wishes of the bishop." I'm leaning back in the booth, staring at my beer. I can feel Tomasetti's eyes on me, probing and poking, and I sense the hard questions coming on.

"Four Amish kids," he says. "Dead parents. Makes it tough."

"Kids always make it harder." But then, Tomasetti already knows that.

"Last few cases you've worked have been tough, Kate."

I look at him. The smile that emerges feels rigid on my face — like if it gets any tighter, the facade will shatter and what I'm really feeling will come pouring out. At the moment, I'm not even sure what that is. "I'm handling it."

"I guess that's why you're here, drinking shots and smoking cigarettes."

"Maybe it is." I look at him, let some attitude slip into my voice. "You going to lecture me now, Tomasetti?"

"That would be hypocritical of me."

"That's one of the things I like about you."

"You mean aside from my animal magnetism?"

"You know when to keep your mouth shut."

"I believe that's the most touching thing anyone's ever said to me."

"You're so full of shit."

Smiling, he finishes his beer. We listen to an old Lou Reed song about Sweet Jane. The young couple at the rear finish their pool game, shrug into their coats, and head

170

for the door. The football game on the tube ends and the local news comes on.

"I've been a cop for a long time, Kate. I've worked a lot of cases. Been to a lot of dark places."

I look at him, not ready to get serious, not wanting to hear what he's going to say next. The urge to spout off something silly and meaningless is strong, but the look in his eyes stops me.

"Whether you want to admit it or not, all of those things take a toll," he says.

"Tomasetti . . ."

He raises a hand to quiet me. "All I'm telling you is, if you want to talk about anything, I'm here."

Some of the ice that has been jammed up inside me melts. The knot that's been in my chest all day loosens. "I'll let you know."

CHAPTER 8

The sun hovers like a fluorescent orange ball above the treetops to the east when I arrive at the station. The storm that rolled through last night is nothing more than a purple line of clouds moving off to the east. The weather system left two inches of snow behind, just enough to cover the tree branches and make the streets slick.

I drank too much last night, and I have the hangover to prove it. Tomasetti followed me home, fixed me a can of soup, then put me to bed. Part of me had wanted him to spend the night, had expected him to ask. He didn't. I'm not sure how I feel about that. I hate to admit it, but my female ego is smarting this morning.

I find Mona sitting at the dispatch station, surfing the Internet, a lollipop sticking out of her mouth. She looks up when I enter and pulls out the lollipop. "Morning, Chief."

"Please tell me you made coffee."

"Figured you'd be in early. It's hazelnut."

I prefer plain old Colombian, but I've learned to choose my battles when it comes to Mona's quirks. "As long as it's hot." I head for the coffee station, snag the largest mug I can find.

Grabbing message slips, she rises and crosses to me. "Thought you'd want to see this ASAP. Tom Skanks down at the bakery came in at about four this morning. I guess he starts his doughnuts about that time. Anyway, he said he heard about the Slabaughs and remembered some guy hassling the wife a few days back."

Coffee forgotten, I take the message from her hand and read "Will be at the bakery until eight." I glance down at my watch. It's just after 7:00 A.M. "I'm going to go talk to him."

"I'll hold down the fort."

The Butterhorn Bakery is two blocks from the police station, so I brave the snow and walk. Originally from Boston, Tom Skanks and his wife, Maureen, opened the shop about ten years ago. It's housed in the storefront of an old brick building that was a funeral home back in the 1970s. Occasionally, Glock or Skid will pick up a couple dozen glazed doughnuts and bring them back to the station. The Skanks have got the best coffee in town and make the tastiest apple fritters I've ever had. I always find myself trying not to think about the old crematorium in the basement.

The aromas of cinnamon and yeast reach me from halfway down the block. Warmth envelops me when I open the door and walk inside, and I know Tom has had the big oven at the rear of the store going since the wee hours of the morning. The customer area is dimly lit, since he's not yet open for business. I look through the service window behind the counter and see Tom in the kitchen area, hovering over a commercial-size deep fryer.

Rounding the counter, I head toward the back and go through the swinging doors. Tom starts when he spots me, sets his hand to his chest. "You trying to give me a heart attack, or what?"

He's a short man with brown hair and a belly that tells me he spends a good deal of his day sampling the fruits of his labor. He wears a white apron over a navy golf shirt and dark slacks. A smear of flour streaks his right cheek.

"I didn't mean to scare you." I motion toward the door. "You might consider keeping it locked when you're not open."

Shaking his head, he goes to the stainless-steel sink and washes his hands. "I'd argue with you, citing the low crime rate here in Painters Mill, Chief Burkholder. But after hearing about what happened to them Amish folks, I don't think I'd have a leg to stand on."

"That's why I'm here, Tom. I understand you saw some kind of confrontation between Rachael Slabaugh and someone here in town."

"Didn't think of it until I heard they might've been murdered." Drying his hands on his apron, he crosses to an industrial-size coffeemaker and pours two cups. "Happened right outside the front door. I saw everything through the window."

"What happened?"

"That Amish woman . . ."

"Rachael Slabaugh?"

"Yeah. Her. She was a pretty little thing. I saw her in town all the time, either with the kids or her husband. But she was by herself that day." He shoves one of the cups at me and motions toward the window. "She tied her horse up to that hitching post, probably to go into the tourist shop next door. Anyway, some guy in one of them little Toyota pickup trucks parked behind her buggy and blocked her in."

"Did you recognize him?"

He jerks his head. "Damn straight. It was that Jerome Rankin character. One of the biggest assholes I ever met."

I've never met Rankin, but I'm well aware of his reputation. My officers have been called to his residence on at least one occasion for a domestic dispute. From what I understand, he's got a temper and a mean streak. "So what happened?"

"Well, the Amish lady was trying to leave, asked him nicely to move his truck. But he refused to let her out of the space. Maureen — that's my wife — was in here waiting on customers, so I stepped outside." He puffs out his chest a little. "I was a decent boxer back in the day." He pats his belly. "Of course, I ain't no more. But I'll tell you, the things he was saying to that Amish lady made me want to knock his block off."

I pull out my notebook. "What did he say?"

"Just horrible things." He glances over his shoulder, then lowers his voice. "You know, like he wanted to stick it in her. Wanted her to suck his dick, stuff like that. Indecent, I tell you."

"Did he touch her?"

"No. Grabbed the buggy reins once, though."

176

"How did it end?"

"I went out there and threatened to call the cops." He shrugs. "Rankin told me to fuck off, then left. The Amish lady was so shook-up, she left without thanking me."

Ten minutes later, I'm in the Explorer, heading toward Jerome Rankin's last known residence. Beside me, Officer Chuck "Skid" Skidmore nurses a Styrofoam cup filled with hazelnut coffee. He works the graveyard shift, which is from midnight to 8:00 A.M., and was the only officer available this early, so I asked him to ride along.

We pulled Rankin's sheet before leaving and checked for priors and warrants. There's nothing outstanding, but the guy's got a colorful history. As we head toward his residence, Skid reads the highlights. "Arrested for domestic violence three years ago. No conviction. There was a stalking incident involving the same woman. No conviction. Got a DUI last year. Get this: He was arrested for sexual assault, but the charges were dropped. Been a busy fuckin' guy."

"Who took the call for the domestic?"

"I did. It was one of my first arrests here in Painters Mill when I came down from Ann Arbor." Skid motions toward the approaching intersection. "Turn right here."

He takes a gulp of coffee. "Let me tell you, Rankin's one crazy son of a bitch, and I ain't the only one who thinks so."

I make the turn onto the township road. "How so?"

"It's weird, Chief. It's like when you look at him, he's not all there. Crazy eyes. You know, like there's something missing."

"Any history of mental problems?"

He flicks the paper. "Nothing shows up here, but this is pretty cursory."

Rankin lives in a small frame house nestled in the woods a few miles from Miller's Pond. When I was a kid, the old place was vacant; some of the English kids in town used to say it was haunted. A few years ago, it caught fire and sustained a good bit of damage. It stood vacant for another year, open to the elements and forest animals, before the owner decided to replace the roof, put in a new furnace and hot-water heater, and rented the place to Rankin. I figure by now he's realized Rankin is a lot more destructive than the animals and elements combined.

"Looks like he's home," Skid says.

I pull into the narrow gravel driveway and park behind an old Toyota pickup truck. "He work anywhere?" I ask.

"I used to see him every so often down at

the gas station off the traffic circle. Ain't seen him there for a while, though."

I find myself thinking of the missing money from the mason jar in the Slabaugh basement. "I wonder where he gets his cash."

"Hard telling with this guy."

I get out of the Explorer. The sun is fully up now. It's getting warmer, and I can hear the melting snow dripping off the trees. "Head around back," I say quietly. "Just in case he decides to take a morning jog."

Grinning, Skid heads around to the back of the house.

I step onto the porch. Wood creaks beneath my boots as I cross to the front door. I'm keenly aware of my service revolver pressing reassuringly against my hip. Using my baton, I knock. "Jerome Rankin?" I say loudly. "This is the police. Open the door."

Silence falls all around. From the woods behind me, a crow caws. It's so quiet, I can hear the wind whispering through the trees. I'm about to knock again, when the door swings open. Rankin appears, looking rumpled and cross. He's wearing low-slung blue jeans and an unbuttoned flannel shirt, which reveals a bony-looking white chest with a big keloid scar that runs from belly button to nipple. He snarls something unintelligible but distinctly nasty, and I realize I've roused him from bed. He doesn't seem the least bit pleased to find me standing at his door.

"You Rankin?" I ask.

"Who the fuck else would I be?"

Frowning, never taking my eyes from his, I hit my lapel mike, let Skid know I have him. Rankin is one guy I don't want to be alone with too long. "You're a real charmer, aren't you?"

"That's what all the chick cops say."

I roll my eyes. "I bet."

A moment later, Skid comes around the corner, his boots crunching through snow and dry leaves. Rankin glances at Skid, then turns his attention back to me. "What do you guys want?"

He's standing in the doorway, squinting as if the light hurts his eyes. I'd like to take a look inside the house, but I suspect he's not going to invite us in. I try anyway. "Can we come in?"

"I'll come out there." I have to back up a step to let him out of the house. "I didn't do anything," he says as he steps onto the porch.

Rankin isn't tall and doesn't have a lot of bulk. But he's got the rangy look of a street fighter, all wire and sinew, with the reflex speed of a rattlesnake. Part of an intricate-looking tattoo runs up the side of his neck like a serpent tail. Despite his diminutive size, I find myself wanting to avoid any kind of tussle.

I hear Skid coming up the steps behind me. "I understand you were involved in a confrontation in town a couple of days ago," I begin.

"Who says?"

"A little bird," Skid puts in.

"Don't remember no confrontation."

Looking at Rankin, I understand what Skid was saying about his eyes. They're vacant. Though he's looking at me, I get the strange sense that he's not really seeing me. There's a blank countenance to his stare, like there's not a whole lot going on as far as thought processes. He's thinking, but I get the uneasy impression they're not the kind of thoughts a normal person has.

"I'm a peaceful fuckin' guy," he adds, looking pleased by his audacity.

Badass or not, he's seriously starting to annoy me. "You harassed an Amish woman outside the Butterhorn Bakery."

Skid eases past us and makes a show of peering through the open door at the interior of the house.

"Don't recall no Amish woman." Rankin

glances over his shoulder, keeping an eye on Skid.

"I have an eyewitness who says you argued with her and verbally abused her." When he says nothing, I add, "In case you missed that segment of *Law and Order,* sport, lying to the cops is against the law."

"Okay. Fine." He raises both hands as if in surrender. But his attention is still divided between me and Skid, and I realize he doesn't want Skid looking in the house. "I might've talked to an Amish woman. Last time I checked, *that* wasn't against the law. Or did I miss that segment, too?"

"You did more than talk to her. You harassed her. Grabbed the reins of her buggy without her permission."

"She pressing charges or something?"

"Or something," Skid echoes.

I frown at him because he's not helping, then turn my attention back to Rankin. "You had an argument with her, and now she's dead. You have a history of stalking women. You were arrested for sexual assault. That puts you on my hit list. If I were you, I'd think real hard about cooperating."

His eyes widen and he takes a quick step back. "You gotta be shitting me. You think . . ." He backs up another step. "I didn't do nothing to that chick, man!"

Skid stops looking through the open door and comes up beside me, his eyes on Rankin. "You got a meth pipe on your coffee table, dude."

"*What?* You're full of shit. That ain't no pipe." Rankin crosses to the door, yanks the knob, and slams it shut. "You ain't got no business looking in my fuckin' house, man."

"It was in plain sight," Skid says amiably.

I glance at Skid. "I wonder what else he has in there?"

"Where there's a pipe, there's usually meth."

"That sounds like reasonable cause," I say conversationally.

"This is a bunch of crap." Rankin breaks in, his voice incredulous. "I ain't got no pipe in there! I ain't done that shit in months. You guys are full of shit."

"Tell us about the Slabaugh woman, and maybe we'll let the pipe go," I say.

"Ain't no damn pipe!"

"Calm down." Sobering, looking a little badass himself, Skid steps toward him. "You're an inch away from getting your ass carted down to the station. You got that?"

"Okay! I'm cool!" Rankin glances over his shoulder, toward the woods. For an instant, I think he's going to bolt. All he'd have to do is vault the rail. Twenty yards and he'd be in the trees.

I sidle right, positioning myself between him and the porch rail. "Tell me what happened between you and Rachael Slabaugh."

"Nothin'! I swear to God, I was just messing with her. You know, flirting."

Flirting. Coming from the mouth of a man arrested for sexual assault, the word pisses me off. A hard rush of anger shakes me, jarring my brain, like a dog shaking a stuffed animal. I envision myself pulling my baton, giving him a couple of good whacks, taking him to his knees. I grapple with my temper, yank it back hard.

"You're a real Romeo, aren't you?" Skid comments.

Rankin turns his head and spits. "Fuckin' hayseed Nazis. You can't come on my property and jack with me like this. I got rights."

"We can do it at the station if you prefer," I say.

Some of his belligerence slips away, but I know it's only temporary. "Look, man, I already told you, I didn't do nothing to that Amish chick. I swear. I just talked to her. That's all."

"I got a witness says you were verbally abusive."

"I mighta stepped over the line a little. I ain't exactly the polite type. But I didn't

184

put my hands on her. I swear."

"Where were you yesterday morning?" I ask.

"I was here. Slept in late."

"Can anyone verify that?"

"My girlfriend."

"The one you beat the crap out of a few weeks back?" Skid asks.

He swings around to face Skid. "She fell."

"So she said."

I hear Rankin's teeth grind, like hard chalk against slate, and I put my hand on my baton. "Rankin," I warn.

"I didn't touch that bitch!" he shouts. "You can ask her."

"What's her name?" I snap. But I already know. I read the emergency room report before leaving the station. Two weeks ago, Rankin's current girlfriend, Lauren Walker, made a trip to the emergency room of Pomerene Hospital with broken ribs and a broken nose. Suspicious, the attending physician asked her what happened. She claimed she fell down some stairs. It's an old story, one that's retold far too often. The doctor notified me, but the next day when I went to her apartment for a statement, she was nowhere to be found.

I look at Rankin, daring him to make a move. "You know we're going to check with

Lauren."

"Go for it. I was here. All fuckin' night. We slept late."

"I find her marked up, and we'll be back for you," I say.

"You guys don't have shit on me." He looks from me to Skid, gives an incredulous huff. "You're fishing. Well, I ain't biting, so hit the fuckin' road."

There's nothing I'd like more than to cuff him and haul him into town. He's a rude, drug-using, woman-beating son of a bitch. Unfortunately, none of those things make him guilty of murdering the Slabaughs.

"Don't leave town," I say.

Muttering obscenities, he yanks the door open, goes inside, and slams it in our faces.

"Now there goes a model citizen," Skid comments.

I glance at him and lower my voice. "Did you really see a meth pipe in there?"

"I saw *something*." He grins. "Might've been a pen."

"I can see how a trained police officer could get those two items confused." I punctuate the statement by rolling my eyes. "Let's go find Lauren Walker."

CHAPTER 9

Skid and I are in my Explorer a few blocks from the station. I'm thinking about swinging by the sheriff's office to talk to Tomasetti, when my radio crackles. "Chief, we got a ten-sixteen out at the Slabaugh place," says Lois.

We use the ten-code system in the department. A 10-16 is the code for a domestic dispute. I've been the chief of police for three years now, and I have yet to take a call for any kind of domestic problem at an Amish farm.

Skid and I exchange *"What now?"* looks, and I pick up my mike. "You got details on that, Lois?"

"CSU guy called it in. Said there was a bunch of Amish people out in the yard and there was some kind of argument. He said it looked like a fight was going to erupt."

"I'm ten-seven-six." Pulling into the parking lot of a Lutheran church, I turn around and hit the emergency lights.

"Well, that's a first," Skid says. "What about Lauren Walker?"

"She'll have to wait a little while."

A few minutes later, we arrive at the Slabaugh farm. Sure enough, a dozen or so Amish men and women are standing in a group between the barn and the house. Quickly, I park and Skid and I get out. As we approach, I identify Bishop Troyer's grizzled form in the center of the group and then see Adam Slabaugh, who's wearing his English work clothes. I notice Salome's slight form in her blue dress and white *kapp*. Several Amish women stand at the perimeter of the group, hovering like nervous hens.

I reach them in time to see Mose Slabaugh charge his uncle. Head down, the teenager butts the larger man like a bull, ramming his shoulder into the other man's stomach. I hear a whoosh of breath, and then the elder Slabaugh reels backward, trips over his own feet, and lands hard on his butt. Snarling, Mose drops down on top of him. He draws back and lands a blow to his uncle's cheekbone. Behind me, Skid mutters, "Shit," and I lunge at the boy.

"Mose!" I bring my hands down on his

shoulders, try to haul him back. "Cut it out!"

It's like trying to wrestle a steak from a starving rottweiler. He twists hard. My hands slide off his shoulders. I see him draw back, hear the wet-meat slap of his fist connecting with his uncle's face. Vaguely, it registers that Adam makes no effort to protect himself.

"Stop it!" I shout. "Right now! Get off him!"

"He killed my *mamm* and *datt!*" Mose screams. *"He killed them!"*

"Mose! You need to calm down."

The next thing I know, Skid is beside me. Simultaneously, we lock our hands around the boy's biceps and drag him back. Mose's head swings around. Blind, furious eyes connect with mine. His teeth are drawn back and his contorted face is the color of raw hamburger.

Lightning fast, he draws back. I duck an instant before his knuckles careen off my left temple. It's only a glancing blow, but it's enough to whip my head around and make me see stars.

Skid thrusts himself between us, jostling me out of the way. I fall to the right and watch in dismay as Skid takes the boy down, flips him onto his stomach, and snaps the cuffs into place. "You just hit a police officer, partner," he says.

"He killed my *datt!*" Mose screams.

"You just lay there a second and cool off." Pressing the boy down, his breathing elevated, Skid turns to me. "You okay, Chief?"

"I'm fine," I tell him, but I can still feel the lingering effects of the blow, glancing or not.

"Katie, are you hurt?"

I glance over my shoulder, to see Bishop Troyer and his wife come to my side. "I'm fine," I say. "Move aside."

Shaking off the aftereffects of the blow, I step around them and focus on Adam Slabaugh. He's standing a few feet away, brushing mud and dried grass from his clothes. Aware that my temper is lit, I point at him. "You. Come here."

Looking like a guilty little boy facing corporal punishment, he drops his gaze and trudges over to me. "It wasn't his fault."

"He slugged you," I snap. "Who else's fault could it be?"

He stares at me, silent.

Realizing we've drawn an audience, I motion toward the Explorer. "Walk."

I start off at a brisk pace, and he falls in beside me. "What happened?" I ask.

Slabaugh tosses me a sidelong look, shakes

his head again. "I don't know."

I stop, another wave of anger cresting in my chest. He faces me and I shove my finger in his face. "I'm getting tired of people not answering my questions. If you don't start talking right *now*, I'm going to haul you to jail and you can tell it to the judge in the morning."

"I came to see the children."

We reach the Explorer and stop. "Why?"

Slabaugh looks at me as if I'm dense. "They are my nephews and niece. I want them to come live with me."

"That's up to the court system, not you."

"I'm their uncle." Looking away, he shrugs. "I'm their only family. They are alone."

Some of my anger begins to dissipate. "Tell me what happened between you and Mose."

"The boy is angry. Understandably so."

"Who threw the first punch?"

Slabaugh doesn't answer, and I get the sense he doesn't want to get his nephew into trouble. "Adam, come on," I say, pressing him. "Tell me what happened."

"The women would not allow me in the house, so I called out for the children to come outside and speak to me," he tells me. "They did, and I asked them how they felt about coming to live with me. Mose made it clear he didn't want that to happen. The younger boys were more open to the idea." He shrugs. "I suppose I may have pushed too hard." His expression hardens. "Solly poisoned them against me. He told them I am a bad man because I am not Amish."

"Why did Mose hit you?"

He shakes his head. I wait him out. After a moment, Slabaugh shrugs. "He says he doesn't want to live with me at the farm." Another shrug. "He got angry. I tried to reason with him, tell him how I felt. . . ." Another shrug. "I didn't intend to provoke him."

"Did you touch him or threaten him in any way?"

"No, of course not. I would never strike a child." He makes eye contact with me. "The anger is part of grief, Chief Burkholder. Mose will change his mind about me once he comes to terms with all this. Once they come to know me, I know I can give them good, happy lives."

I remember the rage I saw on Mose's face. I think of the blind punch he threw at me. Already I can feel the bruise burgeoning at my left temple. "Stay here," I say, and start toward Mose and Skid. Some of the Amish women have gone back to the house. The ones who remain watch me with frigid stares. I feel their eyes upon me as I approach.

Skid meets me halfway. "You okay, Chief?"

"Just pissed."

"Kid's got a hell of a jab." He motions toward Adam Slabaugh. "So what's his story?"

"Says he came to ask the kids to live with him."

"Guess it didn't go down too well." Nodding, Skid looks over his shoulder at Mose. "Kid says he doesn't want to go."

A few yards away, Mose stands alone, his hands cuffed behind his back, staring down at the ground. Ohio doesn't have a mandatory arrest law, though in domestic violence situations a warrantless arrest is the preferred course of action. Since it's my call and there are extenuating circumstances, I probably won't take him in. But I need to let him know this kind of behavior won't be tolerated.

"Keep an eye on the uncle, will you?" I say to Skid. "I'm going to talk to the kid."

"Sure thing, Chief."

I'm midway to Mose when I spot Bishop Troyer and his wife talking with another Amish couple, and I decide to give Mose a few more minutes to cool off while I get some information from them. "Bishop Troyer."

He turns to me, bows his head slightly. "Chief Burkholder."

"Can you tell me what happened?" I ask.

While the bishop isn't above giving me an "I told you so" look, I know he won't lie to me. "Adam Slabaugh arrived about twenty minutes ago and demanded to speak with the children. Of course, we turned him away at the door." He grimaces. "But Adam would not leave. The children ran out to speak with their uncle. Mose and Adam began to argue."

"Did Slabaugh touch the boy?"

"No, he did not."

"What about Mose? Did he strike his uncle?"

The bishop hesitates, struggles with some internal conflict, then gives a minute nod. *"Ja."*

Neither of us is happy with the answer, but I thank him anyway and start toward Mose.

The bishop stops me. "Katie, the children have been through a terrible ordeal. Do not cause them further suffering."

Since it's my policy not to make promises I can't keep, I turn away and continue on toward Mose. Salome is standing beside him, speaking quietly, as if trying to calm him down. Her eyes are red, her cheeks shiny with tears. Mose watches me approach, as if I'm his executioner. He knows he screwed up.

I call out the girl's name. She jerks around. Her mouth opens in surprise, then she looks down at the ground. "Go inside," I say to her.

She looks at Mose, then back to me. "He was only trying to protect us."

"Go inside," I repeat. "Right now."

Something in my voice convinces her I'm serious, because she takes a final look at her brother, then starts toward the house.

I stop a few feet from Mose. The belligerence I saw earlier in his expression slips away, leaving in its wake the expression of a young man who knows he's going to have to own up to what he's done.

"I don't want to live with my uncle," he says without preamble.

"At the moment, where you're going to live is the least of your problems," I say. "You struck a police officer."

"I didn't mean to. I thought you were —"

"You were out of control and itching for a fight."

"I didn't do anything!"

"You assaulted your uncle. You assaulted

me. Give me one reason why I shouldn't cart you off to jail right now."

Glaring in the direction of his uncle, Mose yanks on the cuffs binding his wrists behind him. "He killed my *datt!*"

It's the third time I've heard that statement. Each time, the words sent a chill through me. "That's a serious accusation, Mose. Do you know something about what happened that morning that you haven't told me?"

He stares at the ground.

"What makes you think your uncle had something to do with the death of your father?"

"He hated my *datt,* and my *datt* hated him! I hate him, too!"

"Why?"

"Because he wants us. He wants to be our *datt.* He's not! He won't ever be my *datt!*"

I move closer, lower my voice. "Do you honestly believe your uncle killed your parents and your uncle?"

He doesn't answer, doesn't meet my gaze.

"Did your uncle do something to make you believe that, Mose?"

"No," he mutters reluctantly.

"Then why did you say it?"

Mose doesn't answer, but for the first time he looks remorseful. Looking down at the

196

ground, he drags his toe across the brown grass. "I don't want to go with him."

"You mean to his farm?"

He nods. "Don't make us go with him."

"That's not up to me."

"Tell the social people to leave us alone."

"Why are you so dead set against living with your uncle?"

He raises his eyes to mine. "My *datt* didn't like him. I don't like him, either."

Sensing I'm getting only part of the story, I take a calming breath. "You can't stay here at the farm by yourself."

"It's my farm," he says defiantly. "I know how to care for the livestock. I know how to work the land."

"I'm sure you can. But you're only seventeen years old."

"I'm a man."

"Legally, you're still a minor. I have to obey the law."

"English laws are not for the Amish. I'm not going with him. He is not Amish. *Er hot net der glaawe!*" He doesn't keep up the faith.

There's no translation needed; I'm all too familiar with the phrase. I heard it a thousand times growing up, especially after I'd decided not to join the church.

"I know this is hard," I tell him.

"You don't know anything," he snarls.

I sigh. "I was older than you are, but I lost my parents, too."

"It's not the same."

"You're right. It's not the same." I pause, studying him, trying to figure out how to reach him. "I'm trying to help you, Mose. I'm not your enemy. I just want what's best for you and your brothers and sister. Children Services —"

"No!" Panic flares in his eyes. "The social people will separate us. They'll take the farm and leave us with nothing."

The unspoken nuances of the situation crystallize in my mind, like a tiny puzzle with a thousand pieces flying together to make a picture. One I wish I'd detected before now, because for the first time I realize I'm being manipulated. "This isn't about whether your uncle is Amish, is it, Mose?"

Refusing to meet my gaze, he digs a trench in the mud with the toe of his work boot.

"This is about your wanting to stay here on the farm with your siblings, isn't it?"

When he finally raises his eyes to mine, they're filled with tears. "That's what my *datt* would have wanted."

"Your *datt* would have wanted an adult to care for you until you're old enough to care for yourself."

When he says nothing, I sigh. "Turn around."

He obeys, and I use my key to unlock the handcuffs. "Children Services is not the bad guy, Mose."

"They'll separate us. Take the farm. *Datt* told us that's what the *Englischers* want."

"I don't believe that," I tell him.

"That's because you're one of them."

I don't know what to say to that. Maybe it's because I understand so very well. To the Amish, the *Englischers* — particularly those in the government — are outsiders and not to be trusted. "I won't let anyone harm you or your brothers and sister," I say quietly. But I don't think I'm going to convince him of anything.

His hands curl into fists at his sides. For an instant, I think he's going to slug me again, and I regret removing the cuffs. Instead, his face screws up and he chokes out a sob. "Don't break up what's left of us." He uses his fist to wipe at the tears. It's an embarrassed, angry gesture that makes me feel as if I've just kicked a puppy. "Please don't take my brothers and sister away from me. They're all I have left."

The statement moves me more than it should. I know better than to get sucked into the plight of these kids. I'm a cop, not a social worker. I have faith that Children Services will do the right thing and place these kids with a good family, at least until Adam Slabaugh is cleared of any suspicion. I know they'll do their utmost to keep the children together. But I know from experience that sometimes kids fall through the cracks. I've seen it happen. What's right for one family can mean heartache for another.

I set my hand on Mose's shoulder and squeeze. "Think about what I said, okay?"

He nods, crying silently, humiliated.

I don't want to leave him like this, but I don't have a choice. I have a murder to solve. Taking a deep breath, I turn away and start toward Skid and Adam Slabaugh.

Skid starts toward me. "So which one are we taking to jail?" he asks.

"Neither one." I stop a few feet from Slabaugh. "Don't come back here until an official decision has been made about the kids."

"You cannot keep me from my family," Slabaugh says. "They are my blood."

"If you come back here again, I'll put both of you in jail," I snap. "You got that?"

Slabaugh skewers me with a stare so cold, I look over my shoulder twice on my way to the Explorer.

■ ■ ■ ■

Back at the station, I go directly to my office and call the Holmes County Department of Job and Family Services. I'm put on hold twice before being transferred to the program manager of Children Services. The conversation goes much as I'd imagined. Once a social worker is assigned the case, he or she will drive out to the Slabaugh farm and "assess" the needs of the children. When I ask about placement, I'm told they almost always try to place orphaned children with family members. In the case of the Slabaughs, blood trumps religion. I wonder if Adam Slabaugh knew that would be the case.

I'm barely finished with the call when Glock appears at the door to my office. "A 911 just came in, Chief. Someone out on Township Road 2 says they found a half-naked Amish guy tied to his buggy."

"You're not kidding, are you?" I ask as I hang up the phone.

"That'd be pretty hard to make up." Glock shakes his head. "The motorist who called it in says the victim looks like he's had the crap beat out of him."

Hate crime. The words flash like red neon

in my brain. In an instant, I'm on my feet and grabbing my keys. "Get an ambulance out there," I snap. "And call the sheriff's office." That makes me think of Tomasetti, and I unclip my cell phone, flip it open.

"Sure thing." Glock watches me cross to the door. "Want me to go with you?"

I shake my head and tell him about my earlier conversation with Jerome Rankin. "I want you to go talk to Lauren Walker and verify Rankin's alibi."

He gives me a mock salute. "I'm on it."

Then I'm down the hall and heading toward the reception area. Lois stands when she sees me. "Tomasetti just called for you."

I don't stop. "I'll call him on the way."

Then I'm through the door and jogging across the sidewalk to the Explorer. I hit the speed dial for Tomasetti's number as I slide behind the wheel. He answers just as I crank the engine. "I think we have another hate crime," I say without preamble.

"Where?"

I give him the location. "I'm on my way now."

"I'll meet you there."

Jamming the Explorer into reverse, I back onto the street, put it in gear, then hit the gas.

I'm not sure what to expect at the scene;

hopefully, no one is seriously injured. The one thing I do know is that I won't tolerate any kind of hate crime in my town. The very thought puts my blood pressure into the red zone. All hate crimes are troubling. But the fact that the Amish are being targeted somehow makes it even more insidious. Maybe because I know the culture so intimately. The Amish are kind, hardworking, and deeply religious. They are pacifists, and most just want to be left alone. I can't help but wonder: *How could anyone hate them?*

But I know the answer, and it's as disturbing as the question itself. Some people hate for the sake of hating. They hurt others for the sake of hurting. In the three years I've been chief of police, I've seen both of those things in all their hideous forms. I've heard the explanations, too, and they're as pathetic and ugly as the people who act on them: The Amish are stupid; they only go through the eighth grade. The Amish are dirty. The buggies slow down traffic and cause accidents. The Amish are a cult of religious fanatics. The diatribe goes on and on, as senseless as the people who spew it.

I hit Township Road 2 doing eighty. My rear tires fishtail as I turn onto the narrow asphalt track, so I back it down to sixty. Less than half a mile in, I see the horse and

203

buggy. It's parked at a cockeyed angle in the bar ditch, as if someone ran it off the road. The horse has managed to work the reins loose, but it can't move forward or backward. Judging from the trampled ground, the animal has been standing there for quite some time.

I slide out of the Explorer. Anger is a knot in my chest as I take in the sight of the young Amish man. He's sitting on the ground, his hands stretched above his head, his wrists tied to the buggy wheel. He looks to be in his early twenties. He's not wearing a shirt. Someone — the Good Samaritan driver, more than likely — has draped a coat over him. His shoulders are bare and flecked with blood, and I pray he hasn't been stabbed or shot. He's wearing trousers, and I can see his work boots sticking out from beneath the coat. An older man wearing a navy jacket, dark slacks, and Walmart loafers stands next to him, looking upset.

Going around to the rear of the Explorer, I pull out a thermal blanket and a bottle of water I keep stored next to the first-aid kit, then start toward them.

The driver looks to be in his mid-fifties and has a receding hairline and a paunch. "I was going to cut the ropes, but I didn't have a knife," he tells me. "Poor guy says he's been here all night. Damnedest thing I ever saw."

"How long have you been here?" I don't stop walking, but continue on toward the buggy.

"Just a few minutes. Called you guys before I even got out of the car." He falls in beside me. "You just never know what you're going to run into on the road these days, do you?"

"What's your name?"

"Herman Morse. I run an insurance agency up in Wooster."

I scan the surrounding woods, wondering if the perpetrator is still around, watching with the glee of some high-school prankster. But I know it won't be that easy. "You see anyone else?" I ask.

"No ma'am. Just the Amish guy."

I motion toward the green Cadillac parked behind the buggy. "That your car?"

"Yes, ma'am."

"I want you to go stand by your car and wait for me, okay? Don't move around too much; there might be footprints we'll want to preserve. I'll need to get a statement from you."

"Uh, sure." He lingers a moment, glances toward the Amish man. "He's pretty banged up. Shouldn't you call an ambulance or something?"

"They're on the way." Reaching the young man, I kneel, take a quick visual assessment. He's pale and shivering. His lips are dry and tinged blue from the cold. Probably suffering from hypothermia and dehydration. His left eye is swollen shut. The other is the color of a ripe eggplant. I cringe when I see his hands. Both are swollen and blue. The fingertips are white and hard-looking; I suspect he may have some frostbite. His wrists are chafed and bloody, which tells me he's been struggling to free himself from his binds for quite some time.

"How badly are you hurt?" Snapping the blanket open, I cover him with it.

"C-cold m-mostly." He stares at me with bloodshot and glassy eyes. "I think my hands are frozen."

Tugging my pocketknife from my belt, I cut the rope. He winces when his limbs break free. I can tell by the lack of movement in his hands that he can't flex his fingers.

"How long have you been here?" I ask.

"All night." A groan escapes him when he tries to rise.

I set my hands on his shoulders and ease him back down. "Just stay put a moment."

"I need to unhook the horse. He's old.

206

Been tangled in the harness all night."

"I'll take care of him. You just relax a moment. I don't want you moving around too much, in case you're injured." I motion toward the blood on his shoulders and chest. "Who did this to you?"

"T-two *Englischers.*"

"Do you know their names? Did you recognize them?"

He shakes his head. "I never saw them before."

I look him over, searching for signs of life-threatening injuries — blood, broken bones, stab wounds, bullet wounds. "What happened?"

He shrugs, looks away. "I was on my way to town for some lumber. They came up fast, blocked my way. When I stopped, they ambushed me."

"What kind of vehicle?"

"A truck. Blue. Old, I think."

"Which direction did they go?"

"Toward town."

I hit my lapel mike and put out a BOLO for an older blue pickup truck. "Did they have a weapon?"

He shakes his head. "Just their fists."

"Did they say anything?"

"They called me names." He shrugs, letting me know that didn't bother him. "Took the Lord's name in vain." That bothered him a lot.

I nod, try hard to bank the fury rising inside me. "There's an ambulance on the way." I uncap the bottle of water, put it to his lips, and he takes a sip. "What's your name?"

"Mark Lambright." He looks down at his hands. His face contorts in pain when he tries to flex his knuckles. "I need to get home. My wife will be worried."

"I'll have someone go by your place and let her know you're all right. Where do you live?" He cites a farm a few miles down the road after I give him another sip of water. "Can you tell me what the two men looked like?"

His eyes skate away from mine. "I don't want any trouble."

"You've already got trouble."

He doesn't answer, and a sensation of déjà vu engulfs me. I recall the burning buggy incident, and I know this man isn't going to cooperate, either.

"Mr. Lambright." I take a deep breath, reel in my frustration. "I need to find the men who did this to you so that I can keep them from doing it again. You could have been killed."

He motions toward his body. "As you can

see, I'm okay."

"What did the men look like?"

He stares down at his swollen, frozen hands.

"If you stick your head in the sand, whoever did this is going to get away and do it again. Next time, it could be a woman or child. They might kill someone. Is that what you want?"

He watches me with his one good eye, shakes his head. "I do not wish for anyone to be hurt. I just want to go home."

I sit back on my heels, frustration churning inside me. In the distance, I hear sirens and I know the ambulance will be here soon. The sound of tires crunching through snow draws my attention. I look up and see Tomasetti's Tahoe pull up beside my Explorer.

Rising, I start toward him. He gets out of the SUV, looking tall and dark against the smooth gray sky. He wears the long wool coat, no gloves or hat. His espresso-colored eyes meet mine as he crosses to me.

"You look aggravated."

"Pissed is probably a more accurate description." I tell him everything I learned from Lambright. "Felony assault at least. Maybe attempted murder. The problem is, he's not going to be much help."

Tomasetti cocks his head. "Why not?"

"He doesn't want to get involved."

"What is this, some kind of conspiracy? He just had the shit hammered out of him. How much more *involved* could he be?"

"He doesn't want to deal with the English."

"You tried?"

I nod. "If the passerby hadn't called us, this probably would have gone unreported."

"We need to ID whoever did this. Without it, we don't have shit."

I glance toward the victim. "We could try waterboarding him."

"Probably wouldn't go over too well with the brass."

I heave a sigh. "I'll get my guys out here to canvass, see if anyone saw anything."

"Scene doesn't look too promising."

The ambulance pulls up behind Tomasetti's Tahoe. We watch the two paramedics open the rear doors and unload the gurney. They roll it across the road to the bar ditch and kick down the brake. One of the men kneels next to Lambright and begins a field assessment. The other, a freckle-faced man with a red goatee, approaches Tomasetti and me. "What ya got, Chief?"

"Assault," I say. "Hypothermia. Frostbite, maybe. He's been out in the cold all night."

"Cold night. He's lucky." He shoves his hands into his pockets. "You guys know who did it?"

"We're working on it." That's my standard answer in situations where I don't know squat.

Tomasetti and I stand in the dirty snow and watch the two paramedics load Lambright onto the gurney. The Amish man makes eye contact with me briefly as they roll him across the asphalt. I stare back, letting him know I'm not happy with his lack of cooperation.

That's when I realize I've yet to make good on my promise to take care of the horse. It's been standing all night with nothing to eat or drink. "I need to unhitch the horse," I say.

Tomasetti arches a brow. "Can't help you there."

I cross to the animal, moving slowly, my hand outstretched. "Whoa, boy. Whoa."

It's an old gelding with a sorrel coat and the kind eyes of a working animal. Stepping into the mud, I set my hand against the animal's neck, then run both hands over its shoulder and down both front legs, checking for injuries. Finding none, I go to work on the harness. Having tacked up our own horses many times as a girl, I let the dormant memories come rushing back. I un-buckle the crupper and girth, unfasten the shaft tugs, pull the long reins through the guides, then lift the collar over the animal's head. In a couple of minutes, the horse is free of the buggy. I lead him to a gnarled fence post, use the scissor snap to attach one of the reins to the halter beneath his bridle, and tie him until a neighbor arrives to walk him home.

I turn back to the street, to find Tomasetti watching me. "You're pretty good at that."

"Lots of practice as a kid."

"I'm impressed."

But I can tell by the way he's looking at me that the horse is the last thing on his mind. "What are you thinking?"

"I was just thinking about connections."

"Okay," I say slowly. "You have my atten-tion."

He moves closer, his eyes meeting mine. "You mentioned earlier you had considered the possibility that these hate crimes are related to the Slabaugh case. Do you still think that's a possibility?"

"I'm not sure," I tell him. "They feel dif-ferent."

The statement doesn't need any explana-tion, not for Tomasetti. And he doesn't dispute it. "I agree. But maybe we shouldn't close the door on the possibility."

The frustration I'd been feeling earlier transforms into something edgy and uncomfortable. "What's your angle?"

"What if the Slabaugh murders weren't intentional?" He shrugs. "What if it started out as a hate crime? The situation somehow got out of control. Things went too far."

My mind takes the turn into territory I don't want to venture and runs with it. "Maybe whoever pushed them into the pit didn't know about the dangerous gases. Maybe they didn't realize the outcome would be fatal."

He nods. "Rachael Slabaugh tried to get the two men out of the pit and was overcome by the methane gas."

"Collateral damage." I consider the implications of that. "I don't know, Tomasetti. If the deaths weren't intentional, it seems logical that the person or group responsible would stop now that the police are all over it."

"Unless they *liked* it. Or decided those deaths weren't such a bad thing. A benefit to their cause."

"That puts all of this into a whole new category."

"A really ugly one."

"Not to mention dangerous." I glance over

at the trampled snow where a young Amish man nearly froze to death, and I shiver. Everything Tomasetti said runs through my head like a ticker tape streaming bad news. "Why not just kill him outright, since they've already crossed that line?"

"A few more hours and he might not have made it."

I nod without enthusiasm. "I'm not convinced it's a viable theory, but I'll keep an open mind."

"Something to think about," he says.

Watching the ambulance pull away, I find myself wondering if he's right, if they'll strike again, and what they'll do next time.

CHAPTER 10

An outdoor scene that's been trampled and is spread over a large area is extremely difficult to process. Tomasetti called his office and requested a CSU, but none of us are too optimistic they'll glean anything useful. Sheriff Rasmussen arrived a short while after the ambulance left. We're basically standing around doing nothing, so I call Glock and send him and Pickles out to canvass the area farms, in the hope that one of the neighbors saw *something.* But with the area being heavily wooded and the houses more than a mile apart, the prospect of a witness is not very promising.

It's nearly noon when my cell phone chirps. Pickles says, "Chief, Glock and I are out here at Dickey Allen's place. We were asking him about the buggy incident, and we got to talking about the Slabaughs. He told us Solly Slabaugh used to hire a guy by the name of Ricky Coulter to do odd jobs around the farm. I ain't run him through LEADS yet, but if I recall, he's had some problems with the law."

That's the way cases usually go. You get a break from some unlikely source when you're least expecting it. It's kind of like falling in love, without all the insanity. "I'll go talk to him." I pull out my keys, make eye contact with Tomasetti, and motion toward my vehicle. "Any of the neighbors see anything?" I ask Pickles.

"Not a damn thing."

"Keep at it."

I ring off, clip my phone onto my belt. I'm walking fast, energized by the possibility of a break in the case. Tomasetti falls in beside me. "You get something?"

"The name of a guy who did some work for Slabaugh."

"Sounds promising."

"A break would be nice."

We reach the Explorer. "What about your vehicle?" I ask.

"I'll pick it up after we talk to Coulter."

"Fair enough." We climb inside and I pull onto Township Road.

"Wouldn't be the first time some lowlife killed the guy who signed his paycheck," Tomasetti says.

"Who says crime doesn't pay?"

■ ■ ■ ■

I call Lois for Coulter's most current address as I head toward the highway. She punches his name into LEADS and discovers he did time at the Mansfield Correctional Institution for burglarizing his place of employment, a tire shop, where he stole some tools and two hundred dollars in petty cash.

"Raiding the till to triple murder is one hell of a leap," Tomasetti comments.

"Yeah, but not implausible."

"What's your theory?"

"Maybe Coulter planned to rob Slabaugh. Maybe he wasn't expecting the brother to be there. Abel was visiting, remember? Anyway, let's say Coulter showed up. The three men had a confrontation. Things got physical. Coulter pushed them into the pit, then panicked and ran."

Tomasetti takes over. "Rachael Slabaugh shows up. Tries to save her husband, but the methane gets to her and she falls into the pit."

"What about the missing cash in the mason jar?" I ask.

"Maybe he hit the house on the way out, once everyone was in the barn."

"Pretty cold-blooded."

"Yeah."

We look at each other, our minds churning. It's a good supposition. But is it right?

Coulter lives in a small frame house a block from the railroad tracks and grain elevator. The dank, salty smell of the nearby slaughterhouse wafts into the Explorer as I pull up to the curb. An old Ford Thunderbird with wide tires, aluminum wheels, and oxidized black paint sits in the driveway, a tribute to the muscle cars of the 1970s.

"He work?" Tomasetti asks.

"Third shift at the oil-filter factory in Millersburg."

We disembark and take the cracked sidewalk to the porch. The front yard is mostly dirt and trampled gray snow. A child's tricycle and several toy cars litter the sparse grass. It looks like a toy graveyard.

Standing slightly to one side, I use my keys to knock on the storm door.

A moment later, a plump woman holding a newborn baby opens the door. She wears faded jeans and a Cincinnati Reds sweatshirt. Pale blue eyes dart from me to Tomasetti and back to me. "Can I help you?" she asks.

I show her my badge. "Is Ricky Coulter here?"

"He's in bed." She looks over her shoulder. "Is something wrong?"

"We just want to talk to him," I say. "Can you get him for us?"

"He's only been asleep a couple of hours."

"This won't take long." Tomasetti smiles easily. "Go wake him for us."

I can tell she doesn't want to comply, but she's smart enough to realize she doesn't have a choice. "Okay." Hefting the baby, she steps back. "Come on in."

We step into a small living room. The walls are white and nicked up, evidence of a family that's long outgrown its dwelling. A few feet away, a toddler wearing a diaper and a stained bib sits on well-worn carpet and pounds a pan with a wooden spoon. In the kitchen, a white dog with a cast on its leg lies on the cracked linoleum, watching us, its tail fanning the air. The television is tuned to a soap opera.

"Can I help you?"

I look up and see a thirty-something man shuffle out of the hall. He's wearing pajama bottoms and a white T-shirt. I can tell by the crease marks on the left side of his face that he'd been sleeping. Behind him, the woman clutches the baby, eyeing us with unconcealed suspicion.

"You Ricky Coulter?" I ask.

"Yeah." Rubbing his fingers over mussed hair, he walks toward us. "What's this all about?"

"I understand you did some work for Solomon Slabaugh," I begin.

"I dug some postholes and put in some end posts for him a couple of months ago." His brows knit. "Does this have something to do with what happened to him?"

"Where were you yesterday morning?"

He takes the question in stride, as if I'd asked about the weather. "I was here."

"You work that night?"

"I was sick. Ate something that didn't agree with me."

"Is there someone who can verify that you were here?"

Turning, he motions toward the woman. "Honey, tell them where I was yesterday morning."

She hovers a few feet away, bouncing the baby, dividing her attention between us and the soap opera. "He was home sick. We ate at that burger place down by the speedway, and he threw up half the night."

The baby squirms and begins to cry. Bouncing him slightly, she coos to him. "Shush now, little bear."

Tomasetti looks from the baby to Coulter. "You ever have a disagreement with Slabaugh?"

Coulter shakes his head. "Never. Solly was a real stand-up guy. Honest and nice as could be."

"We know about your record," Tomasetti says.

"I figured that's why you're here."

"You robbed your employer," I add. "Took two hundred dollars and over five hundred dollars in tools."

Coulter's gaze flicks to me. "That was a long time ago. I did my time for that. I'm a different man now."

"Prison rehabilitated you?" Tomasetti's voice is bone dry.

Coulter doesn't notice. "You might say that. I found the Lord when I was in prison. I read the Bible. Started going to services every Sunday. Once I let Jesus Christ into my life, He showed me the way."

Tomasetti gives him a "You've got to be shitting me" look. "He didn't happen to show you the way to Slabaugh's cash or valuables, did he?"

Coulter offers a placid smile, his resolve unshaken. "If someone needed a shirt, Solly would have given them not only his shirt but his coat, too. If I needed something — money, food, *whatever* — he would have given it to me, no strings. He was a staunch

221

believer and a good man. I couldn't believe it when I heard they were killed."

"Do you mind if we take a quick look around?" Tomasetti asks.

Coulter opens his arms, a priest welcoming the lost into his church. "Knock yourselves out. I don't have anything to hide."

I see Tomasetti roll his eyes as he starts toward the kitchen. Searching the home of a private citizen without a warrant can be tricky, but I know why Tomasetti asked. He knew Coulter would give us his permission. Chances are, we won't find a damn thing. Criminals rarely invite the cops into their homes if they've got something to hide. But you never know when a lucky break might present itself.

I start toward the bedrooms at the rear, not quite sure what I'm looking for. I pass a bathroom, flip on the light, peek inside. I see a shower curtain with green fish and little blue starfish; seaside-themed wallpaper. Ratty towels hang neatly on a pitted chrome rack. A plastic boat rests on the side of the tub. A typical family bathroom. Nothing of interest here.

Moving on, I come to the first bedroom. It's a small space with a single window and blue paint on the walls. A bunk bed decked out in Spider-Man sheets sits opposite a crib. Toys of every shape and size lay scattered on the carpeting. The room smells of baby powder and dirty clothes. Stepping over a coloring book on the floor, I peek in the closet. Out-of-season clothes lie folded on an old bookcase. I notice a Sam's Club–size box of disposable diapers, sneakers, a tiny hoodie wadded up on the floor.

I proceed down the hall to the master bedroom. It's larger, with two windows, newish beige carpet, and a fresh coat of paint. The furniture is rustic with a Native American theme. The bed is unmade and I can see the glow of the electric blanket control on the night table. I go to the closet, pull open the sliding door. I see a half dozen pairs of blue jeans, sweaters, and flannel shirts. Work boots and a pair of women's clogs lie on the floor. Moving the clothes aside with my forearm, I check the rear, where an old suitcase, a baseball bat, and an old leather glove are stashed.

I'm about to straighten, when I catch a glimpse of glossy wood behind a long coat. I shove the coat aside. A strange thrill rushes through me when I see the dark patina of a rifle stock. I don't have anything against citizens keeping guns in general. But Ricky Coulter is no ordinary citizen. He's a felon — not to mention a person of interest in a triple murder case — which makes it illegal for him to possess even a hunting rifle.

I pull a pair of latex gloves from my coat pocket, slip them on, and pick up the rifle. Some vague sense of recognition flares in the back of my mind as I drag it out. The rifle is familiar, but I'm almost certain I've never seen it before. It's an older .22 bolt-action with a walnut stock, no scope. I open the chamber, find two bullets inside. Loaded. With little kids in the house. "Idiot," I whisper, and tug a Baggie from my belt.

Plucking out the bullets, I drop them into the Baggie, put it in my coat pocket. Closing the chamber, I carry the rifle into the hall.

Tomasetti and Coulter are standing in the living room. I can tell by Coulter's expression that Tomasetti isn't being very nice. Both men stare at the rifle in my hands as I approach. I focus my attention on Coulter. "Did you forget about this?" I ask.

He blinks at me. "Where did you get that?"

"I didn't pull it out of my back pocket."

"It ain't mine."

"Maybe you could explain how it got in your closet."

His eyes flick from me to Tomasetti to the

rifle. "I've never seen it before in my life."

His wife gasps. "Ricky . . . where'd that come from?"

Tomasetti shakes his head. "And to think I was just starting to like him."

"I'm serious." Coulter's voice is indignant now. "I don't have any guns in this house. I got kids. I'm a convicted felon; I can't have any kind of weapon."

"How did it get in your closet?" I ask.

"I don't know." He takes a step back, his eyes bouncing like Ping-Pong balls between me and Tomasetti. "It ain't mine. I swear. I don't own a twenty-two, and I never have."

In ten years of law-enforcement experience, I've heard every conceivable lie told in every conceivable form and spewed with the vehemence of brimstone and fire. I'm an expert at spotting lies and the liars who tell them. But as I watch Coulter, all I can think is that this guy is a step above the rest, because he's almost believable.

Tomasetti steps closer to him. "So if it isn't yours, how did it get there?"

"I don't know." He chokes out the words like a cough. "I'm telling you: That gun ain't mine."

I glance sideways at Tomasetti, and I can tell he's thinking the same thing I am: *This guy is good.* That's unusual, because Tomasetti is one of those cops who believe 90 percent of the population are pathological liars.

"We're going to have to take you to the station," I say.

"Ricky? What's going on?" His wife rushes toward us. She's still holding the baby, looking at the rifle as if I'm about to shoot her husband with it. "Where did you get that gun?"

The toddler runs to his mother, grabs her leg, and buries his face in the denim. "Mommy."

"It's not mine. I swear!" Coulter chokes out a sound of pure anguish. "Aw, come on . . . my kids . . ."

Maintaining eye contact, I tug handcuffs from my belt and approach him. "Turn around."

"What are you doing?" his wife screeches.

"We're just going to talk to him," I tell her, hoping she stays calm.

"Aw man." Coulter's face screws up. To my dismay, he hangs his head and begins to cry. "Don't do this. Not in front of my kids."

I glance toward the door. "Let's step outside."

With the insouciance of a man taking a Sunday stroll, Tomasetti steps between the wife and Coulter. "We just have a few questions for him, ma'am. Step aside."

"About what?" she cries.

I turn my back on them. Taking Coulter by the bicep, I guide him through the front door. It's colder and the wind has kicked up. A misty rain falls from a murky sky.

Coulter wipes his face with his sleeve, then turns and offers his wrists. "That's not my rifle."

I snap on the cuffs. "We'll get it straightened out at the station."

An hour later, Tomasetti and I are sitting in my office, drinking one of Mona's coffee-chocolate-hazelnut concoctions. I'm wishing I had something a lot stronger. I booked Coulter into jail on a parole violation and contacted his parole officer. She sounded young and inexperienced — and surprised by the news. In the year he's been out of prison, Ricky Coulter has been a model parolee. He holds down a full-time job and has never missed a single appointment. After hanging up, I recap the conversation for Tomasetti, and he tells me she just hasn't been part of the system long enough.

"A few more years and nothing will surprise her," he says.

"That's really jaded, Tomasetti."

"Reality is jaded." He shrugs, unapolo-

227

getic. "One day Citizen Joe's a born-again Christian; the next he slits his neighbor's throat over a parking space."

"Nice." I'm not going to admit there's a part of me that agrees with him.

I sip coffee as I type the serial number of the rifle into an NCIC query to see if it comes back as stolen.

"So what are you thinking?" Tomasetti asks after a moment.

"I'm thinking I don't like this."

"You mean Coulter as a suspect?"

"I mean any of it."

I finish typing and look at him over my monitor. He's wearing a charcoal shirt with a black tie beneath a nicely cut jacket. His trench coat is draped across the back of his chair. I can smell the piney-woods scent of his aftershave from where I sit. He's a nice-looking man, but not in the traditional sense. He's got a severe mouth, and his eyes are too intense. But the overall picture of him appeals to me in a way that no other man ever has. I don't know why, but that scares the hell out of me.

"The kids . . ." I shake my head. "I felt like the bad guy, taking him in the way we did."

"You weren't."

"I know, but it felt that way." I hit ENTER,

sending the query, and lean back in my chair. "He seemed pretty adamant about the rifle."

"You tell a lie enough times and you start to believe it yourself."

For an instant, I wonder if he's talking about more than just Coulter. I've told my share of lies. He knows about most of them, but not all. "Anyone ever tell you you're cynical?"

"All the time." Leaning back in the chair, he extends his legs out in front of him and stretches. "What else is bugging you?"

I think about it a moment. "When I saw the rifle in the closet, I got this strange feeling that I'd seen it before."

"You mean recently?"

"I'm not sure. Maybe." I reach for the memory, but it's not there, like a hand grasping at smoke. "I was hoping to tie up the Slabaugh case with Coulter, but I don't think he's our guy."

"To tell you the truth, I don't like him for this or the hate crimes."

"Where's all that hard-nosed cynicism, Tomasetti?"

"At the risk of ruining whatever image of me you've drawn in your head, I don't think a cop should let cynicism override good old-fashioned instinct."

"Now there's a novel concept."

"Chief?"

I glance toward the door to see Glock standing there, looking excited. "Please tell me you have good news," I say.

"A guy out on Township Road 2 remembered seeing a dark-colored pickup truck hauling ass last night near where you found Lambright. Says he noticed because the driver blew a stop sign, just about hit him."

"Anyone get a plate number?"

He shakes his head. "Witness says he was moving too fast."

"What about a description of the driver?"

"Don't know. T. J.'s talking to the guy now."

"Any word on Lambright's condition?" Tomasetti asks.

"Broken ribs. Broken nose. Hypothermia. Emergency doc says someone worked him over good."

"Just for being Amish," I mutter. "Sons of bitches."

"Maybe the truck will pan out," Glock says.

I'm not as optimistic. "Run all blue and black pickup trucks, Ford and Chevy, registered in Holmes and Coshocton counties," I say to Glock. "Run the drivers through LEADS, see if we get anything

230

interesting."

"I'm on it," he says, and disappears down the hall.

I feel like breaking something, but there's nothing handy, so I look at my computer screen to see if anything has come back on the rifle. Of course, there's nothing there yet. The database is huge and queries take time. Something about the rifle niggles at me. Some insignificant memory on the edge of my brain. Something I thought wasn't important but is. I know I've seen that stock before. But where?

I'm in the process of retracing my every step from the day before when it hits me. "Holy shit." I jump to my feet fast enough to startle Tomasetti. "I think I just remembered where I saw the rifle."

He arches a brow. "Lay it on me."

I look at him, my heart pounding. "The Slabaugh place. Yesterday afternoon. In the mudroom."

"Yesterday? Are you sure?"

"No." But I am. The more I think about it, the more certain I become. I grab my parka. "Only one way to find out."

Standing, he reaches for his own coat and sighs. "Cynicism outstrips faith in mankind once again."

CHAPTER 11

Rain slashes down in sheets when we step out of the station. We hightail it to the Explorer, but we're dripping by the time we buckle in.

"If you saw the rifle at the Slabaugh place yesterday, how the hell did it get to Coulter's house?" Tomasetti asks.

I glance at him as I back out of my parking space. "Good question."

"Are you sure it's the same rifle?"

"I'm not one hundred percent certain. But it's old, similar to one my dad used to own, so it caught my attention." The tires spin on the wet pavement when I hit the gas. "It's too similar not to check out."

"Where did you see it?"

"The mudroom. Salome took me into the basement yesterday and I just happened to notice it." I tell him about the mason jar and the missing cash.

Tomasetti mulls that over. "Any idea when

the money was taken?"

"No idea. I sent the jar for latents."

The windshield wipers wage a losing battle with the deluge as I turn into the Slabaughs' lane. I park behind a buggy I don't recognize, and I realize Bishop Troyer has probably asked another Amish family to stay with the children. I wonder if the social worker from Children Services has been in contact yet. I wonder how it went. . . .

Punching off the headlights, I twist the key and kill the engine. A few yards away, the house hulks, the windows utterly dark, and a strange thread of worry goes through me.

"Kind of early for bed, isn't it?" Tomasetti asks.

"A lot of Amish farmers are up by four A.M. They go to bed early." Still, I can't deny the uneasiness slinking up my spine. The place looks deserted.

"I'd never make it as an Amish guy."

"Yeah, you drink too much."

"I cuss too much."

We smile at each other, and I reach for the door handle. "Let's go wake them up."

We slosh down the walk to the back porch. Opening the screen door, I rap hard with my knuckles. Around me, the farm is dark and still, imparting a semblance of isolation, as if we're the last living people on earth.

I'm in the process of knocking a second time when the door swings open. An Amish man with red hair and a full beard thrusts a lantern at me. "Hello?" He blinks owlishly. "Is there a problem?"

I show him my badge and identify myself. "I'm sorry to bother you so late."

He squints at Tomasetti. "Is this about Solly and Rachael?"

I nod. "Bishop Troyer left you with the children?"

"*Ja.*"

"What's your name, sir?"

"Nicholas Raber."

"May we come in?"

"Of course." Bowing slightly, he backs up a few steps.

I enter the mudroom. Vaguely, I'm aware of Tomasetti behind me, and of Raber shuffling toward the kitchen, probably to light another lantern. The potbellied stove is to my left. I slide a mini Maglite from my coat pocket and shine the beam toward the area where I last saw the rifle. A strand of uneasiness ripples through me when I realize it's not there.

"The rifle's gone," I whisper.

"You sure?"

I turn and frown at him. "There's nothing wrong with my eyesight or my memory."

He smiles, and I know he's messing with me. Rolling my eyes, I glance toward the kitchen, where the yellow glow of lantern light spills into the mudroom. Raber stands in the doorway, watching us.

Looking at him, I motion toward the corner where I last saw the gun. "Did you see the rifle that was here earlier?"

He shakes his head. "No."

Tomasetti comes up beside me and directs his attention to the Amish man. "How long have you been here?"

"Since five o'clock. We fixed the children dinner." His expression becomes puzzled. "Why are you asking about the gun? Is there something wrong?"

"We're not sure yet." I step closer to him. "Is your wife here with you?"

"*Ja.* She's upstairs."

"Can you check with her to see if she remembers seeing the rifle?"

He nods, his expression going from puzzled to concerned. "What's happened?"

"I saw a rifle here earlier," I say. "Now it's gone. I need to know where it is."

"I'll wake Frannie." He nods, keeps on nodding. "Frannie cleaned earlier. Maybe she moved it to another place."

235

"Thank you." I pull my cell from my belt and dial Bishop Troyer's number. He's one of the few Amish in the area who has a phone he keeps for emergencies. I figure this qualifies.

He answers on the tenth ring, and I remember the phone is in the kitchen. He had to get up and go downstairs to answer.

"*Ja,*" he says grumpily.

"Bishop Troyer, I'm sorry to wake you."

"Yes, me, too," he growls.

I tell him about the rifle. "I need to know if you moved it when you were here."

"No," he replies. "I didn't even know it was there."

"Did your wife move it?"

He's quiet for a moment. "I'll wake her and ask her."

"If she did, will you call me right back?"

"Yes," he says. "But I'm certain she didn't move it."

"Thank —"

He hangs up before I can finish. Smiling, I hit END and glance at Tomasetti.

"Any luck?" he asks.

I recap my conversation with the bishop.

"You sure you saw the rifle, Kate?"

"I'm sure."

Raber comes back into the kitchen. "My wife did not see any gun," he says.

I look at Tomasetti. I can tell from his expression that he's thinking the same thing I am. Neither of us likes Ricky Coulter for the murders. Did someone know Coulter had worked for Slabaugh and plant the rifle in Coulter's house for us to find?

I turn my attention back to the Amish man. "Have you had any visitors today?"

He looks confused for a moment, as if the thought had never occurred to him, then slowly shakes his head. "Frannie and I arrived here around five o'clock. We've been busy with the children and chores. Supper and prayer and baths. We've had no visitors."

I nod. There's been a lot of traffic in and out of the house in the last day or so. Almost anyone could have come in and taken it, unnoticed. "Are the children here?"

"Of course they are."

"Could you go get Mose for me?"

His hesitation tells me he doesn't want to do it. The Amish are extremely protective of their young, particularly when it comes to outsiders. "Please," I say. "I wouldn't ask you to wake him at this hour if it wasn't important."

Shaking his head in resignation, Raber turns and starts toward the living room. For a moment, neither of us speaks. Outside, rain pours off the gutters and slaps the ground. It's so quiet inside, I can hear the hiss of the lantern.

"What the hell is going on?" I whisper.

Across the room, I see Tomasetti looking at the potbellied stove. "Who had access to the house?"

"Almost anyone. A visitor."

"I sent the rifle to the lab for latents," he tells me. "Results should —"

Raber bursts into the kitchen. "Mose is gone!"

"Gone?" Tomasetti and I exchange looks. "Where?"

"I don't know." The Amish man looks upset. "He's not in his bed."

"Any idea where he might be?" I ask.

Raber shakes his head. "I do not know."

"Does he have transportation?" Tomasetti asks.

"The horses." He crosses the room, yanks a heavy wool coat off a wooden dowel set into the wall. "I will check."

Tomasetti stops him. "We'll take the barn. You go check the other children."

The man looks undecided for a moment, then his eyes find mine. "Mose and his brothers and sister are my responsibility."

"I'm sure they're fine," I say. "Go check on the others. Agent Tomasetti and I will check the barn."

"*Ja.*" Jerking his head, he spins and disappears into the darkened living room.

"Let's go." I fly into the mudroom, jog to the door, yank it open.

Then we're outside in the cold, sprinting through the rain. I can hear Tomasetti beside me, cursing. Without moonlight, the nights in Amish country are incredibly dark. There are no streetlamps, no porch lights or glowing windows. We splash through a deep puddle, and I'm soaked from the knees down. Fumbling for the mini Maglite in my pocket, I pull it out, turn it on.

I see the behemoth shape of the barn twenty feet ahead. Concern transforms into an edgy uneasiness when I notice that the door is ajar. We pause before entering, not sure what we might be walking into. I'm aware of Tomasetti next to me, pulling his sidearm. I do the same, keep my finger off the trigger. He goes in first, but I'm right behind him.

Entering the barn is like stepping into a long-buried casket. It's dark and dank and dusty. I smell the earthy scents of horses and hay, punctuated by the unpleasant tang of the manure and hogs. I sweep the area with the flashlight. I see huge wooden rafters garlanded with gossamer cobwebs.

The rails of the fence are dead ahead. I can see the glint of the pigs' eyes.

"I can't see shit," Tomasetti whispers.

"I think the horse stalls are to the right," I whisper.

We sidle right ten feet, twenty. I'm keenly aware of Tomasetti beside me, the gun in his hand. My own weapon is heavy and cold in mine. I start when I hear movement ahead and direct the beam forward. Two buggy horses look at us through the bars of their stall, chewing hay.

"Horses are here. Mose has got to be around somewhere," I say.

"Unless he walked into town for a beer."

Considering my own teenage years, I realize it's a possibility. "Let's check the loft."

"Lead the way."

I hand the Maglite to Tomasetti. Spotting the loft ladder, which consists of six short timbers nailed to the wall, I look up into the darkness. "Mose!" I shout. "It's Kate Burkholder."

The unmistakable thud of hurried footsteps on the wood ceiling sounds above us. I glance at Tomasetti. He motions with the light toward the opening, and I begin a too-fast climb to the top.

I feel confident we're not in any danger; I'm more worried about Mose. He's suffered a terrible loss and has been under a tremendous amount of emotional distress. Still, I don't like the idea of entering a place totally blind.

Reaching the top of the ladder, I thrust my head and shoulders into the loft. I hear shuffling to my left and immediately sense a presence. Heart pounding, I heave myself up and lurch to my feet. Tomasetti is right behind me with the flashlight. The beam hits the rafters overhead as he climbs up. Then he's on his feet and the beam sweeps over bales of alfalfa hay. A pink blanket looks out of place spread out on the floor. Then I see Mose. He's standing next to the stack of hay. He's wearing trousers but no shirt, and his suspenders are hanging down to his knees. Using his hand, he shields his eyes from the beam of the flashlight.

"What are you doing here?" he asks.

Tomasetti steps closer, keeping the light on the boy, purposefully blinding him. "You Mose?"

He squints, his gaze skating from me to Tomasetti. "Who're you?"

Tomasetti doesn't answer.

"What are you doing up here?" I ask.

Mose looks uncomfortable. He can't meet our gazes. "I just . . . wanted some quiet."

For an instant, I think maybe we caught

241

him masturbating. Ready to cut him some slack, I glance at Tomasetti. He doesn't look quite as compassionate. Suspicion glints diamond hard in his eyes. "What are you doing up here, Mose?" he asks.

"Nothing."

"You're hiding out here in the dark all by yourself. No one knew where you were."

"I'm not hiding." Mose shifts his weight from one foot to the other. "I'm not doing anything."

I hear movement in the hay. Tomasetti hears it, too, and he jerks the beam left. Salome emerges from behind a tall stack of hay. She's wearing the blue dress but no stockings or shoes. Her brown hair billows about her shoulders. Her *kapp* hangs around her neck. She doesn't meet my gaze, but the guilt on her face is unmistakable.

Shock is like a silent shotgun blast. The concussion pushes me back a step. I stare at her bare feet. I don't want to acknowledge the thoughts prying into my brain. Ugly thoughts that offend some deeply ingrained sense of morality. Thoughts that affront me with the wrongness of what I see, what I feel in my heart.

Holstering his weapon, Tomasetti steps toward her. "What are you doing out here with him?"

Salome steps back and mutters something unintelligible.

Shaking his head in a gesture that looks like disgust, he shines the light on the floor. The beam stops on the scrap of white fabric lying on a bale of hay next to the blanket. Another layer of shock rattles my brain. Panties. Salome's panties. I stare at them, aware of the pound of rain on the tin roof, matching the hard pound of my own heart.

The next thing I know, Tomasetti crosses to Mose. "What the hell were you doing with her?"

"We were just talking."

"Don't bullshit me."

A dozen alarms jangle in my head. "Tomasetti," I warn.

He doesn't look at me, doesn't even acknowledge me. Every ounce of his attention is on Mose. "That girl is your sister!" he shouts.

Mose looks down at the ground.

Tomasetti shines the light on Salome. "How old are you?" he demands.

"F-fifteen." Her voice is little more than a chirp.

"Fifteen?" He gives Mose a dark look, then turns back to the girl. "Did he force you?"

"No!"

Tomasetti's mouth twists. He doesn't believe her. Or maybe he doesn't want to believe her. I see him grinding his teeth. He turns to Mose. "Do you think she's old enough to be out here with you like this?"

"I don't —"

"How could you disrespect her like that? How could you disrespect yourself?"

Mose gulps. "I —"

He doesn't have time to finish the sentence. Lunging at him, Tomasetti clamps his hand around the back of the boy's neck, shoves him toward the ladder. "Get your goddamn ass down there."

Mose stumbles, regains his footing, and shoots a nasty glare at Tomasetti. "Don't do that again."

"Or what? What are you going to do, you perverted little shit?" Tomasetti thrusts a finger toward the ladder. "Get down that ladder before I throw you down." The muscles in his jaw work as he crosses to me, hands me the flashlight. I see him pulling himself back. "Get her dressed and come on."

"Calm down." I make eye contact with him as I take the flashlight. "He's a minor."

"I know what he is," he grinds out.

I watch them descend the ladder, then I direct the flashlight beam toward Salome.

She's sitting on a bale of hay with her head down, sobbing. She holds her *kapp* in one hand, her panties in the other. *Shit,* I think, and go to her.

"You okay?" I ask.

She nods but doesn't look at me.

I shine the light on the panties in her hand. "You need to get dressed, so we can go."

She raises her face to mine. Tears glisten on her cheeks. Her nose is running, but she doesn't bother to wipe away the snot. "I can't go down there. I can't face them."

"Yes, you can," I say firmly. "Get dressed."

Rising, she turns her back to me and steps into her panties, tugs them up. Then she looks down at her *kapp* and begins to wail. "Why is he so mad?" she chokes out.

"You know it's wrong for you to be out here like this with Mose, don't you?"

Plopping down on a bale of hay, she puts her face in her hands. "You don't understand."

"He's your brother," I say. "You're only fifteen. You shouldn't be doing this."

"We weren't doing anything wrong," she says, pulling her hair into a ponytail.

"How can you say that?" When she doesn't respond, I touch her chin, force her gaze to mine. "How long has this been going on?"

She looks away, shrugs. "A few months."

"Have you had sex with him?"

Her silence is the only answer I need. The thought of incest repulses me. It makes me angry and sad, maybe because I don't know how to help. I don't know if they can be helped. What's done is done, and there are some things you can't take back.

"This can't continue," I say. "It's wrong. You know that, right?"

She raises her gaze to mine. She's so young and pretty, so innocent. The loss of that innocence, so fleeting and precious, makes me want to cry. "You don't know everything," she says.

Something inside me goes still, and suddenly I realize she's going to throw something unexpected at me. "What are you talking about?"

She raises her head and begins to work at the knot on the tie of her *kapp.* "I can't tell you," she sobs. "It's too terrible. I can't tell anyone."

"Tell me what?" I watch her, waiting.

She works at the knot, but her hands are shaking so violently, she can't manage to untie it. Finally, I take the *kapp* from her and loosen the knot.

After a moment, she looks me in the eye

246

and heaves a sigh. "I'm going to have a baby."

The words shock my brain, like ice water thrown in my face. For an instant, I can't catch my breath. *I'm going to have a baby.* The words shake me from the inside out. All I can think is that she's too young. That Mose is far from being a man. That they're brother and sister. And the situation is so fundamentally immoral, I can barely get my mind around it.

"Oh, Salome." I struggle to keep my voice steady. "Are you sure?"

She nods. "I'm sure."

Kneeling in front of her, I set the *kapp* on her head and draw it snugly against her hair. It's not until I'm actually tying it at her nape that I realize my *mamm* did the same thing for me a thousand times when I was a girl. It's an unconscious gesture of kindness, a clumsy effort to comfort her. A long-gone memory that never really went away.

"How far along are you?" I ask.

"I haven't . . . you know, for a couple of months."

Here she is, fifteen years old, pregnant, and she can't even say the word *menstruation* aloud. And yet she has had sex with her own brother. The utter wrongness of that makes me want to throw up. I stare at her, not knowing what to say next.

"I know what you're thinking," she says.

"*I* don't even know what I'm thinking," I say drily.

"Mose isn't my real brother," she says after a moment. "He's adopted."

"Adopted?" I repeat the word dumbly, not knowing whether to believe her. Still, relief is like a slash across my belly. This is the first time I've heard of an adoption, and a very big part of me wants desperately to believe her. A teenage pregnancy is bad enough, but for that pregnancy to be the result of incest is unthinkable. "Does he know about the baby?"

She shakes her head. "I was going to tell him, but then *Mamm* and *Datt . . .*" The words trail off.

"How long ago was Mose adopted?" I ask after a moment.

"A long time. I was five, I think, so about ten years. It seems like he's always been my brother."

In the back of my mind, I wonder if the adoption was a legal one. All cultures cherish their children. But in the Amish community, children and family are the cornerstone of life. It would be almost unheard of for an Amish couple to relinquish custody of a child. But there are a few circumstances that would warrant a change of guardianship. If the parents are killed, for example. If financial difficulties, physical health, or certain emotional problems prevent one or both parents from caring for the child.

"Do you know the circumstances of the adoption?" I ask.

She shakes her head. "I was too little to understand at the time. Mose never told me."

I get to my feet and look down at her, my emotions reeling. I can't believe this innocent young girl is pregnant. I can't believe her own brother is the father — even if he is adopted. I wonder how Children Services will handle the situation; I wonder if they'll separate Mose and Salome. I don't have much experience with that segment of the county government, but I suspect the two teenagers will now go to different homes.

"Let's go inside," I say after a moment.

"I can't," she says. "I can't face them. They'll know what Mose and I were doing out here."

"It'll be okay. I'll stay with you."

"I'm . . . ashamed."

"All of us make mistakes," I tell her. "What's done is done. You can't go back and change it." How well I know those words. . . .

She raises her eyes to mine. "Even you made mistakes?"

"Especially me." I raise my hand, brush at the tears on her cheek. "Everything's going to be all right."

Rising, she chokes out a sound that's part sob, part laugh. "It doesn't feel like it," she says, and we start toward the ladder.

CHAPTER 12

Half an hour later, five of us sit at the Slabaugh kitchen table. Nicholas Raber and his wife, Frannie, Tomasetti, and Mose. After leaving the barn, I'd brought Salome inside. She was upset and crying, so I brewed her a cup of tea and we talked for a bit. I asked her about the rifle, and she had no idea it was missing. Afterward, I walked upstairs with her, waited while she took a bath, then put her to bed.

Samuel and Ike are still sleeping. I know this will be the last night these children sleep in their own beds. Come morning, life is going to change for them all in a very big way, especially Mose and Salome. I wish I could protect them from the further upheaval they're facing, but I can't.

The lantern flickers in the center of the table, the gas hissing through the glowing yellow mantle. Nicholas and his wife sit together, staring down at the tabletop, their expressions nervous and troubled. Mose is slumped in a chair, staring intently at his hands on the table in front of him. I can tell by the white knuckles that he's apprehensive. In the dim light from the lantern, I notice the angry red glow of a new acne outbreak just below his cheekbones. Tomasetti is sitting next to Mose, his expression as dark and cold as the night.

After a moment, Tomasetti skewers Mose with a hostile look. "Salome told Kate you're adopted. Is that true?"

Mose shifts uncomfortably in his chair, his gaze flicking from the Amish couple to me, as if we're going to save him from having to answer.

"Don't look at them," Tomasetti snaps. "They can't help you. This is your deal. Why don't you act like a man and level with me?"

Mose wipes his hands on his trousers. "The Slabaughs adopted me ten years ago, when I was seven."

"Why were you adopted?" I ask. "What happened to your parents?"

"They were killed in a buggy accident."

"Where?"

"Indiana. Near Connersville."

"How did you end up here?" Tomasetti asks.

Mose doesn't look at him. "Rachael was

my aunt. She took me in when they were killed."

"Do you have siblings in Indiana?"

"No."

"What was your last name before you were adopted?"

"Hochstetler."

I pull out my note pad and jot down the name. "So Salome is your first cousin?"

He shrugs. "I guess."

All I can think is that a first cousin is too close for a sexual relationship. That's not to mention the problem with her age, and the baby. "You'd better be telling the truth," I say. "You know we're going to check."

"It's true."

For a moment, the only sound comes from the rain tapping on the windows. Then I'm aware of the hiss of the mantle, the high-wire buzz of tension in the room.

After an uncomfortable silence, Tomasetti asks Mose, "Where's the rifle that was in the mudroom?"

The question echoes off the walls like a gunshot. I watch Mose, concentrating on his body language, his eyes, anything that might divulge a lie.

"You mean *Datt*'s hunting rifle?" The boy appears surprised by the question. "It's by the stove in the mudroom."

"No, it's not."

"Then I don't know where it is. Someone must have moved it."

Frannie breaks in. "Perhaps Solly did something with it in the days before his death."

"The rifle was there yesterday," I say. "I saw it."

"That means someone in this house moved it," Tomasetti says. "Or took it."

I look at Frannie and repeat the same question I posed to Nicholas earlier. "Has anyone visited the house?"

"Polly McIntyre brought a cherry pie for the children," she says. "Bishop Troyer was here."

Tomasetti nails Mose with another hard look. "If you touched that rifle, now would be the time to tell us."

"You're not in any trouble," I add. "We just need to know about the rifle."

"I didn't touch it," he says.

I think of Salome's pregnancy. "Maybe you needed money, decided to sell it."

"I didn't touch the gun," Mose replies defensively.

We haven't revealed to anyone that we found the rifle at Ricky Coulter's house or that Coulter is sitting in a jail cell on a probation-violation charge.

Tomasetti looks at me from across the table. "Did you ask Salome about the rifle?"

"She doesn't know anything," I reply.

Tomasetti's gaze lingers on mine a moment too long; then he offers Mose a dark look. "Did you take that rifle, Mose?"

"No."

"Did you plant it in Ricky Coulter's house?"

Mose comes up out of his chair. "I don't even know who that is!"

"Sit down," I snap.

Across from me, Nicholas and Frannie exchange anxious glances.

Mose lowers himself back into the chair. "Stop jacking with me! I didn't do anything wrong."

Tomasetti sighs. "No one ever does anything wrong," he says drily.

I turn my attention to Nicholas and his wife. "You'll be staying here with the children the rest of the night?"

"Yes, of course," Nicholas replies.

I look at Mose. "You're coming with us. Go upstairs and pack an overnight bag."

"What?" He comes out of the chair again. "An overnight bag? Why?"

"Because you're going to stay with Bishop Troyer and his wife tonight."

"I can't leave my family!" he cries. "Not

now. They need me!"

"You mean Salome, don't you?" Tomasetti asks.

"No!"

I cut in before the exchange becomes even more heated. "Taking Salome into the loft was wrong, Mose. You know that. We can't let you stay here."

"We love each other!" he shouts. "I'm going to marry her!"

Across the table from him, Frannie gasps. *"Er is ganz ab."* He's quite out of his mind.

Glaring at his wife, Nicholas raps his knuckles hard against the table and rises abruptly.

I give Mose a warning look. "You need to calm down."

"You can't do this!" Too enraged to listen, he slams his fist against the tabletop, his wild gaze darting from Frannie to Nicholas. "Don't let them do this!"

Shaking his head, Nicholas walks into the living room.

Tomasetti isn't the least bit impressed by the younger man's wrath. "Go pack a bag, or we'll take you without it. As far as I'm concerned, you can spend the rest of the week in those clothes."

By the time Tomasetti and I hand over a

very disgruntled Mose to the bishop and his wife, it's after midnight. We're in the Explorer, heading back to town. The only sound comes from the back-and-forth slap of the wipers as they wage war against the seemingly endless drizzle.

I'm bone-tired, but I can tell by the tension running through me that I won't sleep. I want to think it's the Slabaugh murder case that's weighing heavy on my shoulders. But I'm honest enough with myself to acknowledge my dark mood has more to do with Mose and Salome. It's a terrible predicament, but even more so for the younger kids. When you're Amish, your family is the center of your universe. I feel their pain and upheaval all the way to my bones. I care about them, I realize. Too damn much, if I want to be honest about it.

Caring is a dangerous thing when you're a cop. Police work requires a cool head and objectivity. It requires balance. Care enough so that you're not cynical, but be able to step away and make the hard choices when you need to. I'm not doing a very good job with the stepping away part of it. I know better than most that a cop who lets his heart get tied up in a case is the biggest kind of fool. It's a precarious and vulnerable state, and I wish I could shake it.

On impulse, I pull into the parking lot of McNarie's Bar. Neither of us speaks when I shut down the engine. We know why we're here. We walk inside with the unspoken mutual agreement that we're going to talk about the case, the hate crimes, we're going to talk about the kids, we're probably going to drink too much, and we're probably going to end up at my place.

We find a booth at the rear. We've barely settled in when McNarie approaches with a tray containing four shot glasses and two Killian's Irish Reds. "Judging from the long faces, I figured this is going to be a double-shot night."

Tomasetti picks up his glass. "You're an astute man, McNarie."

"A student of the human condition," the old barkeep replies, and then hustles away.

The place is hopping. Usually, I prefer it quiet. Talk is cheap in small towns, especially if you're a high-profile public servant, and Painters Mill is no exception. Tonight, however, I'm glad for the people and noise. It reminds me that life goes on and there are a lot of happy people out there. The world is bigger than I am. Bigger than the things going on inside my head.

We clink our glasses together and down the vodka. I revel in the burn, realize I'm eager for the next shot, anxious to blur all the sharp edges of my thoughts.

Leaning back in the booth, Tomasetti picks up his Killian's and contemplates me. "Hell of a scene at the Slabaugh place tonight."

I peel at the label on my beer bottle. "Salome's pregnant."

Tomasetti isn't easily shocked, but I can tell by the way he's staring at me that this news does the job. "Shit. How far along?"

"Two months."

"Is Mose the father?"

"She says so."

"Jesus." He tips the beer, takes a long pull. "Fifteen years old."

"And Amish." I sigh. "At the very least, Mose will be placed with a separate family. I hate the thought of the little ones being separated."

"Most of the time, things like that are out of our control."

"Doesn't make it any easier."

"No, it doesn't."

I pick up another shot glass and knock back the vodka. It slides down more easily than the first. Already I feel the foggy pull of the booze, and I know if I order a third shot, it will go down even easier. "What do you think about the rifle?"

"Someone's lying."

"Who?"

He shakes his head. "Don't know yet."

"What do you think about Ricky Coulter?"

"I think someone wants us to think he took the rifle and the money and murdered the Slabaughs."

"You think the killer is trying to frame him?"

"Only he didn't realize you saw that rifle."

"Makes sense." I don't want to say aloud the next logical question, but I know it's one that must be asked. "Do you think Mose is capable of killing two people who practically raised him?"

"I don't know, Kate. Kids . . ." Shrugging, he lets the word trail. "This business with Salome . . . if he can sleep with his own sister, what else is he capable of?" Tomasetti's gaze sharpens on mine. "Does he know she's pregnant?"

"She says no."

He considers for a moment, and I know he's still thinking about Mose. "Sometimes even a good kid can do really bad things if his back's against the wall."

"But why kill them?" I say. "Why not just steal some money and run away?"

"I don't know. Maybe he didn't want to

leave." Another shrug. "Maybe he wanted the farm."

"Tomorrow, I'll check out Mose's story on the adoption. See if everything lines up."

Nodding, he reaches for the shot, raises it, and downs it in a single gulp. "Who else do we have?"

"Coulter," I say. "I don't think he did it."

"Or else he's a pretty convincing liar. I don't think we should rule him out."

I think about Coulter for a moment. The vehemence with which he defended himself. The tears. His wife and children. "It's getting harder and harder to tell the good guys from the bad guys."

Tomasetti stares into his empty glass. "Something like twenty-five percent of the population are sociopaths. People who don't have a conscience. Lying is second nature to them."

"That's a scary thought."

"Keeps us in business."

"True." But all the jagged elements of the case are running through my head. "There's also the hate-crime angle."

He twirls the shot glass between his fingers. "Maybe we just need to find the connection."

The jukebox spits out an old Nirvana rocker. I can feel the alcohol working its dark magic on my brain now, smoothing down the rough edges. I don't need booze to think, but sometimes it helps me cut through the clutter that accumulates in the course of a day like today.

"Maybe it's like you said," I tell him. "The murders were secondary. Someone went into the Slabaugh barn with a hate crime in mind. They went in to rob or vandalize, or both."

"Or kill the livestock," Tomasetti puts in.

"They know the Amish won't go to the police or identify them." The theory gains momentum in my mind, and I run with it. "So these haters are in the barn. Slabaugh and his brother show up. There's a scuffle. Things get out of control. The intruder shoves one of them into the pit."

"Or one of them falls during the confrontation."

"The second brother goes into the pit to help the first, succumbs to the gas."

"Or the second brother gets close to the edge of the pit and the intruder shoves him in."

"That would explain Slabaugh's head wound."

Tomasetti considers that for a moment. "What about the wife?"

"Accidental. Rachael comes out a few

minutes later with the kids and finds the two men in the pit. She succumbs to the gas while trying to help them and falls in herself."

"Kids' stories back that up?"

I nod, trying to put all the disjointed pieces together. "It's a viable theory."

He swigs beer, eyeing me over the top of the bottle. "Let's go back to Coulter a sec." He looks down at his beer, and I know he's trying to work through the details of it, just as I am. "Takes a lot of effort to frame someone."

"He's the perfect candidate. He's worked for Slabaugh. He's been to the house." I shrug. "He's an ex-con. All of that is pretty much common knowledge in a small town."

"That makes him vulnerable. They plant the rifle, knowing we'll follow up on the connection."

"How'd they plant the rifle in Coulter's house?"

"Maybe they broke in. Hell, maybe the Coulters don't lock their doors. Some folks don't around here. The killer went in through an unlocked door or window. I'll check with the wife to see if she remembers anything."

We fall silent. But it's a comfortable silence. We sip our beers, thinking, listening

263

to the music. After a while, Tomasetti says, "How are you holding up, Chief?"

"I'm fine." The words come out a little too fast, and we both notice. I'm not very good at talking about myself, even worse about discussing my feelings. Maybe it's because over the years I've honed my ability to keep secrets, raised it to an art form.

"Cases like this can take a toll on a cop," he says. "Especially if you care." He pauses. "You care, Kate."

"That's kind of ironic, isn't it?"

"What's that?"

"When we first met, I was the one who had my shit together. You were pretty much a walking disaster."

"An attractive walking disaster."

That makes me smile, and I'm thankful I have Tomasetti to help me keep things in perspective.

His gaze sharpens on mine. "So talk to me."

I'm careful about the information I reveal to other people. I don't like anyone knowing too much about what's inside my head. Or, God forbid, in all those deeper, darker recesses. But Tomasetti isn't just other people. He's a friend. My lover. I trust him. I know about his past, he knows most of mine, and we've been through a lot together.

But old habits die hard, and I find myself wanting to close the lid on the can he's trying to open.

"I've guess I've sort of put these kids on a pedestal," I admit. "Because they're Amish. All of it's gotten kind of tangled up inside me."

"Hmmm. Sounds like you might be human. Have you had that checked?"

That makes me smile, because I know he feels a lot more than he lets on. He smiles back, far too comfortable with all this, and leans back in the booth to watch me squirm.

McNarie brings two more beers. Tomasetti passes him a couple of bills and slides a Killian's across the table to me.

"You came down pretty hard on Mose tonight," I say.

"He deserved it."

"You lost your temper with a kid. That's not like you."

"That's exactly like me." He tips the bottle and takes a drink. "I wanted to knock his fucking block off."

"Maybe I'm not the only one who has some emotional stake in this case."

Something flashes in his eyes, some dark emotion I can't quite identify. A warning, telling me not to go there. "My kids were girls," he says after a moment. "Younger, but still . . ."

The statement shocks me. In all the months I've known Tomasetti, he's never broached the subject of his family. What little I know, I've had to pry out of him. It happened back when he was with the Cleveland Division of Police. There was a home invasion. His wife and two young daughters were raped, murdered, and then burned when the house was torched — all this the result of a career criminal seeking revenge. I know Tomasetti spent some time in a psychiatric hospital, but he got through it. He holds his emotional cards close to his chest. Keeps the rest of it locked down tight, off-limits even to those he trusts.

What happened to his family is always in the backwaters of my mind. Only now do I realize that dealing with these Amish kids has brought that part of his past to the forefront, too. "I'm sorry," I say quickly. "I know that. I didn't mean to dredge —"

"You didn't," he says easily. "It's bound to come up from time to time."

I don't know what to say. Copping out, I take another drink of beer, look down at the bottle in my hands.

"Donna would have been eleven this year. Kelly would have been ten." He shrugs. "When I saw Mose in the loft with Salome,

I wanted to take his head off."

"You were a father."

"Yeah." He sighs. "It seems like a lifetime ago. But I still think about it. What it was like. What happened to them. I still miss them every day."

"I can't imagine how hard that was."

He shifts in the booth, and I know he's ready to move on to another subject. Any other subject. "So how is Salome going to fare as far as the Amish? I mean being pregnant and unmarried. That's got to be frowned upon."

"Fornication is a pretty serious offense," I tell him. "But the Amish won't turn her away. That's not to say it'll be easy for her. Salome will have to confess her mistake while kneeling before the congregation." I shrug. "Of course, there will be gossip. There always is. But the Amish will support her and her baby."

"That's something," he says.

"Sometimes I think that's the best we can hope for."

CHAPTER 13

The blast of the phone yanks me from the best sleep I've had in weeks. Even before I'm fully awake, I'm keenly aware of Tomasetti lying next to me, his body warm and solid against mine. He doesn't move, but I know he's awake. We're both light sleepers. Disoriented, I look around, shove the hair from my eyes. The face of the alarm clock tells me it's just after 3:00 A.M. We've been asleep less than an hour.

I grab the phone. "Yeah," I croak.

"Chief, sorry to wake you, but I got a ten-seventy out at the Hartzler place."

That's the code for a fire. I sit up. "Anyone hurt?"

"Ed Hartzler is missing."

"Shit." I fumble for my robe, shrug into it. "Fire department en route?"

"I called them straight away."

"I'm ten-seven-six."

Dropping the phone into its cradle, I rush

to the closet, fling open the door, yank the light cord.

"What is it?"

I turn and see Tomasetti's silhouette. In the dim light slanting into the room from the closet, I see him walking toward me. A small thrill races down my spine when I realize he's still naked. We've been together like this a dozen times now, but I don't think I'll ever get used to seeing him without his clothes.

Stupidly, I avert my gaze, turn back to the closet. "Fire," I say.

He comes up behind me and puts his hands on my shoulders. Bending, he kisses me on the neck. "Does the chief of police show up for every fire?"

I turn toward him, still intent on getting to the scene. But before I realize what I'm going to do, I lean into him, press my mouth to his. As if of their own accord, my arms go around his neck. He kisses me back, and my head begins to spin. *God,* I think, and pull away. "It's an Amish farm." Still stunned from the kiss, I blink at him. "We've got one missing."

In an instant, he transforms from aroused male to cop. "Goddamn it." He's already rushing to the chair next to the bed where he draped his clothes.

269

We dress at a frantic pace, yanking on slacks and buttoning shirts, watching each other, wishing we'd had more time.

"You thinking the same thing I am?" I ask as I throw on my parka and head for the door.

"Yup." Tomasetti grabs his trench coat on the way out. "Let's hope we're wrong."

Ed Hartzler's farm is located on Painters Creek Road. It's one of the larger Amish farms in the area, spanning nearly a hundred acres of rolling hills, impenetrable forest, and a good part of the creek.

To keep any potential gossip to a manageable level, Tomasetti and I take separate vehicles. He follows me in his Tahoe. I drive well over the speed limit, but he doesn't have a problem keeping up.

I see the orange glow of the fire from a mile away, and I know it's bad. By the time I turn into the long gravel lane of the Hartzler place, I can see the flames shooting fifty feet into the air. The stink of smoke is thick, like wet ash in my mouth. Midway down the lane, three wild-eyed horses gallop past my vehicle.

Two fire trucks are in position and three firefighters hose the blaze. A buggy and two ambulances are parked haphazardly in the driveway a bit farther back from the barn. Several members of the Hartzler family, some of the children not much older than five or six years, have formed a chain and are passing buckets of water from the well to a smaller outbuilding to keep it from catching fire, as well.

I park out of the way, about thirty yards from the barn, but even from that distance I can feel the heat. The steady roar of the flames mingles with the rumble of the diesel engines of the fire trucks, forming a deafening chorus. I'm aware of Tomasetti parking behind me, but I don't wait for him. I approach the nearest firefighter, who's manning the water pump.

"Anyone hurt?" I ask.

"We still haven't located Ed Hartzler. Family's pretty upset."

The fire crashes like a giant beast on a rampage. Timbers sizzle and crack. The flames are both hideous and beautiful as they consume the one hundred-year-old structure. "Do you guys need anything?"

"We're good, Chief," he says. "Coshocton County's on the way."

I leave him to his work. I stop next to Tomasetti, who's standing a few feet back, and tell him about Hartzler."

"Hope he's not in there."

"The barn is going to be a total loss."

We turn to look at the human chain. The Hartzler family, still clad in pajamas and nightshirts, try desperately to save what looks like a chicken house. But with a fire this size, their efforts may be futile; nothing can save the structure if the fire chooses to devour it. I only hope Ed Hartzler isn't inside the barn, because there's no way anyone could survive.

I start toward the family. I see a dozen faces, all of them red with tears and sweat and the cold. There are children and teen-agers, a skinny old man, and a pregnant woman. I've met Ed and his wife, Sarah, several times over the years. Twenty years ago, I went to school with Sarah. They have a big, extended family, including at least one set of grandparents. As I take in their frightened faces, all I can think is that this isn't going to end well.

For a moment, I consider jumping in and helping them carry water, but the effort is so futile, I decide against it. Instead, I approach Sarah Hartzler. She's in the middle of the chain. Her face is shiny and wet. She wears a white nightgown that's smudged with dirt and soaked with water at the hem. Judging from the size of her abdomen, she's at least six months pregnant.

"Sarah." I say her name twice before she looks at me. I can tell she doesn't want to stop lugging water. But the skinny old man, the grandparent, I realize, walks over to her. "Sarah, we will haul the water. Go with Katie. Try to get some rest."

"No, Papa. . . ."

Momentarily breaking the chain, he takes her hand and guides her toward the back porch of the house. Tomasetti and I trail behind them, not speaking. The old man stops at the concrete porch steps and orders her to sit. "You rest now. We'll see to the fire."

Sarah collapses onto the step.

The old man turns to me, his expression grave. Knowing he wants to talk to me out of earshot of his daughter, I walk several feet away and he follows.

"Ed was in the barn," he tells me, watching the flames. "Our mare was about to foal, so he took a blanket and slept out there. He thought it would be tonight." Pulling a handkerchief from his pocket, he wipes the sweat and soot from his forehead. "Ed got the horses out. He went back in for the milk cows, but I didn't see him come back out. No one can find him."

I hit my lapel mike and order all available men to the scene for a search of the area

273

surrounding the barn. When I look at the old man, I realize we both fear it's too late for his son-in-law. "Any idea how the fire started?" I ask.

He shakes his head. "Ed is very careful with the lanterns."

"Did you see anything?"

He gives me a look that makes the hair at the back of my neck stand up. "I keep my bedroom window open. Something woke me. When I looked out the window, I saw the flames. Katie, I saw two people running from the barn."

False hope skitters wildly through me. "Edward?"

He grimaces. "At first, I thought so. I called out." His hand trembles when he raises the kerchief to his face. "One of them turned and looked at me, but they kept on running. They were *Englischers*."

He says the word with a hefty note of distaste. "Did you recognize them?" I ask.

"No."

"Did you see their faces? Their clothes? Can you give me a description?" The questions tumble out of me too quickly.

The old man takes it in stride, shakes his head again. "It was too dark. They were running too fast. All I could think about was Ed. . . ." He lowers his head.

Behind me, I'm aware of Sarah crying openly now. "Where's Edward?" she sobs. "Someone find him."

She knows, I think, and suddenly I'm furious. Another family shattered on my watch: eight children left fatherless, a young Amish widow forced to raise them alone. I can't prove it yet, but after hearing what the old man had to say, I'm convinced this was no accident. The hate crimes have officially crossed over into murder.

I look at him and something twists inside me. He looks broken and old. Too hollowed out inside to even shed a tear. I watch him walk away to join the others in the water chain. Deeply troubled, I drift back to Tomasetti and Sarah. The woman holds her swollen abdomen with one hand, wipes the tears from her face with the other. I don't know for a fact yet that this is arson. I don't even know for certain that Ed Hartzler is dead. But I've been a cop long enough to know that's probably the way this is going to play out.

I get on the radio and tell Glock and Skid about the two men the elder Hartzler saw leaving the scene. "Keep an eye out for tracks. If you find anything, preserve it."

"Roger that."

I spend ten minutes on the phone with

the sheriff's office and the fire marshal. When I run out of productive things to do, I look at Tomasetti.

He crosses to me, his expression unreadable. "There's a CSU on the way."

"I'll have the area cordoned off." I grind out the words, only a fraction of my attention on Tomasetti. I'm furious and in no condition to speak to a man I just slept with. The emotions inside me are too ugly, and I don't want to mix them up with the intimacies we shared just hours before. "If they find Ed Hartzler dead . . ." Too angry to finish, I let the words trail.

"Working yourself into a lather isn't going to help."

"Telling me how not to feel isn't going to help, either."

"I just want you to keep your head."

"I'm not like you, Tomasetti. I can't just turn off my emotions when they're inconvenient."

"Is that what I do?"

Knowing I'm being unreasonable, and needing some space, I walk away. I make it only a few feet before he stops me. I spin to face him. "I'm too pissed to talk about this right now," I tell him.

His hand drops away from my shoulder, reminding me that less than an hour ago I was sleeping naked beside him. "We don't even know if we're dealing with arson yet, Kate."

"Bullshit. I know what this is, and so do you."

Sighing, he shoves his hands into his pockets and looks toward the barn. I watch the fire, willing my temper to cool. Yellow flames lick at the night sky, sending out a strange orange glow. The fire has died down some, but the roof has caved in. The structure is a total loss. From where I stand, I can hear the hiss of steam from the water. I smell the stink of burning wood and manure and something darker I don't want to think about.

"I'm not going to let them get away with this," I say.

Tomasetti nods. "Was the old man able to give you a description?"

"No." I want to hit something. There's nothing handy, so I kick the ground with the toe of my boot. "Damn it."

The sky chooses that moment to open up and a cold black rain pours down. Tomasetti and I look up, cursing not because of the water pouring down our collars, but because we know the rain will destroy much of whatever evidence the arsonists left behind.

■ ■ ■ ■

It's just after noon, and I'm sitting in my office sucking down coffee, wishing I had a clean change of clothes because the ones I'm wearing reek of smoke. I'm wishing even more fervently that I'd gotten a decent night's sleep. Tomasetti, Sheriff Rasmussen, and I spent seven wet and cold hours at the Hartzler farm. The CSU and fire marshal were on-site when I left. The firefighters had begun the task of combing through the rubble. I'm praying Ed Hartzler shows up, but I know it's only a matter of time before they find his body — what's left of it anyway.

Earlier, I put a call in to the Connersville, Indiana, Police Department to check out Mose's story about his parents' accident. The officer I spoke with hadn't lived there very long, but he said he'd check the records and call me back. Next, I contacted the Lancaster County Sheriff's Office to see what I could find out about Abel Slabaugh. I spoke to a young deputy sheriff by the name of Howard, who basically didn't know shit about Abel Slabaugh or any of the Amish. He was, however, familiar with the bishop, a man he knew only as Smucker. He didn't know if Smucker had a phone,

278

but offered to drive out to the bishop's farm to put me in touch. I'm not holding my breath.

I'd barely hung up the phone when I received a call from Ricky Coulter's attorney, threatening to sue the township if his client wasn't released within the hour. I assured him we would either charge Coulter or cut him loose, but neither of those things would be happening within the hour.

And so I'm sitting here, smelling of smoke, exhausted, waiting for official word on Edward Hartzler. Outside my window, the rain has transformed to snow. The wind has picked up and the flakes stick to the glass like glitter to glue, obscuring my view. Through the open door of my office, I hear Lois at the switchboard, arguing with some journalist wanting information on the Slabaugh case. My money's on Lois.

The Slabaugh family has been dead for over forty-eight hours now. The case is growing cold, and I'm no closer to knowing who did it now than I was when I walked into that barn and found them dead in the manure pit.

My phone jangles, startling me. Expecting some pushy young reporter — or the fire marshal's office — I glance down at the display. I see Tomasetti's name and snatch it up, hoping for good news. "Yeah."

"You sound like how I feel."

"It's comforting to know someone else is as miserable as I am."

"Glad I could help." He pauses. "Ed Hartzler is dead, Kate. One of the firefighters found his body twenty minutes ago."

I close my eyes, surprised by the hard twist of dread in my gut. "Damn it."

"Looks like one of the big timbers fell on him. Probably knocked him unconscious."

Or pinned him, I think. Images fly at me. A man trapped, screaming, as the flames cook him alive . . . Rising abruptly, I grab my parka off the back of my chair. "I'm going to go talk to the family."

"I already did."

The words stun me. Notifying next of kin is one responsibility I have never delegated, never shirked in any way. That Tomasetti would do that for me brings forth an unwanted rush of emotion so strong that for a moment I can't speak.

"Kate? You okay?"

I clench my jaws, stave off the tears waiting at the gate. "How's his wife?"

"You know. Pretty broken up. But her father's with her. He was going to try to get the bishop out there."

"Damn it, Tomasetti, I want this son of a

280

bitch. I think I could kill him with my bare hands."

"You might just get your chance," he says. "I think we might have our first break."

"Solid?" I'm almost afraid to get my hopes up.

"CSU found a can of Skoal at the scene. Hasn't been there long."

"Amish kids have been known to sneak dipping tobacco."

"We questioned them separately and away from their parents. None of them claims the can. If we can lift some latents and we get a hit, we might have a name."

Mentally, I shift gears, grasp hold of the last shred of optimism. "How long will that take?"

"We couriered it to the lab. Maybe late this afternoon if I call in some favors."

"Do whatever it takes."

"You know I will."

"Any prints on the rifle?" I ask.

"Not even a smudge."

"Someone was being careful."

"Maybe." He sighs. "Glock get anything on the dark pickups?"

"He's still working on it. Nothing yet." The phone jingles again. I look down and see all four lines blinking. "I've got to go."

"You want to grab some lunch later?" he asks.

"I'd like that." I end the call and hit the first blinking light. "Burkholder."

"Katie." It's Bishop Troyer, and his usually unflappable voice is harried. "Mose has been injured."

Concern steamrolls over me. "What happened?"

"One of the Slabaugh boys rode the horse over to my place. He was very upset. He says Mose has been beaten."

"Beaten?" The news jolts me. "How badly is he hurt?"

"I do not know."

"Who did it?"

"I do not know. I'm on my way there. I thought you should know."

My mind spins through what I've just heard. "What was he doing at the Slabaugh place, Bishop?" I can't keep the accusation from my voice.

"I do not know." I can tell by the guilt in his voice that the bishop knows exactly why Mose was there. "He must have left when I was in town earlier."

A hundred questions pound at my brain, but there's no time to ask them now. "I'm on my way."

"I'll meet you there."

CHAPTER 14

My tires send snow flying when I turn into the lane of the Slabaugh farm. The Explorer fishtails when I hit the gas, but I cut the wheel hard, and I don't slow down until the house is in sight. As I ran out the door of the station, I asked Lois to call for an ambulance. To my dismay, it's not here yet. Bishop Troyer's buggy is nowhere in sight; evidently, he hasn't arrived yet, either.

Jamming the Explorer into park, I fling open the door and hit the ground running. I sprint to the house and burst inside without knocking. Ike and Samuel meet me in the mudroom.

"Chief Katie!" Samuel cries. "Mose is hurt!"

"He's all bloody." Ike clings to his older brother's shirt, crying. "He's gonna die just like *Mamm* and *Datt*."

"No one's going to die," I tell him.

"But what if he does?" Ike whines.

"Where is he?" Even as I bark out the question, I move past them into the kitchen.

Mose sits slumped in a chair, his elbows on the table. His shirt hangs like a war-torn flag on the back of his chair. I see blood, stark and red against white skin. I wince upon spotting the pink-purple stripes on his back and shoulders. He looks at me, and I steel myself against a recoil. His lip looks like a fat, purple worm that's been nearly chopped in half by some mean kid. His left eye is swollen. There's more blood on his chest. Someone worked him over good.

Salome stands over him, pressing a towel to his lip. She's been crying. Her eyes are red and wet. She glances over at me, but her gaze skitters quickly away. "He needs a doctor," she murmurs.

I cross to Mose and bend to make eye contact. "How badly are you hurt?" I ask.

He doesn't look at me, doesn't answer.

"Mose," I say, pressing. "I'm here to help. How bad are you hurt?"

"I'm fine," he snaps. "Just . . . shook-up is all."

"What happened?" Pulling out the chair next to him, I sink into it and lean close to him. "Come on. Talk to me."

Mose lowers his head. I look at Salome, aware that her hand is shaking. She drops

284

her gaze. Guilt gouges me when I realize they're more frightened of me and what I might do than they are of whoever did this.

"You're not in any trouble." I struggle to keep the intensity out of my voice. "I just need to know what happened. I need to know who did this."

Mose raises his eyes to mine. He looks miserable, embarrassed and scared. "I was walking on the township road. Two guys in a truck stopped and asked me if I needed a ride. I said no." He drops his gaze to the tabletop and shrugs. "They jumped me."

"Do you know them?" I ask. "Do you know their names?"

He shakes his head. "I never saw them before."

"What did they look like?

"I dunno. *Englischers.*"

"Can you describe them?"

"Not really. They were older than me. In their twenties, maybe. They wore blue jeans. Cursed a lot."

"What kind of truck? What color was it?" The questions trip over themselves, coming out in a rush.

"Uh, I don't know. Red, maybe," he replies. "Not sure what kind."

I stare at him, aware that my protective instincts have been roused. Not the first time that's happened since I've met these kids. Wanting to protect the innocent is a noble endeavor, but not the smartest frame of mind for a cop. After a while, those kinds of emotions just get in the way.

I look at Mose. The outside corner of his left eyeball is bloodred. The cut on his lip gapes like a tiny screaming mouth. At the very least, he's going to need stitches. I can't even imagine the other damage he might have suffered — broken ribs, internal injuries, a concussion. That's not to mention the psychological harm. I'm appalled and ashamed that someone could do this to a teenage boy, Amish or otherwise. I know it's stupid, but I feel somehow responsible, as if I should have been able to stop it.

"How did you get those marks on your back?" I ask.

Mose looks everywhere except at me. "Buggy whip."

"They whipped you?" I can't keep the incredulity from my voice.

"*Ja.* It don't hurt much."

"Where did this happen?" I ask.

Mose stares at the tabletop. "On the road between Bishop Troyer's house and ours."

"How long ago?"

He lifts his shoulder. "I don't know. An hour or two."

Shaking my head, I hit my lapel mike and put out a BOLO for a red pickup truck. When I finish, I look at Mose. "What were you doing on the township road?"

His gaze skates away from mine. "Walking."

"To where?" I ask the question, but I already know the answer.

"Here."

"You know you were supposed to stay away, don't you?"

"I know it." When he looks at me, his expression is so filled with misery that it's difficult for me to hold his gaze. "I had to come. This is my home. You've no right to keep me from it."

I suspect his covert excursion had more to do with seeing Salome than with a sudden attack of homesickness, but I don't press him on it. "Is there anything else you can tell me about the men who did this to you?"

Eyes fixed on the tabletop, Mose shakes his head. "They just called me names. Stuff like that."

I nod, running it through my head. "Where did the buggy whip come from? They were in a truck."

Mose shrugs. "I dunno. Maybe they got horses at home. Had some tack in the truck."

A knock sounds at the door. Before I can rise, Samuel answers and two paramedics walk in.

Mose's eyes widen when he spots them; then he turns his gaze to me. "I don't want to go with them. I can't. I want to stay here."

"You're injured. You need to get yourself checked out at the hospital."

"I'm not hurt."

"Mose —"

"I want to stay here!" Panic flares in his eyes. "Why can't I just stay here?"

Grappling for patience, I squeeze his arm. "Calm down," I say, helping him to his feet. "I need for you to be smart about this. Do you understand?"

"I want to stay here."

"Go with the paramedics. Get yourself checked out. I'll meet you at the hospital later. Now go." I nod at the nearest paramedic.

He gives a small nod back, then smiles at Mose. "You ever ridden in an ambulance before, buddy?" he asks.

"No," Mose mumbles.

"Well then, you're in for a treat. Come with me and we'll get you all fixed up."

Taking a final, lingering look over his shoulder at Salome, Mose lets himself be led out the door.

I spend three hours at Pomerene Hospital in Millersburg while Mose is X-rayed, scanned, and stitched. I try squeezing him for more information about the perpetrators who beat him. He cooperates but isn't able to offer anything helpful in the way of identifying the men. A couple of times, I sensed him holding back, but I wasn't sure so I let it go. In the end, I chalk his reticence up to the fact that he shouldn't have been out on that road to begin with.

By the time I get him back to Bishop Troyer's farm, it's after 6:00 P.M. I was supposed to hook up with Tomasetti for lunch, but somehow the afternoon blew by and we never connected. He assured me he'd call if news came back on the Skoal can, but he hasn't. Prints are a long shot. Still, I can't help but be hopeful.

I should go back to the station, type up my report on Mose's assault, and add it to the growing file of hate crimes against the Amish. I should swing by the house, grab a shower and some food, and empty the trash. Of course, I'm not going to do any of those things.

It's too early for a drink. That's not to

mention the small fact that I need to be sober if we get a break in the case. Neither of those things keeps me from pulling into the lot of McNarie's Bar and walking inside.

The place is quiet this evening. I catch McNarie's eye and take a seat at my usual booth. A moment later, he sets a tray in front of me. Two shots, a Killian's, and a pack of Marlboro Lights. "You're becoming one of my best customers, Chief."

I pick up one of the shot glasses and tap out a cigarette, already anticipating the burn of the booze. "Do me a favor and don't tell anyone, okay?"

"A closed mouth is one thing that separates a good bartender from a great one."

"One of many reasons I come here."

Grinning, he goes back to work.

I down both shots in quick succession. I want another, but I light up instead. The beer is ice-cold and goes down like a cherry slush on a hot day. Around me, the other patrons go about the business of getting drunk. A fat biker in coveralls shoots pool with a skinny guy wearing an FFA jacket. At the bar, an old man with white hair spilling from a John Deere cap sits hunched over a cup of coffee. A long brown cigarette smolders in the ashtray next to his cup. A few booths down from mine, a young couple sits on the same side of the booth, their legs entwined beneath the table, a beer sitting untouched in front of them. They have better things to do than drink.

The sight of the young couple makes me think of Mose and Salome. I still haven't heard back from the police department in Connersville, Indiana, to verify Mose's story about his parents. When I do, I'll ask them to run a cell phone out to the Amish bishop to see if he can fill in any of the blanks about Mose's adoption.

I don't want to sit here and analyze why I'm drinking at a time when I shouldn't be. Of course, that's exactly what I'm going to do. That's when I acknowledge the possibility that Tomasetti's right: I'm too emotionally invested in these kids. I want to think it's because they're young and innocent and Amish. But I've never been very good at lying to myself. Those kinds of lies make life too easy, and some of us are destined to suffer.

I care about those kids. I think about them too often. I feel connected to them in ways I shouldn't, because I know sooner or later those emotions are going to come back to bite me. While those feelings extend to all four children, it's Salome who's commandeered my heart. Maybe it's because she reminds me of myself when I was that age — innocent, impressionable, more vulnerable than she could know, and looking for trouble. I know what it's like to be ravenous for a life you know you can't ever have, to want with such fierceness that it hurts, to feel the initial slap when fate doles out that first heaping portion of disappointment.

Salome is in for some heartache, and most of it will be her own doing. Some people — and I'm at the top of that list — never learn to settle for less. It's all or nothing. We continue butting our heads against brick walls, expecting the bricks to crumble, when most often they remain steadfast.

The Amish community as a whole is the same way — a battle-scarred wall that has withstood centuries of assault — yet their way of life has never faltered. They can be unforgiving of transgressions, but they can also be as welcoming as a mother's embrace. When there is a fall from grace, it's usually long and arduous, with a lot of emotional cuts and scrapes along the way. My own fall was fatal in many ways. It cost me a lot — my family, my standing in the community. It killed a part of me I'll never be able to get back, put me on the path of no return. At the same time, it also opened doors that otherwise would have remained closed and locked down tight. I still had my dreams and hope for the future. I had the drive to achieve them. Those things sustained me when nothing else would.

I want to spare Salome the agonies of my own past, save her from making all the same mistakes I did. I want her to be happy and fulfilled. I can't help but wonder: *Will she find those things with the Amish?* The question makes me realize just how much empathy I have for her. It makes me see a parallel I don't want to see, a connection I don't want to make.

Raising my beer, I make eye contact with McNarie. He gives me a nod, and I know another round of salvation is on the way. But it's not going to arrive quickly enough to keep me from confronting a part of my past I haven't yet faced, a demon taunting me with truths I can no longer avoid.

Salome is only a couple of years younger than the child I would have had if I'd decided not to have an abortion after Daniel Lapp raped me.

"Chief Burkholder."

I'm so immersed in my thoughts, I didn't notice the door opening. I didn't see Sheriff Rasmussen walk in and head my way. Surprise and discomfort take turns punching me when I look up at him. It's after hours; I have every right to be here. Still, all I can think is, *I'm busted.*

"Mind if I join you?"

"Sure." I try to smile, but my cheek muscles feel paralyzed. "You know what they say about drinking alone."

"Yeah." Chuckling, he slides onto the seat opposite me. "It's not nearly as fun as drinking with someone else."

He smells like cold air and sandalwood. We're looking at each other, two contenders sizing each other up. He looks comfortable, glad to be here, ready to wind down with a beer. I feel as if I've been waylaid.

"I didn't know you smoked."

Feeling like an idiot, I snuff out the cigarette. "I don't."

"Okay." He says the word as if he understands. I'm pretty sure he doesn't.

McNarie crosses to the booth and, without looking at me, sets two more Killian's on the table between us, then slides a shot glass in front of me. Eyeing the shot glass, Rasmussen picks up his beer, tips it at me, and then drinks. "Bottoms up."

Feeling only slightly self-conscious, I down the shot. On the jukebox Led Zeppelin's "Down by the Seaside" gives way to Lynyrd Skynyrd's "That Smell." The alcohol chooses that moment to kick in. It makes me feel like a train clattering down rickety tracks, heading toward a ravine without a bridge. That's when I remember I didn't eat lunch, or dinner. Undulating waves of warmth wash over my brain. I go with it, but when I look up at the television above the bar, it dips left and right.

"Been here long?" Rasmussen asks.

"Too long, probably." I smile, hoping it's not as crooked as it feels.

"Been there, done that."

I doubt that, too, but I nod. "Any word on the rifle or the Skoal can?"

"Tomasetti thinks we still might hear something today. He's been on the phone with the lab up there, pushing them pretty hard."

"I guess that means we probably shouldn't drink too much."

He looks at the three spent shot glasses in front of me and chuckles. "Guess that depends on your definition of 'too much.' "

"Good point."

He glances at his watch, shrugs. "Getting kind of late anyway. Don't know if those lab people up there work overtime."

"They do," I say. "Especially if Tomasetti is pushing for something he wants."

"He's good at pushing, that's for sure."

An awkward silence ensues. I look toward the bar. McNarie is drying glasses, frowning at me. I frown back, look down at the bottle of beer in front of me, pick it up and drain it.

"You play pool, Chief?"

I glance at Rasmussen. He's staring at me intently, the way men do sometimes when they're thinking there's a possibility they might get lucky, and I think, *Uh-oh.* I've met him only half a dozen times in the year he's been sheriff. He's got a good reputation. Good cop. Honest. Single. He's attractive, in a boy-next-door kind of way. When I look into his eyes, I don't see much in the way of baggage. Not like Tomasetti anyway. It's one of many things that binds us, makes us so compatible. Sometimes I'm not sure if that's good or bad. It just is.

"I'm not very good at it," I reply, enunciating each word carefully to keep from slurring them.

"You're probably better than you think."

"No, I really suck. Honest."

Smiling, he nods toward the pool table at the rear. "I'll bet you ten bucks you can beat me."

"You could throw the game to win the bet."

"Twenty bucks, and I promise not to cheat."

The next thing I know, he's pulling me from the booth. I'm aware of his hand, large and hot and damp. The crisp, musky smell of his aftershave. My head is spinning like a top. *Shit.* But I let him haul me to the pool table.

He shoves a cue at me, then proceeds to rack the balls. "You break, Chief."

Having been a cop in a large metropolitan city, I've spent a good bit of time in bars just like this one. I've consumed more alcohol than I like to admit. I've even played a few games of pool. But it's one pastime I never mastered. I take a moment to chalk the tip of the cue. Leaning forward, I set my hand on the felt and line up.

"Might help if you do it this way." Rasmussen comes up beside me, nudges me aside. Bending, he demonstrates. "Like this. Keep your hand steady."

"Okay." He steps back, and I imitate him. "Wait."

He moves closer. I start to straighten to give him room, but he sets his hand on the small of my back. "Stay put." Taking my hand, he usurps the cue, wraps his own fingers around it. "Hold it like this. See? You'll have more control."

Putting his arm around me, he takes my fingers and sets the cue in my hand. He's standing too close. His hip is touching mine. I can feel his breath ruffling my hair, his shoulder pressing against mine.

He doesn't know about Tomasetti and me. Maybe because we're not exactly official, for a multitude of reasons. I'm debating whether to fill him in, when he whispers, "Take the shot."

"What are we doing here?" I ask.

"Playing pool." Mr. Innocent.

"I don't think this has anything to do with pool."

"Take the shot," he repeats. "Go on."

I thrust the cue forward. The shot feels good, solid. The balls disperse, clicking together and rolling across the felt.

"Not bad for an amateur."

The baritone voice snaps me away from the game. I look up to see Tomasetti standing ten feet away, watching us the way a pit bull might watch some cocky terrier an instant before he tears it to shreds. I didn't notice him walk in, and the sight of him standing there shakes me. The shoulders of his trench coat are wet and sprinkled with melting snow. As I take in his measure, his attention shifts to me. His expression is oddly amused. But his smile is cold, his eyes hard. Baggage, I think.

"Amateur, hell." Oblivious, Rasmussen leans forward and takes a shot. "Did you see that break? Twenty bucks says I'm about to get my ass kicked."

"As much as I'd like to bear witness to that, I'm going to have to pass." Tomasetti tosses the sheriff a cool look. "While you two were in here getting shit-faced, I got a name from the prints on the Skoal can."

I nearly drop my cue. Game forgotten, I prop it against the wall and cross to him. "What's the name?"

His expression is still amused, but it's laced with another emotion I can't readily identify. Something hard and a little bit cruel. "William Steele."

I know the name. "He goes by Willie," I say. "Troublemaker. Small-time hood. Lives in an apartment over the furniture store in town."

Rasmussen comes up beside me, standing a little too close. "Bigot?"

Tomasetti smiles, but his expression holds not a trace of humor.

Sidling away from Rasmussen, I answer for him. "He beat the hell out of a migrant worker a few years back. Steele was a minor at the time. Seventeen, I think. Judge gave him probation."

299

"Looks like Willie didn't learn his lesson," Tomasetti says.

"Those prints place him at the scene," Rasmussen states. "Anything else?"

Tomasetti's expression isn't friendly. "CSU picked up a couple of footwear imprints. If we can match one of them to his shoes, it would help seal the deal." He turns his stare on Rasmussen. "Why don't you go get the warrant so we can search his place. The chief and I will go pick him up."

I can tell by Rasmussen's reaction that he doesn't appreciate being given orders, especially by an outsider — and in front of me. To his credit, he doesn't balk, just reaches for his cell phone. "I'll give Judge Siebenthaler a call and get out there."

Tomasetti lifts his lip in a poor imitation of a smile, then he turns and strides toward the door.

CHAPTER 15

The cold air slaps me in the face when I go through the door. Tomasetti's a few strides ahead, and I quicken my pace to catch up with him.

"You got an address on Willie Steele?" he asks.

"I know where he lives. But he's probably at work right now. The oil-filter factory down in Millersburg."

"Let's go pick him up."

We reach his Tahoe and climb inside. He doesn't look at me as he starts the engine and pulls out of the parking space. The wheels spew gravel when he turns onto the street. Neither of us speaks as he heads toward town, cranking the speedometer well over the speed limit.

I'm usually pretty good at reading people — their moods, their frame of mind. Tomasetti is one of only a few people I can't. I've tried on multiple occasions. Just when I think I've got him nailed, all those quirks figured out, he lets fly some stunner that has me rethinking everything I know about him.

I look out the window and give both of us a chance to settle. Not an easy task when it comes to Tomasetti. He looks relaxed, but he's driving too fast. He didn't like seeing me with Rasmussen. But I know Tomasetti has too much pride to succumb to petty male jealousy. Still, he's a man, and some things are programmed so deeply, not even intellect or character can totally eradicate them.

I consider waiting him out, but his stony silence is beginning to make me uncomfortable. "How did you know where to find me?"

He glances at me and frowns. "You're kidding, right?"

Nodding, I look out the window, then sigh. "Are we okay?"

"Why wouldn't we be?"

He's going to make me spell it out. *May as well put it on the table,* I think. "I wasn't expecting Rasmussen to show up. He just did."

"That's fine. You're a grown woman, Kate. You're free to do whatever you want with whomever you want, whenever you want and as often as you like."

"I'm really glad you pointed that out." I glance at his profile, notice for the first time the tight set of his jaw. "So why are you pissed?"

"I'm not pissed."

"Maybe we should talk about it."

He takes his time responding. "You two looked pretty cozy. I didn't like it. I'll get over it. End of story."

"It was just a friendly game of pool."

"Did he hit on you?"

I shrug. "He was thinking about it."

Tomasetti sends me a dark look.

I meet his gaze head-on. "You're not one of those guys with trust issues, are you?"

"I just don't like smart-assed cops crossing that line."

"We haven't really told anyone we're . . . together."

"Is that what we are?" he asks. "Together?"

"We haven't talked about exclusivity." I stammer the words, trying not to screw this up. I sense it's an important moment. But I'm not much better at talking about my feelings than he is.

"We're talking about it now." He makes a turn, and I realize we're pulling into the parking lot of the Farnam oil-filter factory. "For future reference, I don't share."

I nod, trying to appear calm, but inside my heart is pounding. This is as close to a relationship talk as we've ever had. "Just don't go all caveman on me, okay?"

"I'll try not to."

"So does this mean we're, like, going steady?"

He parks illegally at the building's entrance, puts the Tahoe in park, shuts down the engine, and turns to me. "That means the next time Rasmussen puts his hands on you, you should tell him to fuck off."

"Since he's sheriff of this county, I'll probably try to be a little bit more diplomatic."

"As long as he gets the message."

We leave the Tahoe and enter through a door below a sign marked EMPLOYEES ONLY. The factory is huge, has bright lights, and smells like a combination of rubber and paint. A security guard sitting in a booth eyes us through a window as we approach. Leaving the booth, he swaggers toward us. His badge says his name is Tony. He raises his hand like a traffic cop. "You're going to have to get visitor passes from the office before you can come in here."

Tomasetti tugs out his ID. "We already have our passes."

The security guard stares at the badge, and for an instant I think I see longing in his eyes. "That'll work." He hikes up his pants. "What can I do for you?"

"We need to see Willie Steele," I tell him. "He works here."

"Willie? Sure. I saw him come in earlier." He motions toward the booth. "I think he's on line 7-W. Let me call, make sure he's there."

We wait while he makes the call. Beyond, huge machines rumble and grind and hiss. The second shift is in full swing. I see a young woman in blue jeans and an Ohio State sweatshirt feeding accordion paper into a massive cutting machine. At the end of the line, another person sends the cut papers down a conveyer belt.

The security guard emerges from his booth. "Okay, I just talked to the supervisor. Steele's working tonight." Tugging up his pants, he points. "I can't leave my post. Just follow this walkway to where it tees, then go left. Line seven-W is midway down to the Paint Room there at the end. Lines are clearly marked. Willie's on the glue wheel tonight. Supervisor's name is Bob Shields. He's expecting you." Tony looks at me, and I see the burn of curiosity in his eyes. "What'd Willie do?"

"We just want to ask him some questions," I reply.

He looks disappointed. "Let me know if you need any help with him. I never liked that guy."

"Thanks," I say.

The walkway is delineated with bright yellow tape. We follow it to the T junction, then turn left. Tony gave good directions, because midway to the end, we see a sign that says 7-W. Beyond, a conveyer belt with huge steel bins on either side rumbles like some massive engine. The accordion papers I'd noticed when we walked in have been cut and formed into cylinders. Held together with springs, they're moving toward a rotating contraption where metal disks are glued onto the top and bottom. The operator then places each cylinder back on the assembly line and they make their way toward a huge oven.

A man with curly blond hair approaches us. Wearing black slacks and a white shirt with the sleeves rolled up, he looks more like a waiter in some upscale restaurant than an assembly-line supervisor. "Can I help you?"

We show him our badges. "We need to speak to Willie Steele," I say.

"He do something wrong?" Shields asks.

"We just want to talk to him," Tomasetti responds.

"Let me pull him off the glue wheel. Gotta get the break operator to replace him or things'll pile up. Can you hang on a sec?"

Frowning, Tomasetti looks at his watch.

I smile inwardly. "We'll wait."

Shields rushes over to his desk, slides to a stop with the verve of a figure skater, picks up the phone. I see him looking at the man working the rotating machine, and I recognize the guy as Willie Steele. "That's him right there," I tell Tomasetti.

"Big guy."

I think of the beating Mose took. "Big coward. Let's see how tough Mr. Steele is when we haul him to the station."

I see amusement in Tomasetti's eyes. "I'll give you the honors."

"Hopefully, he knows I used to be Amish."

"This is going to be a lot more fun than I thought."

Shields comes back looking harried. "Break operator is on the way. Can you hang for a couple of minutes?"

Tomasetti sighs, shifts his weight from one foot to the other. I'm about to reply, when I notice Steele looking at us. He's frozen, his mouth open. The cylinders moving down the conveyer belt begin to pile up in front of him, and I realize he's thinking about running.

The woman working next to him notices and stands up. "Hey!"

"We just got made," I hiss.

Steele bolts.

"Shit," I hear Tomasetti mutter, and then I'm running toward Steele.

"Halt! Police!" I shout. "Willie Steele! Stop!"

At the assembly line, a dozen faces turn to watch me as I sprint past them. Twenty feet ahead, Steele knocks over a stool, tosses a trayful of cylinders at me. "Fuck!" he shouts.

For such a big guy, he's fast and agile. I'm running full out, but he's still pulling away. Tomasetti is slightly ahead of me now. Wishing I hadn't done those shots earlier, I hit my lapel mike, call for backup. If Steele gets out of the building and to his vehicle, he could get away.

Tomasetti and I are at an added disadvantage because Steele knows the layout of the building and we don't. As long as we keep him in sight, we should be okay. Not an easy task when the guy runs like a freaking rhinoceros on speed.

He takes us toward a huge overhead door marked PAINT ROOM at the end of the walkway. He makes like he's going to go right. I veer in the same direction, my arms

308

pumping, my feet pounding the concrete. At the last minute, he goes left, and I lose another yard.

Out of the corner of my eye, I see employees coming off the lines to watch. The conveyer belts don't wait, and oil-filter cylinders pile up and fall to the floor.

We're running down another walkway now. A forklift backs into Steele's path. Cursing the driver, Steele slams his fist into it, but he keeps moving and veers left. Tomasetti darts around the other way. I follow Steele, but I'm losing ground. Then we're back on the walkway. Steele looks over his shoulder, spots Tomasetti.

"Fuckin' cop," he snarls, and darts right. Remembering what he did last time, I take a chance and veer left. At the end of the walkway, he darts left, too. I gain ten feet, almost close enough to tackle him. I'm focused, running as hard as I can, ready to take him down.

He cranks his head around. I'm so close, I can see his eyes widen when he spots me. I'm aware of Tomasetti off to my right, a few feet behind me. The forklift comes out of nowhere. Steele doesn't have a snowball's chance of avoiding it. At the last instant, he puts his hands out. The momentum of his body collapses his arms. His forehead clangs hollowly against the steel cage that protects the driver. Steele reels backward two steps, then goes down like a big rodeo bull. He slides along the concrete on his back, coming to rest against a support beam.

I reach him just as he raises his head. "Stay down!" I snap, tugging the cuffs from my belt. "On your belly! Now!"

"Wha . . ."

Grabbing his arm, I flip him over and kneel. "Shut up and give me your wrists." Shoving my knee into his back, I reach for his hands. "Don't move."

"My fuckin' head . . ."

"Serves you right." His wrists are slick with sweat as I pull his hands behind his back and snap the cuffs into place.

Tomasetti slides to a stop next to me, kneels, and rams his knee against Steele's back. "I'll bet no one ever accuses you of being smart, do they?" he says to Steele.

The downed man groans. "What'd I hit?"

I rise and look around. A dozen factory workers have formed a circle around us, their eyes alight in anticipation of some late-night entertainment. Across from me, Tomasetti brushes dust from his trench coat. He's breathing hard. I can tell by the look in his eye that he enjoyed the chase.

"You okay?" he asks.

310

"I'm good. How about you?"

"Most fun I've had all day."

I'm smiling when I bend and grasp Steele's arm. "Come on. Up and at 'em." He outweighs me by a hundred pounds, but he feels as wobbly and frail as an old man when I pull him to his feet.

"I'm dizzy. I think I need a doctor." Steele shakes his head, makes a show of blinking. He's got a bump the size of a hen's egg in the center of his forehead.

I look at Tomasetti. He rolls his eyes, then addresses Steele. "You ever hear the Chinese proverb about the steel dragon?" he asks.

"No, man."

"Didn't think so." Taking Steele's arm, he guides him toward the exit on the opposite side of the building.

I address the group of line workers. "Sorry for the disturbance, folks. Show's over, so you may as well go back to work."

A collective groan of disappointment emanates from the crowd.

I catch up with Tomasetti just as Steele asks, "So what's the proverb say?"

"Translated, it says don't ram your head into forklifts."

Steele gives him an incredulous look. "That's the stupidest fuckin' proverb I ever heard."

■ ■ ■ ■

Two hours later, Rasmussen, Tomasetti, and I sit at the conference room table with a downcast Willie Steele. At first, he was belligerent, so we let him stew in a cell for an hour or so in the hope that when we started questioning him, he would be ready to talk. It worked. The earlier belligerence has given way to reticence. Or maybe he's being coy. *That's all right,* I think. *It's still early in the game.*

The bump on his forehead now resembles a baby eggplant. I'm starting to wonder if we should have him transported to the hospital to make sure he doesn't have a concussion. Not because I'm unduly concerned about Steele's physical well-being, but I've learned that if a suspect's health is in the hands of the police, they'd damn well better make sure he emerges in the same condition as when he came in.

A few minutes earlier, the warrant came through from Judge Siebenthaler. I dispatched Skid and Glock to pick it up, then head over to Steele's apartment for a search. Hopefully, they'll come back with some shoes or boots we can match to the footwear impressions from the scene.

When everyone's ready, I hit the RECORD button on the digital machine and take a moment to identify all present and recite the date and time. Then I read Steele his Miranda rights. "Do you understand these rights?" I ask.

"Yeah."

Everyone holds their collective breath, anticipating that Steele may exercise his right to an attorney, which would bring this to a grinding halt. Five seconds pass, then Tomasetti dives in with a harsh summary of Steele's predicament, using the "We have a bunch of evidence against you, so you may as well start talking" approach. "We have a Skoal can with your fingerprints on it that places you at the scene of a murder."

"What? *Murder?*"

"We've got footprints that are going to match those boots we took off you."

Steele gives him a red-eyed glare. "I didn't kill anyone! What the fuck are you talking about?"

"The barn you torched? We found a dead guy inside."

"What? We didn't —"

"We've got you dead to rights," Tomasetti points out. "We could charge you with first-degree murder right now. If the prosecutor wants to be a hard ass about it, he might even go for the death penalty."

"Fuck you! I didn't kill no one!"

"You're going down, my man. You'll be *lucky* to get life in prison. It's a done deal. End of story. You getting all that?"

"I didn't do no murder!" he cries.

"So if you're feeling lucky today, go ahead and keep your big fat mouth shut."

Steele jumps to his feet, slams his fists against the tabletop, jangling the cuff. "This is bullshit! I didn't kill anyone!"

In an instant, Tomasetti is on his feet. Clamping his hand around the back of Steele's neck, he shoves him back into the chair. "Sit the hell down, you piece of shit."

Steele sits there, breathing hard, glaring up at Tomasetti. "You guys are railroading me."

"Shut up." Tomasetti says the words through clenched teeth. I know him well, probably better than anyone, but even I can't tell if it's an act. Either he's a better actor than I'd imagined, or he's genuinely pissed off.

Tomasetti bends, gets in Steele's face. "I'm going to give you one chance to save yourself," he says in an ominous tone. "Are you ready to listen?"

Steele struggles to get himself under

control. After a moment, he says, "I'm listening."

"We know you were working with someone. Give us the name or names, and we'll cut you a deal."

"I wasn't with no one! I swear!"

I fold my hands in front of me and sigh. "Willie, there's no such thing as loyalty when it comes to doing hard time. When we find your partner, you can bet he's going to roll over on you. Even if you were only along for the ride, you're going to fry."

Steele gapes at me, his mouth opening and closing like a big fish. "I-I think I want a lawyer. I know how you fuckin' cops operate. You're trying to trick me into incriminating myself."

Tomasetti scowls at me. "Book this piece of shit. Murder one. Arson. Felony assault. Attempted murder. And be sure to tack on the hate-crimes designation. That's good for an extra five years." He looks at his watch. "I've got to get back."

I rise quickly, look at Steele. "You just blew the best chance you're going to get."

"Wait!" Steele screams the word. His face blooms brick red. He's sweating profusely. The bump on his forehead seems to throb beneath the stark fluorescent lights.

We look at him, wait. He stares back.

"Okay," he says. "I'll talk."

Tomasetti looks at his watch, shifts his weight from one foot to the other. "We don't have all day."

Steele blinks rapidly. "What's in it for me?"

Rasmussen speaks up. "Give us the names of the people who were with you and we'll recommend manslaughter to the prosecutor."

"I don't know what that means."

"Best-case scenario," the sheriff says, "you get probation."

"No jail time?" Steele asks hopefully.

Rasmussen shrugs. "We can't make any promises, Willie. All we can do is let the court know you cooperated and make a recommendation."

"Juries like it when defendants cooperate with the police," I add.

Steele looks like a trapped animal, one that's thinking about chewing off its own leg to get free. One more small push and he's going to start gnawing.

Tomasetti removes the handcuff key from his pocket and bends to unfasten the cuffs. "Better?" he asks.

"Yeah." Rubbing his wrists, Steele flexes his fingers and stares down at his hands as if wondering what they're capable of.

Taking Tomasetti's cue, I rise and go to the coffee station, pour coffee into a Styrofoam cup, and slide it across the table to Steele. "You need creamer?" I ask.

"Black's fine." After a couple of minutes, he raises his head, looks at Tomasetti. "You sure you guys aren't trying to fuck me over?"

"We need your help," Rasmussen says. "Do the right thing. Help us out here. And we'll help you as much as we can. You have my word on that."

Steele picks up the cup and slurps. His hands shake so violently, he ends up spilling some. No one seems to notice.

We wait.

After a moment, Steele raises his gaze to Tomasetti. His forehead is so swollen and misshapen that his eyes look slightly crossed. "We didn't mean for no one to get hurt."

"I understand," Tomasetti says. He's the good cop now, the guy you can confide in without worrying that he'll use it against you.

Steele blows out a breath. "We killed them sheep. The ones that belong to that nasty old Amish broad." He goes silent.

"What else?" I ask.

He stares at his hands. "Tossed a Molotov cocktail into a buggy." Incredibly, he laughs. "You shoulda seen that fuckin' horse go."

317

At the last moment, he remembers whom he's dealing with and sobers.

"Willie," I say, pressing. "Tell us the rest."

"We beat that fat Amish guy. Tied him to his buggy." He shifts in his chair. "Every time we hit him, that fuckin' guy spewed Bible shit. Like God was going to swoop down from heaven and rescue him."

I stare at him, wondering if he's so stupid that he doesn't realize that kind of commentary isn't exactly inspiring our collective sympathies.

"What about the barn?" Rasmussen asks.

Steele's gaze snaps to his. "That wasn't my idea. I swear to God. I didn't want to do it. It was a nice damn barn."

Tomasetti's eyes glint. He looks like a predator toying with some half-dead prey. "Whose idea was it?" he asks.

Grimacing, Steele touches the bump on his forehead, checks his fingers for blood. "James Springer."

Recognition sparks in my brain. I've heard the name before. Some long-buried memory tugs at me. I turn the name over in my head, churning through the years. That's when I recall going to school with a boy by the name of James Springer. An *Amish* boy. He was nearly ten years my junior. I remember him because I always thought he looked like a cute little puppy. "He's Amish?" I ask.

"He ain't no more," Steele replies. "They kicked him out. For doing drugs, I think. You know, meth got ahold of him, so it wasn't really his fault. Now he's broke. Family won't talk to him. Can't get a girl. He's pretty pissed. Blames the Amish for everything that's happened to him."

"Who else helped torch the barn?" Tomasetti asks.

Steele's gaze skitters away. "Ain't no one else."

Tomasetti slams his hands down on the table so suddenly, Steele jumps. "I'm an inch away from throwing your lying ass in jail."

Steele hangs his head, looks down at the tabletop. "Aw, man."

"Protecting someone isn't worth going to prison for the rest of your life," I tell him.

Cursing under his breath, Steele lifts his gaze to mine. "This ain't fuckin' easy."

"You should have thought of that before you started your own personal crime wave," Tomasetti snaps.

Steele's face screws up and he begins to cry. "My brother, man. My fuckin' kid brother. He's only seventeen." He presses the heels of his hands to his eyes. "Don't tell him I told you. I don't want him to hate me."

"Nothing you say will leave this room." Tomasetti, I realize, is a master liar when he's got the law to back him up. I wonder if he's as good when he's in rogue mode.

The room falls silent, the only sounds the buzz of the fluorescent lights overhead and Steele's nervous fidgeting. We watch him, giving him a chance to pull himself together.

"Did you and your buddies murder Solomon and Abel Slabaugh?" Tomasetti's voice is low, but the question echoes like a gunshot.

Steele looks as if he swallowed his tongue. I see his throat working. His hands clench into fists on the tabletop in front of him. When his voice finally comes, it's a strangled sound I barely recognize. "We didn't kill no one. You can't pin that on us."

"Don't lie to me," Tomasetti says in an ominous tone.

"I ain't fuckin' lying!" Steele jumps to his feet. "I swear!"

Next to me, Rasmussen puts his hand on his baton.

"Sit down and calm the hell down," Tomasetti says.

"How can I calm down when you're accusing me of something I didn't do? That's some serious shit!" Steele is literally frothing at the mouth. Spittle flies from his lips, a speck landing on his chin. "I didn't kill them people! Don't try to put that on me!"

"Is it possible your brother or Springer did it?" I ask.

He turns his attention to me. For an instant, I think he's going to attack me, and I wonder about the wisdom of removing the cuffs. "They ain't killers, neither," he says. "They just want to cause problems for those dirty Amish pricks."

"Where were you three nights ago?" Tomasetti asks.

Steele snaps his gaze to him. "I worked a double. You can fuckin' check."

"I fuckin' will," Tomasetti replies smoothly.

"You cops can't pin them murders on us. We didn't do it." Steele makes a strangled sound, getting himself worked up again. "You said if I talked, you'd help me out, not railroad me."

"If you're telling the truth, you don't have anything to worry about," Rasmussen says.

"What about the Amish boy?" I ask. "The teenager?"

Steele raises his gaze to mine. His face is red and blotchy from crying. "What Amish boy?"

"The teenage boy you beat the crap out of this afternoon."

"We didn't beat no Amish kid."

"For God's sake, Willie, you've already confessed to manslaughter, arson, and felony assault. A misdemeanor beating is the least of your worries."

"It's a lesser charge," Tomasetti explains.

"Kid probably won't even press charges," Rasmussen puts in.

"I don't know anything about no Amish kid," he insists. "I swear."

I stare at him, wondering why he would lie about a misdemeanor charge when he's already confessed to multiple felonies. "You need to think real hard before you start lying to us."

"I ain't got no reason to lie. I told you what we done. I ain't going to say I did something I didn't just to get on your good side. I got enough fuckin' problems."

I consider that for a moment. "What about Springer and your brother? Could they have done it without your knowledge?"

"I don't think so." But he doesn't seem quite so sure of himself now. "Me and Springer . . . we're some kind of unit. We done most of it. My brother . . . not so much."

Tomasetti crosses to him, sets his hand on

Steele's shoulder. "Well, Willie, I'm glad you and Springer are pals because chances are you're going to be cell mates for the next couple of decades."

CHAPTER 16

By the time we round up James Springer and Kevin Steele, it's 4:00 A.M. They weren't very happy when we rolled them from their beds and slapped on the cuffs. Unlike their counterpart, both men refused to talk to us without lawyers, so I handed them off to Rasmussen, who booked them into the Holmes County Jail.

Tomasetti, Skid and I are sitting in my office. On the credenza behind me, my desktop computer rattles like an old refrigerator. I've got a couple of reams of arrest-related paperwork spread out on my desk, but I'm too tired to finish reports tonight.

But it's a good tired, the kind that comes in the wake of a righteous bust and the knowledge that we got three criminals off the street in a single fell swoop. I don't like the idea of letting Willie Steele off on lesser charges; he's no less guilty than the other two men. But if that small concession will guarantee his cooperation and convictions for the other two, then it's a compromise I'm willing to make.

"I think I'm going to head back out." Skid rises and stretches. "Leave you two all the fun paperwork."

"Should be quiet now that the three-man crime wave is off the street," I tell him.

"Hell of a bump on Steele's forehead," Skid comments. "Never seen anything like it in my life."

"The moral of the story is, Never ram your forehead into an immovable object," Tomasetti says.

"Going to have to remember that." Giving us a mock salute, he saunters out of my office.

For a moment, neither of us speaks. I shut down my computer and arrange the paperwork into a couple stacks. "I'll tackle these reports first thing in the morning," I say.

Tomasetti eyes me from across the desk. "It already is first thing in the morning."

I smile. "Postsleep."

He doesn't move, and I get the impression he's got something on his mind. "What do you think?" he asks.

"I think you're welcome to sleep at my house." The words come with surprising ease.

"Do we have to sleep?"

"We probably should."

"*Should* usually doesn't stop us."

Despite the comfortableness of the moment, I blush. When he smiles, the now-familiar thrill moves through me, and it shocks me all over again that two people as wounded as we are have come this far in a relationship neither of us believed possible.

"What do you think about Steele?" he asks after a moment.

"I think he might be telling the truth."

"Leaves us with a couple of loose ends."

"Leaves the Slabaugh case open."

He sighs. "You think Steele and friends did the Slabaughs?"

I consider the question, let it roll around in my head a moment. "I think they're at the top of the suspect list."

He nods, but I can tell my words didn't alleviate whatever it is that's troubling him. I don't think we're going to solve it tonight, so I reach for my coat and rise.

Tomasetti stands, too, and we start toward the door. "So if Steele and his goons didn't beat the crap out of Mose, who did?" he asks as we pass through the reception area.

I wave at Mona. "Maybe James Springer and Kevin Steele did it. Maybe we'll get more out of them after they've spent the night in jail."

Tomasetti nods, but as he leaves me and starts toward his Tahoe to follow me home, he still looks troubled.

The events of the day follow me into the disjointed world of my dreams. I'm at the Slabaugh farm, in the barn, standing a few feet from the manure pit. I'm holding a baby in my arms, and though I've never had a child, I know the baby is mine. I feel the connection as surely as I feel my heart beating in my chest, the blood running through my veins. James Springer stands before me. Only this apparition is not Springer. His eyes are the color of blood, and I see hatred in them, a barely controlled rage.

"Dirty Amish bitch," he says.

He's looking at my baby. His eyes burn red, and I see the veins pulsing in his face. I'm aware of the child's warmth against my breast, and I know Springer wants to take him from me. He wants to hurt him. Kill him. I'm willing to die — or kill — to keep either of those things from happening.

When he lunges, I'm not fast enough to get away. I'm not strong enough to stop him. I feel hands on my arms and look over to see Willie Steele and his brother, Kevin, on either side of me. They yank me back, so violently that my head snaps forward and my teeth clack together. I lose my footing. Springer jerks the baby from my arms. Then the baby is falling into space. I struggle against the talonlike hands, fingers digging into my skin. I hear my own scream, so loud that it rattles my brain. But the hands that catch the baby are not mine.

Springer grins and looks down at the baby in his arms. I see rotting black teeth. He smells of death and decay. He stares down at the baby as if he wants to tear into it with his teeth, devour it, consume it. And in that moment, I know I'm going to kill him.

I reach for my sidearm, but my fingers fumble the grip. I grapple with my holster. I know my .38 is there, but I can't get my hand around it. My certainty that I have the upper hand evaporates. Ten feet away, Springer holds the baby by its tiny foot, dangling it over the manure pit. The infant's face is red. His cries ring in my ears, shatter my heart.

"Don't kill my baby!" I scream.

Then I'm running toward them, but I'm not moving. When I look down, I see that my feet are immersed in black muck. And I know I'm not going to get there in time to save the baby. Already I feel the horrific loss the child's death will cause; it's like a baseball bat slamming into my body. The terrible shock of that is almost too much for my mind to bear.

Don't kill my baby!

It's Salome's voice screaming the words. I look around, but she's not there. When I look down, I'm wearing her blue dress. *Don't kill my baby!* It's Salome's voice, but my thoughts. It's my heart that's breaking. My life that will end with the death of that child.

Springer's fist opens. The child flails, then tumbles headfirst into the black muck of the pit. I scream out a name I don't recognize. Then I hear the terrible splash, and I tell myself my baby can't be gone, because I know God would never be that cruel. Not twice in one lifetime.

Then I'm falling. Above me, I see the rafters of the old barn. I smell the stench of the liquid manure. I feel the methane gas stealing the oxygen from my lungs. Then the black ooze rushes up and slams into me, as cold and black as death. The noxious liquid sucks me down, like a huge, voracious mouth swallowing me whole.

Blackness closes over me, but it doesn't silence the baby's cries. Nothing will ever silence that tiny voice, because it's inside me. Hearing those cries and not being able to reach the child is like dying a thousand tortuous deaths. I thrash and struggle against the muck. But it sucks me down, smothering and digesting me until I cease to exist.

"Kate."

I'm still thrashing when I wake. Tomasetti is leaning over me. Even in the dim winter light slanting in through the window, I see concern on his face, and I realize I must have cried out. I blink at him, shaken and embarrassed. A cold slick of sweat covers my entire body. My hands and legs are shaking, and I can still feel the dark grip of the nightmare. For several disorienting seconds, I think I can still smell the muck of that terrible pit.

"Jesus." Sitting up, I shove the hair from my face. "I'm sorry."

"You okay?"

I draw a deep breath, willing myself to calm down. "I haven't decided yet."

"Must have been a bad one." He sets his thumb beneath my chin and forces my gaze to his. "If I ask you how often that happens, would you tell me the truth?"

"Probably not."

"Kate . . ."

I look at him, not liking the way he's staring back at me, as if I've just been diagnosed with some fatal affliction. "It's been a while," I say after a moment.

He nods. "You want to talk about it?"

I try to smile but don't quite manage to. "Think you could check under the bed first?"

"There's no monster here."

"Just you."

"A monster with a heart."

That makes me smile, and I feel the dream tumble into the backwaters of my mind.

Dipping his head, he kisses me, and I'm amazed that such a small thing can have such a profound effect.

A glance at the alarm clock tells me it's not yet 7:00 A.M. We have a few minutes, so I lie back and snuggle close to him. He puts his arm around me, and in that instant his embrace is the safest place in the world. I love the way his arms feel when they're around me. I give him a condensed version of the nightmare. When I'm finished, we go quiet, thinking, listening to the rain outside.

"Sigmund Freud would probably have a field day with that," I say after a moment. "You know, baby envy and all that."

"Freud was full of shit."

That makes me grin. "I'm glad I have you to help me keep things in perspective."

"Probably just the case working on your mind," Tomasetti says. "Mixing it up with your past. Stress does that."

"My sister, Sarah, had a baby," I blurt. "Two months ago. I don't know why, but I haven't been able to make myself go to see the new baby. I've driven by their farm, but I never go inside. I just . . . sit out on the road like some weird stalker. I know my not showing up is hurting my sister. And there's a part of me that wants to see my little niece. But . . ."

Lying next to me, Tomasetti goes still. I sense his mind sifting through everything I've said, and I kick myself for unloading on him. "I'm sorry," I say quickly. "I shouldn't have —"

"Kate." He says my name with a slight reproof.

We fall silent. I can hear rain dripping off the eaves, slapping down on the ground. I know Tomasetti's about to say something wise and profound. I know it's going to hurt a little bit, but I'll be better for it afterward. "This case has a lot of themes running through it," he tells me. "Amish kids. The deaths of their parents. Babies. Pregnancy." He pauses. "Might be dredging some things up for you."

"I thought of that."

"I know you have."

"Salome is about the age my child would

have been if I hadn't —" Even after all this time, I have a difficult time saying the word, but I force it out. "Abortion," I finish, but the word feels thick and greasy coming out of my mouth.

"Maybe dealing with these kids is bringing some of that back for you," he says. "You didn't get a chance to deal with it right after it happened."

"Maybe."

"Your new niece represents something you lost, Kate. Sometimes things like that are hard to face."

He's right, and the truth of his words hurts. But I don't let myself flinch. I'm tougher than that, and I want him to know it. "Will you do me a favor?"

"Well, since you're naked . . ." He smiles at me. "You know I will."

"Don't ever feel sorry for me. I think that's the one thing I couldn't stand."

His expression turns puzzled. "Why would you say that?"

"Because you know what happened to me. Because I've . . . let you in. I mean, I've let you inside me. Inside my mind." I swallow, not sure how much to tell him. Trust is so damn hard to come by. "My heart."

"I don't feel sorry for you. Not by a long shot."

"You know a lot about me. Probably more than anyone else in the world."

"I promise not to blackmail you."

A tension-easing laugh bursts from my throat. Gathering my emotions, I punch his shoulder. "We're having a serious talk here."

He feigns offense. "I'm serious."

Leaning close to him, I press a kiss to his mouth, then start to rise. "I've got to go."

He stops me. Shifting in the bed, he turns me to him, then sets his hands on either side of my face. "I've let you inside, too, Kate. Don't forget that. This relationship thing is a two-way street, and I'm right there with you."

I blink at him, stunned, and a little bit thrilled. "So I could blackmail you, too?"

"You could, but then I'd have to kill you. That would be a shame, because I really like you."

We're staring at each other. He gives me a small smile. I'm keenly aware of his closeness. I smell the lingering remnants of his aftershave, remember all the impressions his body made on mine during the night. "We'll figure out this relationship thing sooner or later," I tell him.

For a moment, I think he's going to say something else. I don't know what that might be, but I see it in his eyes. And in that instant, I want to hear it more than anything else in the world.

The phone on my night table interrupts, and the moment evaporates. We stare at each other a few seconds longer, not speaking, wanting more time but knowing it's not to be.

"I've got to get that." Rolling away from him, I grab the phone, put it to my ear. "Burkholder," I snap, trying to sound as if I'm not in bed, sleeping or otherwise.

"Chief Burkholder, this is Chief Archer from Connersville, Indiana." He clears his throat. "Sorry to call so early."

It takes my befuddled brain a moment to place the name. Then my intellect clicks in, and I realize he's returning my call. Mose had told me his family was from Connersville and I wanted to check out his adoption story. "Thanks for returning my call, Sheriff."

"Sorry I didn't call sooner, but I was out of town. Big conference over in Richmond on the meth problem." He sounds harried, as if he's back in town and pounding through a whole collection of messages. Mine wasn't very high on his list, and he's anxious to move on to the next.

"I'm calling to verify some information about a young man by the name of Moses

335

Slabaugh."

"Slabaugh . . ."

"His name would have been Hochstetler. He's living here in Painters Mill, but he's originally from Connersville."

"Yeah, I know that name. Amish folks?"

"That's right. Mose claims his parents were killed and he was adopted by another family shortly thereafter."

"I remember that," the sheriff says. "Hell of a thing. Nice Amish family, too."

"How long ago did it happen?"

"Oh, gosh, I'd say it's been ten years now. One of the worst accidents I've ever seen."

In the three years I've been the chief of police here in Painters Mill, I've investigated one fatal buggy accident. A logging truck from Pennsylvania crossed the yellow line and hit a buggy head-on. It was a triple fatality, and I was first on the scene. The images ran through my head for months.

"We require all buggies to have 'Slow Moving Vehicle' signs here in Painters Mill," I say. "Some of the more conservative families balk, claiming the signs are ornamentation."

A too-long pause ensues, and I get a prickly sensation on the back of my neck. "Sheriff Archer?"

"The Hochstetlers weren't killed in a

buggy accident," the sheriff tells me.

The prickly sensation augments to a stabbing suspicion. "Mose told me his parents were killed in a buggy accident."

"The Hochstetlers died in the manure pit out on their farm. You know, methane gas. I ought to know; I was first on the scene. First damn week of work and I got two dead Amish on my hands."

His voice fades as the words hit home. *The Hochstetlers died in the manure pit out on their farm.* I almost can't believe my ears. All I can think is, *Why would Mose lie to me about something like that? He was seven years old at the time. Why would he lie?* Muttering a thank-you, I hang up the phone, then sit there, my head reeling.

"What is it?" Tomasetti asks.

I look at him, feeling shell-shocked, and tell him what I learned from Sheriff Archer. "Why would Mose lie about something like that?" I ask.

Tomasetti's expression is dark. "Because he's lying about something else," he says. "Or covering something up."

"Or both." My mind spins through the possibilities, and I hate all of them. I don't want to say aloud what I'm thinking. Of course, I don't have a choice. As much as I don't want to confront those possibilities, they're there, staring me in the face. Until this moment, I've been too blind to see them.

"My God, he would have been seven years old," I say, and another chill runs through me.

Tomasetti nods, knowing what I'm thinking. "We need to get out there."

I'm already up, rushing toward the shower. "Could Mose be the one who pushed his parents into the pit? Has he done it before?"

"I think it's time we asked him."

CHAPTER 17

Twenty minutes later, I whip the Explorer into the Slabaugh lane and zip toward the house. I called Bishop Troyer on the way and asked him to check on Mose. Sure enough, the boy was nowhere to be found. Concern notches up into worry as I park at the rear of the house. It doesn't elude me that the buggy is gone, and I wonder if Mose took it, or if the Rabers went into town.

Praying it's the latter, I swing open the door and get out. Drizzle floats down from a slate sky as I jog toward the rear porch. Around me, fog hovers like wet ghosts, turning the farm monochrome. It's like walking into an old black-and-white movie.

I hear the crunch of gravel behind me and turn to see Tomasetti park the Tahoe beside my Explorer. I don't wait for him. Reaching the door, I rap hard with the heel of my hand.

"Mr. and Mrs. Raber?" I shout. "Police! Open up!"

A hard-edged uneasiness steals through me as I wait. The seconds seem to tick by like minutes. I know it's premature, but I can't shake the feeling that something is wrong.

"They home?" Tomasetti strides toward me, his expression sober.

I motion toward the gravel area. "Buggy's not here."

"Maybe they went into town, took the kids with them."

"I called Bishop Troyer on my way over. Mose is gone."

"Shit." Sighing, he leans past me, twists the knob. The door eases open, and we look at each other. "Reasonable cause," he says.

"Let's go." In an instant, I'm through the door, running past the mudroom and into the kitchen. "Salome!" I shout. "It's Kate. Are you here?"

Tomasetti takes the steps two at a time to the second level. I clear the downstairs bedrooms, the bathroom, and the basement, but none of the Slabaughs is there.

We meet in the kitchen a few minutes later. Tomasetti looks pissed. "That little fucker lied to us."

I nod, hating it that I agree with him.

"The question is, why?" I sigh. "Where the hell are they?"

"Hiding," he growls. "Let's check the barn."

We move through the mudroom. Before realizing it, I'm running at a steady pace down the sidewalk. Light rain is falling now, cold on my face, but I barely notice.

"Kate."

I look at Tomasetti and see him motion toward a small outbuilding — a shed. That's when I realize the overhead door is ajar. We veer left. Bending, he rolls up the door. I duck beneath it before it's fully up. The first thing I notice is the truck. It's an old white Chevy with bald front tires and a broken headlight. It looks out of place here.

I glance at Tomasetti and he shakes his head. "Where the fuck did that come from?" he mutters.

"It wasn't there last time I was here," I say.

"I bet he's been planning to run for some time." Hands on his hips, he crosses to the truck, looks in the window. "Suitcases."

I think of Salome. A sweet Amish girl. Pregnant at the age of fifteen. She thinks she's in love. The situation is a disaster waiting to happen. "I bet he talked Salome into running away with him," I say.

"Probably." Tomasetti yanks at the truck's door, but it doesn't budge. "Locked," he says. "No keys."

"Where are Ike and Samuel?" I ask.

"Maybe they're with the Rabers."

A thread of worry twists through me, a hot wire melting through flesh, touching nerves. "We need to find them."

"The Rabers, too." He starts toward the door. "Let's check the barn."

Then we're outside and running, and I realize we both feel a sense of urgency. Something's wrong, but we're not sure what. Tomasetti slides the big door open. The smells of pigs, hay, and the wet ammonia stink of the manure pit wafts out. We enter as a single unit.

"Salome!" I shout. "Mose! It's Kate!"

"Ike! Samuel!" Tomasetti goes right, toward the steps that will take him to the loft.

I go straight. "Salome!" I check the stalls to my left, but they're empty. Moving faster now, I duck through the rails. The concrete beneath my feet is slick with manure. The ammonia stench burns my nose, makes my eyes water. "Salome!"

I walk to the manure pit, cast a cursory glance toward the oily bottom. Absently, I note someone has used the hose to partially fill the pit. Several objects float on the oily surface — a red inflatable ball, a length of two-by-four. Shock freezes me in place. I almost can't get my mind around the sight of two small pale faces in the ooze. Samuel and Ike, I realize with a burgeoning sense of horror.

"Tomasetti!" The panic in my voice shakes me from my momentary stupor. Looking around wildly, I spot the hose coiled on a wood dowel on one of the support beams. I lunge at it, yank it off.

"Kate!" I glance up and see Tomasetti sprinting toward me. "What is it?"

"The kids!" I shout. "They're in the pit."

"What?" He rushes to the pit, looks down. "Aw, man."

I loop the end of the hose around the support beam, tie it in a double knot. The same way I did it the night I found Rachael and Solly in that pit. But all I can think is that I'm going to fail these two little boys the same way I failed their parents.

"I've got a cable in the Tahoe," Tomasetti says.

"No time." When I turn to Tomasetti, he's already got the other end looped around his hips. "John, you can't go down there."

"And you can?" he snarls. "Fuck that. Get on the horn. *Now.* Get the fire department out here. Open all the doors."

Hitting my lapel mike, I put out the code. I rush to the door, throw my weight against it, shove it open. I break two windows for a cross breeze. But there's not enough wind to help.

When I turn my attention to Tomasetti, he's yanking off his coat. I watch, feeling helpless and terrified as he tosses it to the floor. Next, he rips off his shirt, tears off a sleeve, then takes the scrap of fabric to the trough and wets it.

I rush to him. "You can't go down there."

"No choice, Kate." He ties the wet fabric around his nose and mouth. We both know it's not going to help. Methane gas displaces oxygen.

"Damn it." I choke out the words. "If you pass out, I'm not strong enough to pull you out."

I can tell by his expression that he's already thought of that. "Tie the hose to the bumper. I'm going down."

"John . . ."

"Go!"

Spinning, I lurch into a sprint, burst through the barn door. Then I'm in the rain, running like I've never run before in my life. I hear roaring, but I don't know if it's my heart or thunder or the hard pound of the rain. I hit the locks from twenty feet away, yank the door open, slide inside. I twist the key, and the engine turns over. Jamming it into gear, I floor the gas pedal. Gravel and mud spew. The Explorer fishtails, then jets toward the barn. I hit the brake. *Too hard.* My hand shakes as I cut the wheel, grasp the shifter to back it through the open door. *Too fast. Going to screw it up if I don't slow down.* I clip the barn door with my bumper as I back through. Wood splinters and cracks, but I don't slow down.

Glancing in the rearview mirror, I see Tomasetti standing at the pit, motioning for me to hurry, the hose looped around his hips. I throw the door open, grab up the other end of the hose, scramble back to the Explorer, loop it around the bumper, and tie it off. I know it's silly at a time like this, but I want to touch him before he goes down there. Of course, he doesn't wait. Grasping the hose like a rappelling rope, he drops into the pit.

In that moment, I know what it's like to go crazy. It's like a current running through my body, causing every emotional circuit to overload, until I can't form a single coherent thought. It takes every bit of concentration I have, but I make myself go to the pit and look down.

He descends quickly, reaches the bottom within seconds. His feet disappear into the tarlike muck. He grasps the closest child by the coat, drags him through the muck and up onto his lap. So far so good.

"Bring me up!" he shouts.

I run to the Explorer, put it in gear, and ease the gas pedal down. I have to resist pulling too fast; I don't want to topple him from the hose. I move forward ten feet, fifteen feet. Tomasetti emerges over the top of the pit. Jamming the Explorer into reverse, I back up to feed him a few feet of hose. Then I shove the shifter into park, get out, and run back to him.

He's breathing hard. Above the fabric tied around his nose and mouth, his complexion is deathly pale. He shoves the unconscious child at me. "He's breathing," he croaks. "Get him outside."

I take Samuel into my arms. His body feels cold and wet and utterly lifeless. I want to make sure Tomasetti is all right before he goes back down, but when I look back at him, he's already dropping into the pit.

Choking out sobs, I carry Samuel through the barn door and outside to the fresh air. I stop on the sidewalk and place him on his side, in case he ingested some of the liquid into his lungs. The rain is coming down in earnest, so I remove my coat and drape it over him.

"Samuel?" I pick up his hand and rub it between mine. "Are you okay, kiddo? Can you open your eyes for me?"

Relief sweeps through me when I notice him shivering. That's a good sign. Bending, I put my ear to his nose. His breathing is elevated but strong.

I don't want to leave him like this — in the rain and all alone. But I have no choice. I've got to pull Tomasetti out of that pit. "Hang tight, baby. I'll be back." Giving his hand a final squeeze, I rush back to the barn, push myself through the rails, look down into the pit. Adrenaline punches me when I see Tomasetti struggling to lift Ike. Ike weighs less than Samuel. That tells me the lack of oxygen is already affecting him.

I scream his name. "John! Grab him and get out of there!"

Nodding, he signals for me to pull him up.

In an instant, I'm through the rails, sprinting to the Explorer, sliding behind the wheel. I take it easy pulling him out, thinking, *If he loses consciousness he could fall back in the pit. . . .*

I check the rearview mirror. Relief sends a

sob to my throat when I see their heads and shoulders emerge. As I pull them out, I notice the way Tomasetti's clinging to the hose, and I realize he's struggling. Ramming the Explorer into park, I rush back to the pit. Tomasetti is facedown on the filthy concrete. At some point, the fabric has come off his face. He's covered with muck and shivering uncontrollably. Next to him, Ike is as still as death.

"Get up! Come on!" Nudging Tomasetti, I grab Ike beneath his arms. "John! Get up! Please!"

Gripping Ike beneath his arms, I drag him toward the door. But I don't take my eyes off Tomasetti. Midway there, I see him struggle to his hands and knees. Head drooping, he disentangles himself from the hose with one hand, supports himself with the other. I place Ike on the sidewalk next to his brother, pull my coat partially over both boys. They're shivering and wet. But they're alive. Tomasetti's alive. Right now, that's all that matters.

I'm on my way back inside to help Tomasetti when I see him crawling toward me. Somehow he made it through the pen rails, and he's trying to reach the door and fresh air.

Rushing to him, I kneel at his side. "Can

you stand?"

"Just need some air," he says.

"Come on." Bending, I slip his arm over my shoulder, help him to his feet, and we stumble through the door. "Ambulance is on the way," I tell him.

Tomasetti goes to his hands and knees, gulping air.

"Hang on." Rising, I go back to the Explorer, pull a thermal blanket from the trunk. When I get back, Tomasetti is sitting beside the two boys. He's conscious and aware, but his eyes are glazed. He's looking down at the boys. Samuel is crying. Next to him, Ike is moaning, beginning to stir.

I kneel next to the children, reposition my coat so that both of them are covered. "You're going to be okay," I say.

Ike reaches for me, clings to my leg. "I'm scared."

"Honey, can you tell me who did this to you?"

Sobbing, the boy presses his face against me. "He was going to come back and get us out."

"Who?"

He hesitates.

"Was it Mose?" I ask. "Did he do this to you?"

Mouth open and trembling, he nods.

"Don't tell him I told."

"I won't. You're safe now. No one's going to hurt you." I glance toward the barn door. "Honey, can you tell me where the Rabers are?"

"They took the buggy to town," Ike tells me.

"What about Salome and Mose?"

"I dunno. They ran."

I nod, relieved that no one else has been hurt. I hate to leave him like this, but I disconnect him from my leg. "I've got to go, honey."

"Don't leave us!" he cries, trying to hang on.

I squeeze his small shoulder. "Everything's going to be okay. Stay here with Agent Tomasetti, and I'll be back. I promise."

Inching closer to Tomasetti, Ike buries his face against his shoulder. I catch a glimpse of Tomasetti's face, and I know this moment is something I'm going to have to think about later. For now, I need to find Mose before he hurts someone else.

"You did good," I say to Tomasetti.

"Go get that fuckin' Mose," he grinds out. Then I'm up and sprinting toward the house. Rain patters my face and shoulders as I run. I can't stop thinking about how close those boys came to death. How in the name of God could anyone be cold-blooded enough to kill their younger siblings?

I'm midway to the house when I remember the truck and suitcases in the shed. Knowing Mose and Salome are going to make a run for it, I change direction, head toward it. Rain stings my face and streams into my eyes. The thought that I should pull my weapon flashes, but I resist the idea. Then I remind myself Mose tried to murder his two younger brothers. He may have killed his parents. Cursing, I pull out the .38, crank back the hammer.

I'm angling toward the shed when I realize someone has closed the overhead door, and I know Mose is inside. Salome probably is, too. They could have seen Tomasetti and me in the barn, gone out the back and circled around. . . .

The truck engine rumbles to life. I pick up speed, decide to approach through the small door on the side, as opposed to the overhead door in front. Before I can swing left, the big door explodes. Wood splinters and flies at me. Through sheets of rain, I see the grille of the old truck. The slash of a single headlight blinds me. The engine screaming like a beast. The vehicle is nearly on top of me. I catch a glimpse of Mose behind the wheel. Salome in the passenger seat. They're ten feet away and closing fast.

I raise my weapon. "Stop!"

The vehicle is moving at a high rate of speed. Rear tires fishtailing, it comes at me. I dive left. The ground rushes up and slams into me. Breathless, I roll, trying to get out of the way. Glancing up, I see the red smear of taillights, wheels slinging gravel and mud. He's heading toward the road.

"Son of a bitch!"

Gripping my pistol, I scramble to my feet, sprint toward the Explorer parked in the barn. My boots pound through puddles and mud, but I don't slow down. Vaguely, I wonder where the hell my backup is.

I'm aware of Tomasetti getting to his feet, shouting at me as I blow past. Inside the barn, I yank open the driver's door, slide behind the wheel, hit the ignition. The wheels spin and grab. I hear the hose snap, then I'm bumping down the lane. I see the red blur of the truck's taillights ahead. Mose is driving erratically, veering toward the bar ditch, then back onto the gravel. It's a dangerous game; he's an inexperienced driver, scared and out of control. But I find myself worrying more about Salome and her unborn child.

He decapitates the mailbox at the end of the lane and whips left onto the township road. Sludge from the truck's tires spatters my windshield. I hit the wipers and emergency strobes. A hundred yards down the road and I'm nearly on top of him. I'm lining up for a PIT maneuver in an effort to spin out his vehicle, when a hole the size of my fist explodes my windshield. A hollow *thunk* sounds; then a thousand diamond capillaries spread out like some bizarre road map. The son of a bitch is shooting at me.

Blind, covered with shards of glass, I cut the wheel right. The tree comes out of nowhere. I try to avoid it, but I'm on the muddy shoulder and the Explorer responds sluggishly. The impact knocks me so hard against the shoulder harness that I swear I can hear my clavicle snap. Simultaneously, the air bag punches me in the face and chest like a huge boxer's glove.

Gasping in pain, I extricate myself from the air bag, reach down, and unlatch my safety belt. Steam spews from the engine. Looking through the shattered safety glass, I see the crinkled steel of my hood. Shoving away the deflating bag, I unlatch the door. When it sticks, I swivel and kick it open.

I slide from the vehicle, but my legs are like rubber and I go to my knees. I know I'm hurting, but there's so much adrenaline, I can't pinpoint where. Groaning, I force myself to my feet, look around. Mose's truck is stopped fifty yards down the road, facing me. Ten feet away, the Explorer sits at a cockeyed angle, wrecked and useless.

That's when my temper kicks in. Operating on instinct now, I hit my lapel mike, put out a 10-33. This is exactly the kind of situation that can spiral out of control and end very badly. I don't know if Salome is a willing participant or a hostage. If Mose feels he has nothing left to lose, he might harm himself. He might harm Salome. Or both.

I should wait for backup, but I'm not going to follow protocol. Pulling my .38, I move to the bar ditch, where I have some measure of cover, and start toward the truck. "Mose!" I call out. "Put down the gun!"

No answer. I don't stop walking. "Put it down, and come over here and talk to me!"

Dead silence.

I try another approach. "You're frightening Salome! Come on! Talk to me! Is she okay?"

The passenger door opens. An instant later, Salome stumbles out. She's wearing the blue dress and only one shoe. No *kapp,* her hair flying. "Chief Burkholder!" she screams. "Don't hurt us!"

"Come here!" I shout. "Run! I'm not going to hurt you."

She breaks into a run, arms outstretched, her eyes wild with terror. I continue toward her. The knowledge that I'm in plain sight should Mose start shooting never leaves my mind. I'm scared, more scared than I've been in a long time, but I don't stop. *Don't let me down, Mose,* I silently chant.

I'm twenty feet from Salome now. She's hysterical, choking out sobs, her arms wrapped around her as if she's holding herself together.

"It's going to be okay," I tell her. "Take cover on the other side of the Explorer. You'll be safe there."

"Don't hurt him," she cries.

The truck's engine revs. Adrenaline jolts me like electricity. Gravel shoots out from beneath the tires. Then the vehicle jumps toward me. I shove Salome toward the bar ditch. "Run!"

"Moses!" she screams. "Don't!"

I face the truck, raise my hands. "Mose! Stop!" I scream the words, but it's too late. I know he isn't going to stop.

"Goddamn it!" Dropping into a shooter's stance, I raise my .38. "Stop! *Stop!*"

The vehicle is ten yards away, engine screaming, gaining speed. I fire five rounds into the windshield. The glass splinters and spreads. The engine emits a final roar. The vehicle jerks right, slides sideways, and then nose-dives into the bar ditch and goes still.

"Moses! *Moses!*" Salome's screams are bloodcurdling.

I spin, point at her. "Stay put!"

Covering her face with her hands, she drops to her knees and bends, her body racked with sobs.

I turn my attention to the vehicle. Somewhere in the back of my mind, I'm aware of the sirens. I can't see the fire truck or ambulance yet, but they're nearby, probably turning onto the township road from the highway. Just a few more minutes . . .

Hold on, Mose, I think. *Don't be dead.* My brain chants the words like a mantra as I approach the passenger door. *Dear God, let him be alive.* I don't want the death of a seventeen-year-old boy on my conscience. The irony of that is almost too much to bear.

The truck is nose-down in the ditch. The driver's side looks difficult to get to, so I approach from the other side. The first thing I see is blood spatter on the door window, and I know in my gut this isn't going to have a good ending. I try the door, but it's jammed, so I hold down the latch and yank it as hard as I can. Steel groans as I pry it open.

Mose is slumped against the driver's door. I know immediately he's dead. He's suffered at least one gunshot to the face, probably two. There's a lot of blood. Brain matter on the headrest. More blood on his shoulders. Blowback on the side window. A clawlike hand still grips the wheel.

"Aw, Mose. Aw, God. Mose."

I barely recognize my own voice as I stumble away from the truck. I feel sick to my soul. Guilt is a swirling black hole inside me, and I'm barreling toward it, an Olympian sprinting toward a false finish. Or maybe the edge of a cliff. I'm already spinning into that awful free fall.

My hand shakes uncontrollably when I hit my lapel mike. My voice sounds foreign to me when I put out the call. I'm standing in the bar ditch. I can't stop looking at Mose. Minutes ago, he was healthy and alive, with his entire life ahead of him. Now he's dead. No matter how badly I want to jump in some time machine for a redo, it's not going to happen. Death is forever. Some kinds of guilt are forever, too, and I'll be feeling the killing edge of this day for the rest of my life.

I can hear Salome screaming, but I'm not

sure if it's real or inside my head. I should go to her. She's been through hell, more than any fifteen-year-old should have to bear. The last thing she needs to see is her lover's shattered body. But I can't make myself move. I can't do anything because I'm frozen in a hell of my own making, staring at the dead body of the seventeen-year-old Amish boy I just shot.

"Chief Burkholder?"

I turn to see a young paramedic standing a few feet away. His partner stands next to him, his eyes going to the body in the truck. "We're going to have to get in there and check his vitals."

I blink and step aside quickly. "I think he's gone."

"Looks that way, Chief, but we still need to verify."

"Of course."

The other paramedic glances at the .38 in my hand. "You okay, Chief Burkholder?"

My collarbone aches, but my own pain seems so minuscule in comparison to what's happened here, I can't bring myself to mention it. "I'm fine."

"Don't go anywhere. We're going to need to check you out. Make sure you're okay."

Only then to do realize I've got tears on my cheeks. I'm gripping the gun so hard, my knuckles ache. When I look down, my hand is shaking as if I suffer from some form of palsy. I know the sheriff's office will be taking my weapon from me. Cops never like that, but it's protocol whenever there's a fatality shooting. The BCI lab will test it, make the official determination that my bullets caused the death of Mose Slabaugh. I'll be put on administrative leave. Not because I did anything wrong, but because I killed someone. They'll urge me to seek counseling. I'll resist. There will be a hearing. But it was a righteous kill.

A righteous kill. Right.

One of the paramedics goes around to the driver's side. I didn't notice the fire truck arriving, but they're here, because there's a firefighter in full gear next to him. I know there are things I should be doing. But I'm not capable of much at the moment. My brain is misfiring, like an engine missing most of its spark plugs. I can't stop shaking. I watch the two men pry the door open. Mose's body nearly falls out, but the paramedic catches the dead boy by his shoulders. I see blood on blue latex gloves. Gray skin and staring eyes. And then the two men lower the body to the ground. The paramedic checks the carotid for a pulse, then places a stethoscope against the boy's chest.

Not wanting Salome to see the body, I glance left, where I last saw her. She's crumpled on the ground, her face and hands in the dirt. Her body quakes with sobs that sound more like screams. She looks small and pale and broken lying there. Her dress and hair are wet. Her fingers are curled in the mud, black under her nails. I want to go to her, comfort her, tell her it's going to be all right. But I don't know what to say. I'm not sure I'm capable of saying anything at the moment.

I'm relieved when I see Glock striding toward her, bending, setting his hands on her shoulders. But his eyes are on me. "I've got her," he says, and it's as if he's reading my mind. "I'll take care of her."

"Kate."

I turn at the sound of my name. Tomasetti stands a few feet away, looking at me as if I might shatter into a million pieces and he's not sure he can contain them all. More than anything, I want to go to him. I want him to put his arms around me and make all this pain go away. I want to sink into him and never leave, because right now I know that's the only safe place in the world.

"He's dead," I tell him.

He looks down at the gun in my hand and crosses to me. "Are you okay?"

"I don't think I am."

"I don't think you are, either." Never taking his eyes from me, he reaches out and eases the .38 from my grasp. "They'll need your weapon."

"I know."

"Rasmussen will want to talk to you."

I nod. "That's fine."

Sighing, he looks past me at Mose's wrecked truck. Both doors of the vehicle are open, and I know he can see the paramedics preparing to load the corpse onto a gurney. "He try to run you down in the truck?" he asks.

"I should have run. Let him go. I should have taken cover in the —"

"That's a crock of shit, Kate. He would have killed you if you hadn't stopped him, and you know it. Don't tear yourself up over this."

"God, Tomasetti." I lower my face into my hands. "God."

"You didn't do anything wrong."

When I don't look at him, he wraps both hands around my wrists and gently pulls them from my face. When I still don't make eye contact, he puts his hand beneath my chin and forces my gaze to his. "You didn't do anything wrong," he repeats. "You got that?"

I look into his eyes. He stares back. He's so solid and unflinching and kind. It's a huge comfort knowing that he's not judging me, that he doesn't blame me. "It feels like I did," I say.

"I know it does. It's not easy taking another person's life. But that's part of the job sometimes."

"I don't know if I can handle that."

"You can."

I feel the burn of tears behind my eyes. The last thing I want to do is cry. Talk about bad form for a female cop. I swipe frantically at my eyes. "How are Ike and Samuel?"

"They're going to be fine. Ambulance took them to the hospital. They'll probably spend the night."

When I close my eyes, I see their small bodies floating in the manure pit. "How could Mose do that to his little brothers?"

Tomasetti shakes his head. "That's probably something we'll never know."

"I didn't see this coming," I tell him. "Why didn't I see it coming?"

"Because you're human." He sighs. "None of us saw this."

That's not what I want to hear, but I let it go. "I want to talk to Salome."

"Glock is with her."

"I need to talk to her." I start to move around him, but he stops me.

"Kate, paramedics are going to check you out, then I need to take you to the sheriff's office. Rasmussen is obligated to talk to you." He sighs. "So am I."

Only then does it dawn on me just how difficult the next hours will be. There will be interviews and forms and a thousand questions. I don't care about any of it. All I want to do is see the children, Ike and Samuel and Salome. I want to be the one to tell them what happened to their brother. At the very least, I want to be there when they get the news. But I know that won't be the case. As of five minutes ago, I'm no longer a cop. Not until the shooting is fully investigated and I'm cleared of any wrongdoing.

I barely notice when the young paramedic crosses to where we stand. While Tomasetti looks on, he runs through the standard emergency medical protocol, taking my blood pressure and asking about any pain. My collarbone hurts plenty, but I don't mention it. There's no way I'm going to the hospital.

When he finishes, he looks at Tomasetti and proceeds to talk about me as if I'm not there. "She looks fine, but you might want to run by the ER before taking her home."

"I'll do that."

I wait until the paramedic is out of earshot before saying, "I'm not going to the hospital."

Tomasetti sighs. "Why am I not surprised?"

"I want to see the kids," I say.

"I know. You can't. Not right now."

"I'm fine, damn it."

"We need to talk to Rasmussen. File a report."

When I don't respond, Tomasetti motions toward his Tahoe, which is parked haphazardly twenty yards away. "Come on. I'll drive you to the sheriff's office."

That's the last place I want to be. Of course, I don't have a choice. They're going to take my badge, my weapon. Strip away my title. They're going to pass my caseload to my subordinates. I know it's temporary. But it doesn't feel that way.

"I hate this," I say.

"I hate it, too," Tomasetti concurs. "But it's going to be okay."

As we walk toward his Tahoe, I glance over at Salome. She looks like a sad little ghost sitting in the passenger seat of Glock's cruiser, a blanket around her shoulders. Her eyes meet mine, and I see a clutter of terrible emotions in their depths: grief, betrayal, hopelessness. But there are other emotions, too — thoughts and feelings I can't even fathom — too many for me to sort through at the moment. For a crazy instant, I'm tempted to break free of Tomasetti, run to her, and tell her I didn't have a choice.

Instead, I get into Tomasetti's Tahoe, and we start toward the sheriff's office.

CHAPTER 18

Killing someone changes you in ways most people can never understand. It stains your soul with an ineffaceable darkness. It burdens your psyche with a weight that will crush you if you let it. It adds a disconsolate component to your persona that shadows every facet of your life, like the total eclipse of a good sun by a bad moon, and you're stuck in that darkness forever. And no matter how much good you do in an effort to make up for that black transgression, you know it will never be enough.

I'm standing alone in that darkness tonight. It's unforgiving and covers my soul from end to end. That my victim was a child only deepens the black crevasse that's split my mind right down the middle. The weight of it is slowly smothering me.

The degree of dysfunction a cop experiences after the use of deadly force depends on the cop. Some are capable of distancing themselves completely. Others can't handle it and turn to alcohol or other vices. More than a few cops' marriages end up in divorce. Others end up eating a bullet to end their misery. I'm one of the lucky ones; I fall somewhere in the middle. I don't feel very lucky tonight.

The first night is always the worst, when you're alone and tired and the images from the day are fresh in your mind. The instant you made the conscious decision to kill runs through your head over and over again, like some bad movie with a skip. That's when the second-guessing begins, and you ask yourself, *Could I have done something differently?* The *if onlys* usually follow. If only I'd seen it coming. If only I'd waited a few more seconds. If fucking only. I can't escape it. Mose is still dead, and his blood is still warm on my hands.

He isn't the first person I've killed. When I was fourteen years old, an Amish man by the name of Daniel Lapp came into our farmhouse and raped me. I grabbed my *datt*'s rifle and shot him in the chest. It was a clear case of self-defense. Of course, when you're fourteen and traumatized beyond anything you've ever imagined, it doesn't matter. I had committed the consummate sin, and I would pay for my offense against

God the rest of my life.

My *datt* covered up the crime, swore all of us to silence, and the entire incident was swept under the rug. I've learned to live with my demons, but it's not a comfortable cohabitation. To this day, I can't drive past the old grain elevator where Lapp's bones are slowly turning to powder without remembering what he did. Without remembering what I did. What all of us did.

After the shooting this morning, Tomasetti drove me to the sheriff's office in Millersburg. Rasmussen, Tomasetti, a representative from the Ohio State Highway Patrol, and I spent four hours in an interview room, where they took my statement. Though the men did their best to reassure me that I hadn't done anything wrong, I felt as tainted and guilty as a criminal. I had, after all, taken the life of a seventeen-year-old boy. The irony that he was Amish doesn't elude me.

For four hours, I answered the same questions a hundred different ways, a hundred times over. I ranted and cursed and slammed my fist down on the tabletop. I did everything cops do in situations like this. Everything but cry, anyway. That's the one thing I haven't been able to do.

They stripped me of my gun and relegated

me to administrative duty. With pay, of course. After the debriefing, Tomasetti drove me home. Wise to the ways of guilt, he did his best to keep me talking. I didn't cooperate and fell into a black silence that echoed inside me like a scream. He wanted to stay with me. *I* wanted him to stay, too. More than I could admit, more than he could know. But the case had just busted wide open; we both knew he had to work.

The Slabaugh case now takes precedence over the hate crimes, though Tomasetti will work both with equal fervor. The cops will want to know if Mose killed his adoptive parents and uncle. They'll want to know if Salome was involved. If she was, they'll want to know to what extent. Good luck with all that, Tomasetti.

It killed me to stay behind. More than anything, I *needed* to see this through. This is my case. My town. It was my goddamn bullet that killed Mose. I wanted to finish this. Too bad, Kate.

Of course, none of that matters, because when a cop is on leave, he's basically no longer a cop. He's a civilian and is treated as such. The only thing Tomasetti asked of me before he left was that I lay off the booze. I figured we both knew he should have taken the bottle with him. Thank God he didn't, because the demons came knocking the instant he closed the door.

It's almost 10:00 P.M. now. The pain in my shoulder is back, so I took three aspirin from a bottle that expired two months ago. So far, it's not helping, but then maybe I deserve to hurt tonight. I've showered and put on a ratty pair of sweats and a T-shirt from my academy days. I turned on the TV, turned it back off. Did the same with the radio. I wish I could do it with my mind. Turn it off, crank down the volume, unplug the damn thing. I'm wired, but exhausted. I can't sit. Can't stand. Can't eat. Can't sleep. It's like my skin is too tight. My mind is wound like a top and at any moment it's going to spiral out of control.

For the first time in a long time, I wish I could cry. It's as if the tears are stuck in my throat and they're slowly choking me. At the same time, the fist lodged in my chest is twisting my heart and lungs into knots, until I can't draw a breath. Even though the temperature hovers around freezing outside, I throw open the kitchen window and stand by the sink, sucking in great mouthfuls of air. I need Tomasetti, but I won't call him. I swore long ago the one thing I would never be is the clinging-vine female.

On a brighter note, in the last couple of

hours every member of my small police force has called at least once: Glock, Mona, Lois, Pickles, T. J., even Skid, who doesn't have a compassionate bone in his body. We ended up talking about the weather. They're my officers, but they're also my friends. My family. They believe me when I tell them I'm all right. I say it so often, I almost believe it myself. Then that fist inside me tightens and I realize I'm about as okay as a dog that's just been run over by a bus.

By midnight, my resistance wears down, and I go to the cabinet above the fridge and pull out the bottle of Absolut. The intellectual side of my brain knows alcohol won't help. In fact, I'm pretty sure it's going to make everything worse. But some nights are simply too dark to face without the sustenance of booze.

Snagging a glass from the cabinet, I set it on the counter and pour. Cold air spills in through the open window. That reminds me I can still breathe, and I'm comforted by that. I barely taste the vodka when I drink, so I pour again.

After the second shot, I take my tumbler and the bottle to the living room. Settling onto the sofa, I top off my glass. I'm a woman on a mission, bound for oblivion, and by God I'm going to get there. I tip the

371

bottle, fill the glass halfway, and take a long pull. Pour and drink. Pour and drink.

But when I close my eyes, I'm back on that dirt road. Mose is in the truck. Silver rain slashes in the beam of the single headlight. I'm aware of the gun in my hand, the roar of the engine in my ears. Salome's screams echoing in my head.

You could have let him go, a little voice says. *You could have let him run.*

"Kate."

The sound of Tomasetti's voice yanks me back to the present. I open my eyes. He's standing above me, his expression concerned. That's when I realize I'm lying on the floor, with absolutely no idea how I got here. I see my glass a few feet away, lying on its side in a puddle of vodka.

The first thought that registers is that I don't want him to see me like this. I don't want him to know I've been drinking. I struggle to a sitting position and the room dips violently right and then left.

He kneels beside me. "I'm sorry I was gone so long."

"S'okay."

"Sure it is." He sets his hand on my back. "Are you all right?"

"I'm good," I reply, but my words are slurred.

372

"How did you get on the floor?"

"Uh . . . no idea."

"Are you hurt?"

"I don't think so."

Grasping my biceps, he rises and pulls me to my feet. The room does a single sickening spin and then tilts left. My quadriceps feel weak. I'm nauseous, and my head pounds like some bad rock song.

"I told you to lay off the booze," he says, but there's no reprimand in his voice.

"It was pretty good advice."

"Easy to give when you're on the outside looking in, I guess."

"I think I'm going to be sick."

Putting his arm around me, he helps me into the bathroom. He flips up the seat on the commode. I slide to my knees and throw up twice. I set my hands on the floor, but my arms are shaking. A flash of heat rushes over me and a cold sweat breaks out on my neck and face. "I'm sorry," I say.

"It's okay," he replies softly. "I shouldn't have left you."

That brings me back to the reason behind all this misery. Thinking of Mose and Salome, I struggle to my feet. "Did you talk to Salome?"

Tomasetti helps me to the sink and lets me lean against him while I splash water on my face and rinse my mouth. "Rasmussen and I took her statement."

Leaning heavily against the sink, I turn to him, ask the question I've been dreading. "Did Mose kill the parents?"

His gaze searches mine, then he nods. "She thinks he might've done it."

Even through the haze of my drunkenness, the news hits me like a punch. I didn't want Mose to be guilty of that. It's not how I want to remember him. "That must have been awful for her."

Tomasetti nods. "She's pretty broken up."

"How are Ike and Samuel?"

"They're going to be fine." When I continue to stare at him, he sighs, knowing I want more. "The doctor at the emergency room says they were both suffering from hypothermia."

"Hypothermia?"

"Evidently, they'd been in the manure pit for quite some time when we found them."

"But how did they survive the methane gas?"

"Well, we drained the pit after the parents were found. Whoever pushed the boys in refilled it with water, in the hope they'd either suffocate or drown. But because of the added water, the muck was diluted and the methane wasn't as concentrated."

For the first time, I remember seeing the child's ball floating on the surface. "They clung to the ball," I murmur.

He nods. "Salome thought Mose might try to harm the boys, so she tossed the ball into the pit."

"She saved their lives."

"Looks that way."

I nod, trying to digest the cold-bloodedness of Mose's actions. "My God, Tomasetti, he tried to kill his little brothers."

"Yeah."

"Is Salome substantiating that?"

"She didn't actually witness it, but she was obviously concerned about her brothers' well-being."

"How is she?"

"Sedated. But she's going to be okay."

All I can do is shake my head.

"Get this," he says. "The day we found Mose beaten?"

"What about it?"

"It never happened. Mose gave Salome a buggy whip and forced her to mark him up." She used a shoe on his face so she wouldn't leave marks on her knuckles.

Recalling the extent of Mose's injuries, I shudder. "Why?"

"Who knows. Maybe he'd heard about the

hate crimes and decided he might be able to divert our attention from the Slabaugh murders. Make himself look like a victim. Garner our collective sympathies."

"Jesus," I say, reeling. "It almost worked."

Tomasetti looks away in an uncharacteristic manner, which snags my attention despite the fact that I'm looped. "If it's any consolation, Kate, I didn't see this coming, either," he admits. "Not this." His tone reveals that bothers him a lot. "None of us did. It was staring us right in the face. Here we are, seasoned cops, and we didn't even consider him a suspect."

"Some things are almost too damn disturbing to consider," I tell him.

"Yeah."

I wish I could clear my head, wish I could think. But my mind is fogged. My thoughts are still circling around Mose and Salome and everything that's happened. "Where is Salome?"

"Children Services placed her back with Adam Slabaugh for now."

"Probably the best place for her." But I sigh. "Samuel and Ike, too?"

He nods.

Relief swamps me that the three siblings are together. "Amish brothers and sisters are close. I'm glad."

I feel Tomasetti's eyes on me as I walk back to the living room. My balance is skewed, but I do my best to hide it. When he tries to help me, I shake off his hands. Twice I have to lean against the wall before making it to the kitchen. At the sink, I fill a glass with water and drink it down. A breeze wafts through the window, and I revel in the cold air on my face.

Tomasetti pauses at the doorway, his arms crossed, watching me in a way that makes me feel self-conscious.

Setting the glass in the sink, I face him. "I really am okay now."

"I didn't ask."

"Then stop looking at me as if I'm going to fall apart. And don't bother lecturing me about the booze."

He takes my tone in stride, doesn't even bother looking away. "I'm the last person to lecture, Kate. You know that."

I do, but the knowledge doesn't help. Drinking myself into a stupor was not only self-destructive but counterproductive. I'm stumbling drunk, but far from numb. The pain is still there, like an arrow sticking out of my back.

"Do you want to talk about it?" he asks after a moment.

"No." I raise my gaze to his. "Thank you,

but I really don't."

He crosses to the table, pulls out a chair, and sits down. After a moment, I join him. I can't look at him, so I put my face in my hands.

"I think you had a lot of emotions tied up in this case," he says. "Too many. And not just with Salome. You were getting close to Mose, too."

The words hurt, as if he reached out and twisted the arrow, drove it in a little deeper. "I appreciate what you're trying to do, but I can't talk about this right now."

"We don't have to talk about it tonight. You don't even have to talk to me about it. But at some point you'll need to talk to someone."

For the span of several minutes, the only sounds come from the rain pattering the windows, the water dripping off the eaves outside, the hiss of wind through the screen.

After a while, I raise my gaze to his. "I should have let him go."

"You could have done that. Of course, if you had, Mose might've killed you. He might've killed Salome and her baby. He might've taken off in that truck and killed some family out for a drive, too."

The logic behind his words should make me feel better, but it doesn't. We fall silent.

Even through the booze, I feel the tension in the room rise. "He was only seventeen years old," I say in a small voice.

"That didn't make him any less dangerous."

"He was Amish. I can't reconcile myself to that. He'll never get the chance to live his life. Because of me, he'll never —" The emotions grip me and shake me. Shocked by the power of them, I set both hands on the table, aware that my heart rate is elevated. Hoping Tomasetti doesn't notice my distress, I walk to the window and gulp the wet winter air.

"Kate."

Tomasetti's voice reaches me as if from a great distance. I jump when he puts his hands on my shoulders. My first instinct is to shake him off and tell him I'm fine. The truth of the matter is, I need him. I'm a thousand miles from fine, and so far gone that I'm afraid I might never find my way back.

He squeezes my shoulders. "You're going to be okay."

I don't turn to him. I feel as if I'm inching closer and closer to some precipitous edge. "I killed a kid today. How can I be okay?"

"If you hadn't made the choice you did, a fifteen-year-old girl might be lying dead in the morgue instead. You might have been killed, too. You made a tough call, but it was the right one."

"Nothing feels right about this case."

"Sometimes that's just the way it is. Sometimes no one wins, and people like us, the ones who are left to pick up the pieces, have to suck it up and move on."

Everything I know about him scrolls through my mind: the murders of his wife and children, the vengeance he doled out in the aftermath of their deaths. I want to ask him how he lives with it. But I already know the answer. He doesn't. The things that happened to him — the things he did — eat at him the same way my guilt and regrets eat at me. Now he's trying to save me from suffering the same fate.

He runs his hands up and down my arms. I'm hyperaware of his proximity, the warmth of his skin against mine. His fingertips are electric as they skim, and gooseflesh traces down my arms. When I shiver, he turns me to face him.

I don't want to look into his eyes. I don't want him to see the ugly things I'm feeling. I feel stripped bare, and I know if he sees my face, he'll know something about me that I've been trying to hide. That dark stain that's spread over my soul. The one that's been there since I was fourteen years old. The one I made darker and larger today.

When I don't look at him, he puts his palm against my face and forces the issue. "I know it doesn't feel like it now, but you're going to be all right," he says softly.

I try to pull down that thick curtain I'm so good at keeping in place, but I don't know if I manage to. I feel exposed and vulnerable beneath his gaze. So much so that I begin to tremble. I sense this is a profound moment, but I'm not sure why. I've had this man in my bed. He's been inside me — my mind, my body, my heart. But now he'll know all of those other facets. The ones I've never shared with him. The ones I've never shared with anyone.

"Maybe it's just the getting there that's so hard," I whisper.

I see a rare compassion in his eyes, and it strikes me that he's done time in the same dark place that haunts me tonight. And I realize he already knows about the other side of me. The imperfect part prone to dark moods and fits of rage. The part of me that drinks too much and courts danger and lies about it when I have to. In that moment, I know he gets it. He gets me. I'm thirty-one years old, and this is the first time anyone has ever given me the gift of true understanding. The knowledge moves me profoundly, relieves me because I finally know I no longer have to hide that.

"You need to get a handle on the booze." There's no reproach in his voice, and he makes no attempt to soften the words with platitudes or euphemisms. That's one of the things I love about Tomasetti. You get what you get, no frills.

"Don't let it get ahold of you, Kate. It'll ruin your life. I don't want that to happen to you."

I don't have anything to say about that. Maybe because he's right, and I've known for quite some time this talk was coming. Known that I needed it. I'm glad it came from him, because I probably wouldn't listen to anyone else.

"I know," I say. "I will."

We fall silent. The tempo of the rain has increased, slapping the ground, splashing against the brick. I feel the cold air wafting in through the open window behind me. Tomasetti is standing in front of me, as warm and solid as a promise — the kind I know can be counted on.

"So are you okay?" he asks after a moment.

"Almost." I meet his gaze, hold it. "I'm glad you're here."

He smiles. "That's what all the women tell me."

I release a laugh, and the burden I'd been holding most of the day lightens just a little. "You're an ass, you know that?"

"That's why you can't get enough of me."

Being with Tomasetti like this is like a healing balm for all the parts of me that are broken. Tonight, he's a light at the end of a long, dark tunnel. He's the warmth of dawn after the endless cold of a winter night. He is laughter in the face of grief. Honesty when life is a jumble of lies. Sanity in a world gone mad.

I don't know if I love him. I'm not sure what love is or if I'm qualified to make that proclamation. One thing I do know is that I care for him more than I've ever cared for another human being. He moves me; he shakes up my world. When I'm with Tomasetti, I don't see myself as a scarred creature with a past. I'm whole and new and the world is full of possibilities. The future is mine for the taking if I just hang in there.

Tonight, I need him. I need him with every cell in my body. I need him on so many levels, I couldn't begin to sort through them or make sense of any of it. I need him with an urgency that scares me, because control is the one thing I will never relinquish, even to him.

Standing in the kitchen with the rain misting in through the window above the sink, I rise up on my tiptoes and brush my mouth against his. It's a small thing, barely a kiss. But that moment of intimacy moves me profoundly. I'm keenly aware of all the things that are unique to this man I've come to care for. The piney scent of his aftershave. The scrape of his whiskers against my face. The solid warmth of his body against mine. His quickened breaths against my cheek. The restraint of a man who is more concerned about me and my frame of mind than getting me naked beneath him.

A thousand sensations rise inside me, like a riptide dragging me out to the deep, dark waters of a tumultuous sea. The reckless heat burning my body clashes with the caution of my intellect, warning me to take it slowly. Caution is so damn overrated.

Breaking the kiss, I look up at him. "I think this is the point when you're supposed to kiss me back."

He pulls away slightly and gives me a crooked half smile, but I can tell he's assessing me. "I appreciate your clueing me in."

"It's not like you to miss a cue."

"I want to make sure you're doing this for

the right reason."

"I am," I tell him. "I'm okay."

Another smile, this time with a hint of skepticism. "Would you tell me if you weren't?"

I stare at him, my pulse keeping tempo with the rain outside. I can feel the cold mist against my back as it comes through the window. "I'd tell you if I didn't want this."

Lifting his hand, he smoothes a strand of hair from my face. "One of these days we're going to have to talk about this."

"You mean about us."

He laughs. "I didn't mean to terrify you."

"You didn't."

"Liar."

I laugh, but it's a nervous sound. "Okay, maybe a little. But *terrify* is a strong word."

"If the shoe fits . . ." Setting his hands on the counter on both sides of me, he leans close and brushes his mouth across mine. "There're no pretenses here, Kate. It's just us. You and me."

"Just us wounded souls, huh?"

"That's right." Taking my hand, he lifts it to his mouth and kisses my knuckles. "You can talk to me. About anything."

"I know." I sigh, surprised when my breath shudders.

His eyes find mine. I stare back, wondering how much he sees, if he'll find what he's looking for.

"I think this is starting to get complicated," he says.

"It is."

"So is that good or bad?"

"It's good. Too good, probably. That's what scares me, Tomasetti. We both know how quickly things can get snatched away."

"It doesn't always happen that way."

"Sometimes it does."

He nods, considering me, weighing my words. "I'm not going anywhere, Kate."

I want to say something more, but I can't speak over the knot in my throat. Because I'm supposed to be tougher than that, I give him a nod, look away.

Taking my hand, he leads me toward the hall that will take us to the bedroom. I pause at the doorway. "I should probably close the window."

"Fuck the window," he whispers, and takes me into his arms.

CHAPTER 19

I wake to the hard thrum of a pounding head, the smell of bacon, and an all-consuming need to throw up. Trying not to moan, I roll over and reach for Tomasetti, but he's not there. That's when I realize he's probably the one doing the cooking. Moving with the caution of a woman who knows that at any moment her head could explode, I crawl out of bed and stumble to the bathroom.

Four aspirin and a long, hot shower later, I walk into the kitchen and find Tomasetti sitting at the table. His laptop sits in front of him next to a steaming cup of coffee. He glances up when I enter and I see him quickly assess my frame of mind.

"Don't say it," I mutter.

"I was going to tell you that you look nice," he says.

I can't tell if he's pulling my leg, so I go directly to the coffeemaker without responding, find the largest mug in my arsenal, and pour.

"I don't usually see you out of uniform," he adds. "You have really nice . . . toes."

After everything we shared the night before, a comment like that shouldn't bother me, but it does. I'm wearing a comfy old sweater and jeans, no socks. I don't understand why he's commenting. I wish he'd cut it out.

Cup full, I join him at the table. "I'd rather be wearing the uniform."

"I'm sure you'll get the go-ahead in a few days."

I motion toward the laptop. "What are you working on?"

"Final reports. We should be able to close the case today or tomorrow."

With those words, all the things I've been trying not to think about rush at me like a volley of spears: finding Samuel and Ike in the manure pit, Tomasetti's risking his life to rescue them, the ill-fated car chase, pulling my weapon, finding Mose dead by my own hand. . . .

"You sleep okay?" he asks.

It's a silly question, because we didn't get much sleep. I'm not complaining. I'm closer to him than I've been to anyone else my entire adult life. It's new territory for both of us. A good place to be. I don't know why that feels so fragile this morning. Maybe because we both know how easily the good things can slip away.

"Thank you for staying," I say.

His mouth twitches as he slides the laptop into its case. "How do you feel?"

"Better." I sip the coffee, nearly moan as the elixir swirls around my tongue. "You make good coffee."

He smiles. "Wait till you try the bacon and toast."

"Bring it on."

"You're out of eggs. You don't keep much food around, do you?"

"Probably a good thing, since I'm a terrible cook."

The rare domestic moment is interrupted when my cell phone chirps. Finding it charging on the counter, I glance down at the display, surprised to see the number of the Lancaster County Sheriff's Office. "Burkholder," I say.

"This is Deputy Howard. Sorry it took me so long to get back to you, Chief Burkholder. Last time we talked, you mentioned you wanted to speak with the Amish bishop out here. Well, I'm out at Amos Smucker's place now, and he says he's happy to talk to you."

I'd nearly forgotten about my request to speak with Abel Slabaugh's former bishop. With the case about to be closed, I almost tell the deputy it no longer matters. But I know from experience that information is the one commodity a cop can never have too much of, even if it's after the fact.

"Thank you," I say. "I'll only take a moment."

The line hisses as the deputy passes the phone to the bishop. "Hello?"

Bishop Smucker has an old man's voice with a strong Pennsylvania Dutch inflection. Quickly, I identify myself and get right to my question. "How well did you know Abel Slabaugh?" I begin.

"I've known Abel since the day he was born. I was very sad to hear of his passing. He is with God now, and I know he will find peace in the arms of the Lord."

"Do you know why he drove to Painters Mill, Ohio?"

The bishop sighs in a way that tells me he wasn't happy about Abel driving a motor vehicle. "Driving is against the *Ordnung*. Of course, Abel asked for my blessing." Another sigh. "He said Painters Mill was too far to travel by buggy. If it hadn't been for the problem with the boy, I would not have agreed to it. In the end, I did."

"What boy?" I ask.

"His nephew, I believe."

"Moses?"

"Yes, I believe that was his name."

He doesn't elaborate, and I sense the bishop clamming up. "Was there some kind of problem with Mose?" I ask, pressing.

The old man hesitates. "Abel confided in me, told me there was a family crisis."

"Bishop Smucker, I'm the chief of police here in Painters Mill. I'm trying to close a case. In order to do that, I need your help."

"It is a private matter, Chief Burkholder."

"I understand. But I still have to ask you why Abel drove to Painters Mill."

"Abel spoke to me in confidence."

"Abel is dead," I say. "So is the boy."

The old man gasps. "The boy, too?"

"Why did Abel drive to Painters Mill?" I repeat.

He is silent for so long, I think he's not going to answer. I'm about to try a more forceful tactic, but then he says, "Abel told me his nephew was having . . . confused feelings for his sister there in Painters Mill. Abel's brother and sister-in-law were concerned. They asked Abel to drive down and bring the boy back here to live."

Premeditation and motive, I think. Mose murdered his parents because they were going to send him away to live with his uncle in Pennsylvania. "Thank you for speaking with me, Bishop Smucker."

I clip the phone to my belt. When I look at Tomasetti, he's staring intently at me. "What do you have?" he asks.

I recap my conversation with the bishop.

Tomasetti nods. "Mose knew his parents were going to send him to Pennsylvania. He didn't want to leave Salome, so he killed them."

The coffee goes sour on my tongue, and I set down my cup.

Rising, he goes to the counter and slides two strips of bacon and a piece of toast on a plate. He carries it to the table and places it in front of me.

"Thanks." I don't want the bacon, but I pick up a piece and take a bite.

His cell phone rings. He glances down at it, then sends the call to voice mail. "That was Rasmussen. I've got to go."

The words send a hard rush of panic through me. I know where he's going — to speak to the kids. Get their final statements. I hate the thought of not being there.

"I want to talk to Salome," I say.

"Kate . . ."

"I mean it, John. I need to see her."

"I don't have to remind you that you're

on leave."

"I know it," I snap. "Damn it, I want to see her. It doesn't have to be in an official capacity."

Muttering beneath his breath, he picks up his laptop case and starts toward the living room. "You know that's not a good idea, don't you?" he says over his shoulder.

"Since when has that stopped me from anything?"

"Good point."

"If you don't take me with you, I'll go on my own."

"I know you will." He growls the words as he goes to the closet, yanks out his trench coat.

"I just want to talk to her, make sure she's okay."

"You're a pain in the ass, you know that?" he says, but he hands me my coat.

"All the guys tell me that," I respond, and we go out the door.

I don't want to be nervous about seeing Salome, but I am. This will be the first time I've spoken with her since Mose's death. I have no idea how she will respond to me. She witnessed the shooting, after all; she watched me gun down her lover. Though I'm sure she realizes I was defending myself and probably saved her life in the process, hearts are rarely as logical as our intellect. I can't help but wonder if she blames me.

But I won't apologize for what I did. If faced with the same choice, I'd do the same thing a second time. I am, however, sorry Mose is dead. I'm sorry I was the one who killed him. More than anything, I want her to know that. I want her to know I care about her and her two young siblings, that I'm here for them. But then, life is full of wishes, most of which are left ungranted.

I'll never admit it to anyone, but I wish there was a place in my life for these kids. I'd like to watch them grow up. Keep an eye on them. Make sure they don't get into trouble during their *rumspringas.* The thought makes me smile. But I know all of it's a fantasy. The truth of the matter is, there's no room in my life for children right now. Just an empty spot that might once have been filled.

"Are you ready for this?"

I glance over at the sound of Tomasetti's voice, realize we're pulling into Adam Slabaugh's lane. Ahead I see the old white house with its green roof and shutters, like an aging patriarch looking out over his legacy of plowed fields and pastures.

"I'm ready." My words come too quickly,

and I see his mouth tighten. "Do the boys know what happened to Mose?"

"I'm sure they probably know Mose is dead. I don't know if they were told how it happened."

I nod, thinking about that. "What if they hate me?"

His gaze lingers on mine. "You saved their lives, Kate. If it wasn't for you, those two boys wouldn't be here." He shrugs.

He's being logical, of course. But it's not helping. By the time we park in the gravel area between the barn and the house, my heart is pounding and my palms are wet with sweat.

"Chief Katie!"

Tomasetti and I turn simultaneously and see Ike and Samuel bound from the house, a Border collie and an obese yellow Lab on their heels.

Ike doesn't slow down before running into me and throwing his arms around my legs. "Daisy's going to have puppies!" he shouts.

"I was going to tell her!" Samuel complains.

This is not at all what I expected, and several thoughts strike me at once. First and foremost, despite losing their parents and brother in the last days, and nearly dying in that pit themselves, they're not broken up or crying or even moping around. The next thing that registers is that the boys are genuinely pleased to see me; they don't hate me. The realization moves me, shakes me up just a little bit.

They no longer look like Amish farm boys. Both are wearing newish-looking jeans, sweatshirts, and coats, and I realize their uncle probably took them shopping at the Walmart in Millersburg.

I set my hand on Ike's skinny shoulder. "Hey, kiddo."

He looks up at me and grins. Only then do I see the remnants of grief on his sweet face. He looks fragile and sad, but he realizes neither. "Hi."

When I look down at the two dogs, I'm shocked to find my vision blurred with tears. "Which one is Daisy?" I ask.

"Daisy's the black-and-white one." Samuel motions toward the Border collie. "The other one's a boy dog, and boy dogs can't have puppies."

"Oh," I say.

"Daisy's really smart!" Ike exclaims. "Uncle Adam said we get to keep all the puppies no matter how many she has. I hope she has a hundred."

I'm aware of Tomasetti coming around the front of the Tahoe and kneeling to pet the dogs. "Your uncle home?" he asks.

"Uncle Adam's in the kitchen," Samuel replies.

"He don't know how to make pancakes, so we had to go to McDonald's."

"Yeah, but we like McDonald's," Samuel adds, nodding.

Ike crosses to Tomasetti and looks down at the Border collie. "She likes it when you scratch her like this."

I laugh outright when he does a spider thing with his little-boy fingers and the dog groans and growls and begins to wriggle. "See? Ain't she funny?"

"Can I help you?"

I look up to see Adam Slabaugh coming down the sidewalk, shrugging into an insulated jacket. He looks even thinner than the last time I saw him. But his blue eyes are alive this morning, and I know that despite the grief of losing his brothers, sister-in-law, and nephew, the three surviving children have filled him with optimism and hope.

Giving Daisy a final pat, Tomasetti straightens and crosses to Slabaugh, and the two men shake. "Looks like you've got your hands full."

Slabaugh sighs. "I wish it could have happened another way."

"I understand," Tomasetti responds.

I join the men and motion toward the two boys, who are a few yards away, playing with the dogs. "How are they?"

Adam grimaces. "Surprisingly good, considering. I didn't know what to tell them about Mose, so they don't know yet. They cried themselves to sleep last night, especially little Ike. I walked into their room at bedtime and they both said prayers for their parents. It breaks my heart."

The picture he paints is incredibly sad, and for a too long moment, I can't speak because I'm afraid I'm going to cry. Kids need their parents, especially when they're young. I want to tell him that, but I don't trust my voice not to betray me.

"I know it's a cliché," Tomasetti tells him, "but kids really are amazingly resilient."

"They're lucky to have you," I say. And then I ask the question that's been tearing me up inside. "How's Salome?"

He offers a grim look. "She hasn't stopped crying. Barely speaks to me. Stays in her room. Last night, she woke up screaming." He shrugs, looking lost. "I didn't know what to do, so I just hugged her."

"She'll probably need some counseling," Tomasetti offers.

I nod in agreement. "I can call you with some names and numbers," I add.

"I sure would appreciate that." Slabaugh looks relieved. "She worked herself up so bad, she threw up."

That makes me think of her pregnancy, and I wonder if he knows. I wonder how she'll manage at such a young age without a woman in her life. "Do you know she's going to have a baby?" I ask.

"She told me." He shakes his head, looks down at the ground. "I don't understand, but I'll support her." His gaze meets mine. "This is all so new to me. I'm doing my best, but I just don't know if it's enough."

Silence falls over us, and Tomasetti gets us back on track. "We're here to get final statements."

"You need to speak with the children?" Slabaugh grimaces. "I really hate to put them through anything more."

"I'll do my best not to upset them," Tomasetti assures him.

Slabaugh glances at me, and I know he's wondering why I'm here. "I'm on administrative leave," I explain. "I just wanted to see the kids. See how they're doing."

Nodding, Slabaugh motions toward the house. "Well, we may as well get this over with. I'll make coffee. I think Salome's in her room. Ike and Samuel —" He looks over where the two boys were a moment ago, cups his hands around his mouth, and calls out their names. "It's like trying to keep up with a tornado." But he smiles. "They're probably in the barn. Go on to the house while I fetch them."

He starts toward the barn; on impulse, I stop him. "I'll get them," I say. "You two go ahead and get started."

He nods. Tomasetti gives me a knowing look, then the two men start toward the house. I stand there on the sidewalk and watch them disappear inside. I'm not sure why I'm delaying my meeting with Salome. I want to see her. But I don't know how she will react. I'm afraid she'll blame me for Mose's death.

Knowing there's not a damn thing I can do about any of it, I head for the barn. Around me, a light rain has begun to fall. A flock of crows caws from the plowed field to my left. Beyond, cattle are bawling. Inside the barn, one of the dogs is barking.

The sliding door stands open a foot or so. I walk in and pause. The interior is dim; little light comes in through the dirty windows. The smell of hay and damp earth mingles with the odor of motor oil and rubber from the tractor that sits to my right. I'm about to call out to the boys, when I hear them whispering. Smiling, I start toward the wood steps that will take me to the loft. Something in their voices stops me. I stand there, listening to them over the rain pinging against the tin roof. Inexplicably, the hairs at my nape stand on end.

I'm too far away to make out individual words, but close enough to discern that Ike is crying and that there's fear in Samuel's voice.

Moving to the foot of the loft stairs, I look up and listen. I hear more whispering. I'm about to start climbing, when I realize the boys aren't in the loft, but hiding in the niche beneath the steps. They've built a fort out of hay. The opening is about a foot square and covered by a burlap bag. Rounding the steps, I pause outside the opening and squat. I'm about to shove the burlap bag aside and peek in, when I hear words that freeze my blood.

"She'll put you back in the poop pit!"

"I don't care. I'm gonna tell Uncle Adam." The fear in Ike's voice drives a stake right through my heart. He's crying openly, his voice trembling with each word. "I'm scared."

"You can't tell," Samuel hisses. "You heard what she said. No one will believe us."

"But I'm scared, Sammy!"

"If we tell, they'll send us to the jail for bad *Englischer* kids. They hate Amish kids. They take away your clothes and make you run around naked. Is that what you want?"

"No," Ike sobs, sounding miserable and hopeless. "I want *Mamm!* Why did *Mamm* have to die? Why can't she be here? I want her back."

"Shhh. Quiet. You're acting like a big baby."

"Salome is bad, Sammy."

"She is not!"

"I saw her steal *Datt*'s money outta the jar."

"Did not, you big liar."

"She said if I told, she'd cut my head off while I was asleep." Ike cries so hard, he begins choking and coughing.

"Come on, Ikey." Samuel's voice softens. "Salome ain't all bad. She promised to take care of us and let us do whatever we want."

"She promised to come back for us after throwing us in all that poop, but she didn't! It's her fault we had to go to the hospital!"

"She said Mose wouldn't let her come."

"She blames everything on Mose! She's mean! I hate her!"

"Stop crying, you big fat baby. We got to go inside."

"I ain't going! I don't ever want to see her

again." Another round of sobs. "I want *Mamm!*"

I don't hear the rest of the tirade. My mind is still trying to absorb the words I heard earlier. *She promised to come back for us after throwing us in all that poop, but she didn't!*

The words pummel my brain, but I resist their meaning. All I can think is that the boys are mistaken. They're grieving and confused, and their imaginations have gotten the better of them. Squatting outside the small fort, I'm vaguely aware of my heart knocking against my ribs, my breaths coming short and fast. Disbelief is a vortex inside my head. More than anything, I want to believe I've misinterpreted what I just overheard. Surely there's a logical explanation. All I have to do is call them out here and ask them to explain.

But deep inside, I know I didn't misunderstand. Those two boys just revealed that it was Salome who pushed them into the manure pit, not Mose. The truth of that is almost too much to bear. Grief slashes at me, a clawed animal trapped inside me and trying tear its way out. The pain is so tremendous that I press a hand to my abdomen, grab hold of a beam with the other.

"God," I whisper. "God."

Squeezing my eyes shut, I push myself to my feet. I take several deep breaths, stifle the emotions rampaging through me. "Ike? Samuel? It's Kate. Can you come out here, please?"

The burlap is yanked aside and Samuel's pale face appears. The look he gives me makes me feel like I'm the Grim Reaper and his time has come. Fear and guilt swim in his eyes. "Yes, ma'am?" he squeaks.

"You're not in any trouble, honey," I say. "Just come out here. Tell Ike to come, too. Okay?"

" 'Kay," he says, and ducks back inside.

Rubbing my hand over my face, I walk around to the steps and collapse onto the lowest one. With numb hands, I unclip my phone from my belt and hit the speed dial for Tomasetti. "John," I whisper.

"What's wrong?" he says without preamble.

"Come out to the barn." He knows something's happened; he hears it in my voice. "Leave Salome and Adam inside."

I hear rustling on the other end, and I know he's coming, no questions asked. Relief sweeps through me. "I'm on my way."

Closing my phone, I clip it back onto my belt and lower my face into my hands. I feel sick inside. Sick for these children who've

404

already been through so much. But I also feel guilty because I did nothing to protect them. How could I have been so remiss?

Ike and Samuel sidle up to me. I raise my head and look at them through my fingers. "Hey," I say.

Ike is still crying. His cheeks are red, and I can see clean stripes where his tears made a path through the dirt. Samuel looks guilty and scared, like maybe he's on the verge of tears, too. They know I overheard them.

"Are you mad at us?" Samuel asks.

"Of course not," I tell him. "I could never be mad at you guys."

The reassurance doesn't seem to help. Ike cries harder, his little chest heaving as he sucks in great gulps of air. Samuel's lower lip trembles. They stare at me as if I'm going to do them physical harm.

"Why are you guys so upset?" I begin.

Ike is too overcome with crying to answer. Samuel looks down at his Walmart sneakers, and I see a single tear fall to the dirt floor.

"We just miss our *mamm* and *datt*," Samuel says bravely.

"I think it's more than that," I say, keeping my voice soft. "Isn't it?"

"We didn't do anything wrong," Samuel proclaims.

"We didn't," Ike chimes in. "Please don't send us to the jail for bad kids. We didn't do anything!"

"No one's sending you anywhere," I say, trying to calm them. "I know you didn't do anything wrong. But I heard what you guys were talking about."

For an instant, I think Samuel is going to throw up. Ike looks like he's going to run back to the hay fort and hide. But neither boy moves a muscle, two little soldiers standing tall, waiting for the firing squad to cut them down.

"We didn't say nothing." Samuel tries to lie, but his trembling voice reveals his ineptness. "We were just playacting. Making up stories."

I reach out and run the backs of my knuckles over his soft cheek. "Honey, I'm not mad. Okay? And you're not in any trouble. But you need to tell me what happened. I'm the chief of police, so you can tell me the truth. I'll protect you and keep you safe."

"You'll send us to jail for bad kids!" Ike blurts. "Salome said so!"

Samuel elbows his brother hard enough to make him grunt.

Realizing what he said, Ike slaps his hand over his mouth, stares at me over the tops of his fingers.

I divide my attention between both boys. "Listen to me. You're not going to jail. And you're not in any trouble. Do you understand?"

Tomasetti appears at the barn door. I glance over, watch his expression as he takes in the scene and walks over to us. "Hi, boys," he says. "Everything okay?"

The kids look at the ground and mutter a greeting.

I scoot over and Tomasetti sits on the step next to me. "Where's Salome?" I ask.

"Inside with Adam."

I nod toward the boys. "Samuel and Ike have some things to tell us," I say.

Tomasetti sets his elbows on his knees and folds his hands. "All right."

I turn my attention to Samuel, holding my breath because I'm afraid the boys will clam up now that Tomasetti is here. Or maybe they'll deny what I heard so clearly just minutes before. I turn my attention to Ike. "Tell Agent Tomasetti who put you and your brother in the pit."

"Mose did it," Samuel says quickly.

I turn my attention to the younger boy. "Ike, who put you in the pit?"

The little boy begins to cry. "Mose."

Reminding myself of the horror and

trauma these two boys have been subjected to, I rein in my impatience. "That's not what I heard you say a moment ago."

Neither boy can meet my gaze. They're not very good at lying, and I'm certain Tomasetti sees that as clearly as I do. Up until now, no one had even considered the possibility they had been threatened — or worse.

"Ike?" I press. "Who put you into the manure pit?"

"No one." But he looks at his older brother. I see an apology in his eyes, and I know he's going to come clean.

"Someone put you there," I say. "You didn't get down there by yourself."

After a moment, Ike wipes his nose on his coat sleeve. "She told us not to tell," he says between sniffles.

"Ikey!" Samuel hisses.

I ignore the older boy. I sense Tomasetti's attention zeroing in on Ike. "Who told you not to tell?" I ask.

He hesitates for so long, I think he's not going to answer. I'm in the process of formulating my next question when he whispers, "Salome."

A profound silence sweeps over us. Abruptly, I'm aware of the high-pitched hiss of drizzle falling on the tin roof, the two dogs snuffling over by the water trough, the cows in the rear part of the barn.

"Salome pushed you in the pit?" Tomasetti asks.

Ike gives a giant nod. "Don't tell! She made us promise not to tell. She'll be really mad."

Next to him, Samuel screws up his face and begins to cry. "Now we're going to go to the jail for bad kids!" he cries. "They do stuff to Amish kids!" He looks at his younger brother. "You ruined everything!"

"No one's going to jail," Tomasetti says.

I'm not so sure. Someone's going to go to jail. But it won't be these two little boys.

CHAPTER 20

I've never been good at sitting on the sidelines. That's especially true when it comes to my job. This morning, the fact that I've been effectively locked out of the investigation is excruciating. Two hours have passed since Tomasetti, Ike, Samuel, and I sat in the barn and the boys shocked us with the revelation that Salome was complicit in the attempt on their lives.

I'm still reeling inside. Hurting, if I want to be honest. But most of all, I'm angry. Angry because I was lied to and manipulated by someone I trusted, someone I cared about. But I'm angriest with myself. Because I allowed this to happen on my watch. Because I so willingly believed the lies I was spoon-fed. I stood by while two little boys were brutalized by their older siblings. Worse, I felt sympathy for their would-be ᴇrer.

at the police station, feeling out of

place because I'm not in uniform, pacing the hall outside the interview room, pissed because the goddamn door is closed. Tomasetti, Adam Slabaugh, Sheriff Rasmussen, and a young attorney who doesn't look old enough to have graduated from law school are inside, questioning Salome. The need to know what's happening is like a bamboo sliver being slowly wedged beneath my fingernail.

I've just reached the end of the hall, and I'm staring, unseeing, into the reception area when the door clicks open. I spin and see Rasmussen emerge, looking like he's just been roused from a nap. His hair is mussed, as if he's been running his fingers through it. "I figured you'd have a path worn in that floor by now," he says.

Trying to turn down my intensity, I cross to him. "No budget for new flooring."

He's looking at me a little too closely, the way people do when they know something isn't quite right about you. "How are you holding up?"

I'm so focused on learning the outcome of the interview with Salome, it takes me a moment to realize he's asking about the shooting. "I'm fine." I say the words with a little too much attitude. But no cop is going to admit she's spent the last twenty-four hours bouncing off the walls. That would be the ultimate bad form after a shooting. You can drink and you can fight, but you can't admit it's messing with your head.

"Good to hear."

I don't waste any time getting to the point. "What did Salome have to say?"

"Jesus, Kate. That kid's been through hell, that's for sure."

That isn't what I expected to hear. "Did she incriminate herself?"

"Every time she started to talk, that fuckin' attorney shut her down." He sighs tiredly, gives me a grim look. "She claims her dad was molesting her. Going into her bedroom at night and raping her since she was twelve. She confided in Mose about it. She thinks Mose confronted their father and they might have gotten into an argument the morning Slabaugh ended up in that pit."

"That doesn't explain why her brothers told Tomasetti and me that she's the one who pushed them into the pit. It doesn't explain how the uncle got into the pit. Or why she started having sex with Mose."

He looks at me as if I should have a little more compassion for a girl who's been through so much, and I get a bad feeling in the pit of my stomach. "She says she doesn't know how any of them got in the pit. She

412

hinted around that maybe the uncle went in to rescue Solly and that Mose couldn't get him out. That's how it usually happens. One person goes in, the would-be rescuers succumb to the lack of oxygen and follow suit. An unconscious man would be very difficult for a seventeen-year-old boy to extract from that pit." He shrugs. "If Mose had gone in after them, he probably would have ended up dead, too."

"Do you believe that?"

"It's hard to know what happened, since everyone is dead."

"Not everyone." I can't keep the sarcasm out of my voice. "How did the two little boys end up in the pit?"

"Salome says Mose did it. She was afraid he might, so she threw in the ball for them to use as a floatation device just in case. But she didn't know Mose had actually done the deed until after the fact."

"That's not what those boys told me and Tomasetti."

"Look, Kate, they're just kids. They've been through a lot. They've been traumatized, lost their parents, their brother. They're confused. Hell, maybe they're looking for someone to blame." Rasmussen motions toward the closed door. "I'm inclined to cut that poor girl in there some slack. I think the judge will, too. I think there were some awful things going on in that house that no one knew about."

I shouldn't be surprised by this, but I am. I stare at Rasmussen, realizing with a keen sense of dismay that he's been sucked in by Salome's innocence and beauty, just like everyone else. *Just like me.* And all I can think is, *She's good.*

"She blamed everything on Mose?" I say, hearing the incredulity in my voice.

"Not at first. In fact, she *defended* him."

"Deception is a lot more effective when you initially defend the person you intend to hang."

"I'm not reading it that way, Kate. She says she loved him and that he was only trying to protect her from being raped."

I stare at him, unsettled by the news, because neither Mose nor Solomon is here to defend himself. "You realize Mose is the perfect scapegoat, don't you?"

"I don't think that girl in there killed her parents. Do you?"

"I think she's capable. I think she manipulated Mose into doing it for her."

"We don't have any proof."

"So why did those boys tell us Salome is the one who put them in the pit?"

The sheriff is ready with an answer.

414

"They're confused. Mose probably coached those boys. He beat them to keep them in line. Hit them in places where the bruises wouldn't show. He threatened them constantly. Those boys were afraid of him."

"That's bullshit. Mose is dead. They know he can't hurt them now. I think they're afraid of *her*."

"Look, Kate, I'm not saying the girl isn't in this pretty deep. Sure, she made some bad decisions. She probably knows more than she's letting on. But I don't think she's a cold-blooded killer."

"She's a classic sociopath. Those tears she's crying all over you? They're called 'crocodile tears,' in case you missed that day in the Academy."

Rasmussen flushes red. "With all due respect, Chief, maybe you ought to take a big step back from this. I think you're a little bit too emotionally involved."

My jaw clamps and I hear my teeth grind. "She's playing you. She's playing all of us."

"I don't understand why you're chomping at the bit to fry a fifteen-year-old Amish kid."

In that instant, the terrible moments leading up to my shooting Mose replay in my mind's eye: the truck roaring toward me, raising my weapon and firing, the wind-

415

shield splintering. Then I turned and looked at Salome. Initially, I misinterpreted her expression as horror. It wasn't until this morning that I recognized it for what it was: a chilling smile of secret satisfaction.

She was *getting off* on playing the role of victim. Getting off on seeing Mose gunned down after he'd served his purpose and she no longer needed him to further her goal. The scenario is so bitter and cold, I can't wrap my brain around it. But I trust my instincts; I know I'm right. The question is, How do I prove it?

"I just want the truth," I say.

"Sounds to me like you want to hang all this on an innocent girl."

"She's not innocent. I think she killed her parents. I think she's capable of killing anyone who gets in her way."

"She's as much a victim as those two little boys." He laughs, but there's no humor in it. "Or maybe you think they're in on this big conspiracy, too."

"I think she's got just about everyone snookered, including you."

His flush is darker this time, and I realize behind all that good-old-boy charm, the sheriff has a temper. His gaze searches mine, as if he's looking for some ulterior motive for the view I've taken on this. "We

416

have no evidence to support anything you've said."

"The word of those two boys."

"Thoughts you may have inadvertently planted to suit your own agenda."

I know arguing with him about this isn't going to help my cause, so I reel in my temper and mentally shift gears. "Did you get anything back on the fingerprints found on the shovel?"

"The only prints found were Mose's."

I nod, but I know in my heart that was by design.

As if my thoughts are reflected in my expression, Rasmussen sighs. "In any case, we're finished with her for now. We're not going to charge her —"

"Not going to charge her?" Alarm shoots through me.

"She's being remanded to the custody of her uncle. Social worker from Children Services interviewed him last evening. They did some kind of home study. He's probably going to get approved for permanent custody."

"Her brothers are terrified of her. I told them they'd be safe. Now she's being sent home to her uncle?"

"The judge doesn't want to separate the siblings. He spoke with those boys, Kate.

They're no more afraid of their sister than I am."

"I overheard the boys talking. I'm telling you: They're afraid of her."

"Well, you're entitled to your opinion, but I'd say this one is out of your hands."

Frustration is like a sizzling charge of dynamite inside me. "Damn it, she's a danger to those kids."

"I've got to go." Looking annoyed, not wanting to deal with this monkey wrench on a golf day, Rasmussen glances at his watch. "She asked to see you. Her attorney said it would be okay so long as you're in there as a civilian."

Surprise ripples through me. I figured I'd be the last person she wanted to see. "Sure."

He sighs. "To be perfectly honest, Kate, maybe you shouldn't go in there."

"I'm glad that's not your decision to make."

Shaking his head, he turns and walks away.

I watch him disappear into the reception area; then I turn toward the interview room. I can feel my heart thrumming in my chest. Nerves tie my stomach in a knot. Over the years, I've conducted hundreds of interviews. I've faced people who would just as soon have slit my throat as look at me. It's strange, but I don't ever remember being as

418

apprehensive as I am today.

All eyes sweep to me when I enter the room. Tomasetti sits at the head of the table, slouching in his chair, doodling on a small spiral pad. Adam Slabaugh sits to his right, staring into a Styrofoam cup as if it holds the secret of the universe. Salome sits beside him, clutching a tissue, looking small and pale and . . . lost. She's wearing blue jeans and a white sweatshirt that's two sizes too big. She looks inordinately out of place here — too young, too pretty, and far too innocent to be surrounded by cops asking questions about murder.

A few feet away, her attorney leans against the wall with a BlackBerry stuck to his ear, a shepherd keeping watch over his accident-prone flock. I've met him at some point, but I don't remember his name. He's a nice-looking young man with a ruddy complexion sprinkled with freckles, reddish hair, and a matching goatee. He's overdressed in a gray suit that looks custom-made, but it's matched with a Walmart tie. I can smell the Polo aftershave from where I stand.

He offers me a cocky smirk as he shoves the BlackBerry into an inside pocket. "Chief Burkholder, I'm Colin Thornsberry, Miss Slabaugh's attorney."

Since I'm not pleased to meet him, I

simply nod.

"Normally, I wouldn't allow an officer with your kind of . . . personal involvement to speak to my client, but she asked to see you. Her uncle agreed it would be okay. Since this is an informal meeting . . ." He shrugs. "Here we are."

I give him my best "Eat dog shit" look as I cross to the table and sit across from Salome.

"Nothing inappropriate, please," the attorney adds. "My client has had a tremendously difficult couple of days."

Not as difficult as her parents, uncle, and brothers, I think. But I don't say the words.

He brushes his fingertips across Salome's shoulder. She offers him a faint smile. Then he withdraws his BlackBerry and strides over to the window, texting like a fixated high school student.

I turn my attention to Salome. Myriad emotions rush through me in a torrent when our gazes meet. She's been crying; her eyes are red-rimmed and swollen. Even knowing everything that I do about her, there's a part of me that's moved. A part of me wants to go to her, believe in her, protect her from all these big bad cops and an attorney who looks at her as if she's a piece of meat. But with four people dead, I don't have the luxury of sticking my head in the sand.

I'm aware of Tomasetti watching me, but I don't look at him. I hear the lawyer speaking with quiet authority into his BlackBerry. But all of my attention is focused on the girl sitting across from me. She doesn't know about my conversation with her brothers. She has no idea I suspect her of cold-blooded murder. She still believes I've come here to beg her forgiveness for killing her lover.

"Thank you for seeing me," I begin.

She sends me a small, uncertain smile. "I didn't know if you'd come. I'm glad you did."

I match her smile. "How are you feeling?"

"Fine." She looks down at her hands, little-girl hands. For the first time, it strikes me how incongruent they are with the rest of her, with everything that's happened, everything she's done.

"Do you need anything?" I ask.

She raises her gaze to mine. Her eyes are soft and benign and so utterly lovely, I can't look away. "I just wanted to tell you . . . I mean, about what happened . . . with Mose." She visibly swallows, blinks back tears. "I'm not mad. And I don't blame you. I know you were only doing your job."

"Thank you," I tell her. "I'm glad you

don't hold it against me." Silence weighs heavy for a moment, like the electrically charged air right before a crack of thunder. "I was afraid he was going to hurt you."

"He never hurt me. He would never do that. He loved me."

"I know."

"He was trying to protect me. He was . . . confused."

"I understand."

Thornsberry passes close, listening, so I pause.

Salome struggles for composure. "I just want this to be over so I can go home and see my brothers and all of us can get back to normal."

I wonder what normal is for her. Killing her parents? Manipulating a lover? Threatening children? Eliminating anyone who gets in the way of her goal? The thoughts make me so angry, my hands begin to shake. "I saw Ike and Samuel earlier this morning," I tell her. "They seem to be doing okay. They asked about you. I thought you'd want to know."

She sends me a grateful smile. "Mose was really mean to them. I'm so sorry for that. Ike and Samuel loved him so much. They looked up to him." Two huge tears break free of her lashes and run down her cheeks.

Using both hands, she quickly wipes them away, but not before Thornsberry notices and sends me a frown.

Salome continues. "Samuel and little Ike are so confused right now. I just want to hug them both and tell them everything's going to be okay."

"I bet you do." Remembering how terrified the boys were of her, I suspect the only reason she wants to see them is so she can threaten them and tell them not to open their mouths.

"They've been through a lot," I say.

"I still can't believe all of this happened," she whispers. "*Mamm* and *Datt.* Uncle Abel. And now Mose. I think my heart is broken."

Next to her, Adam Slabaugh leans toward her and pats her shoulder awkwardly. "It's going to be all right."

At the window, Thornsberry blabs on about some other client's pretrial-hearing date. I use that moment to catch Tomasetti's eye. Not hard to do, since he's been staring at me since I entered the room. He returns my gaze, his eyes warning me to behave.

I turn my attention back to Salome. "Did you know Mose's parents were killed in a manure pit accident ten years ago?"

She blinks at me. The look of surprise that crosses her face seems so genuine that, not for the first time, I find myself believing its sincerity. "I didn't know."

"That's odd. He didn't tell you about it?"

Her eyes flick nervously to her uncle, then to Tomasetti, and back to me. "He told me they were killed in a buggy accident."

Leaning forward, I put my elbows on the tabletop and lace my fingers. "You know what, honey? I think you *did* know. I think Mose told you all about it. And I think that's how you conceived the idea to murder your parents."

"What?" She chokes out a sound of pure shock. "That's . . . crazy. I would never do that."

Next to her, Adam Slabaugh stiffens. "What are you saying, Chief Burkholder? What is this? What are you doing?"

I give him a hard look. "Did you know Solly called Abel and asked him to drive down to pick up Mose and take him back to Pennsylvania?"

He looks baffled and doesn't respond.

I turn my attention back to Salome. "You knew, didn't you?"

"I don't know what you're talking about."

"Your parents found out you and Mose were having sex, didn't they?"

"No!"

Thornsberry crosses to me, slaps his

hands down on the tabletop in front of me in a dramatic gesture designed to intimidate. "What the hell do you think you're doing, Chief Burkholder?"

I ignore him, never taking my eyes off Salome. "When they threatened to send Mose away, you decided to kill your father. Mose had told you about the manure pit accident and you manipulated him into carrying out the plan, didn't you?"

"No!" she cries.

"Your uncle was expendable, too, wasn't he? When he fell into the pit, it was no big deal, was it?"

"Stop it!"

"Only the plan went wrong, didn't it? Your mother fell in when she was trying to help. You hadn't counted on that."

"Chief Burkholder!" Thornsberry shouts. "That's enough!"

Shock waves reverberate through the room. Across from me, Adam Slabaugh shifts uncomfortably in his chair. "Why are you saying these things?" he cries.

"Because they're true." I stare hard at Salome. "Aren't they?"

"Kate." Tomasetti practically growls my name. "This is not an appropriate time to discuss this." But he doesn't sound very convincing, and he makes no move to stop me.

"Maybe we should wait until Ike and Samuel turn up dead," I snap. "Would that make this more appropriate?"

Salome opens her mouth. This time, the shock I see is real. She can't believe I'm talking to her like this, can't believe her act isn't working on me. She can't believe no one in the room is coming to her rescue, protecting her from the bad bitch cop.

"You controlled Mose with sex. You manipulated and abused your little brothers by threatening them with violence," I tell her. "You told them if they didn't do exactly as you said, they'd be sent to jail."

"I did not! I'm the one who saved their lives! I was afraid Mose would try to hurt them, so I threw the ball into the pit for them!"

"Is that why Mose's prints were on that ball, not yours?" I snap.

She makes a choking sound, her mouth and eyes wide. "You're lying!"

Adam Slabaugh rises abruptly. "Stop this! Right now!"

"Chief Burkholder, you are out of control." Jabbing a finger at me, Thornsberry snarls the words to Tomasetti. "Get her out of here!"

Tomasetti doesn't move, doesn't even acknowledge him.

I barely spare them a glance. I can't take my eyes off of Salome. I'm waiting for that initial chink in her armor. I want to see the innocent facade crumple and watch the monster emerge. I know better than anyone: Not all monsters are ugly beasts with horns.

"Your brothers told me everything, Salome. *Everything.* The beatings. The secrets. The sex. The fights. And then they told me about the murders."

"They're lying." She says the words quietly, but her composure is beginning to slip.

"That's how Solly got the wound on his head, isn't it? You hit him with the shovel."

"Stop it." Salome manages to look crushed. "None of that is true."

"Your *datt* didn't rape you, did he?"

"He came to my room. I was afraid to tell. It went on for months! Years!"

Across from her, Adam Slabaugh covers his face with his hands. "Solly would not," he says in a broken voice.

"He did!" Salome screams. "I told Mose about it, and he went crazy." She looks wildly around the room, seeking an ally, any ally. For the first time, Adam Slabaugh doesn't look prepared to jump in to defend her.

"Miss Slabaugh." Thornsberry puts his hands beneath her arms, pulls her to her feet. "You don't have to answer any of her questions. In fact, don't say another word." He jabs a finger at me. "What the hell's your problem? I'll have your goddamn job for this."

I hold Salome's gaze, pushing her hard. "Samuel and Ike overheard you and Mose talking about the murders. *They told me everything.* It's over."

"No!" She raises her hands as if to fend me off. "You're lying. They didn't hear anything." Allowing her attorney to pull her away from me, she looks wildly around the room. "She's lying. I'm a juvenile. She can't treat me like this."

I don't relent. "You made one mistake, though, didn't you?"

"Leave me alone!" The facade is breaking away, the rabid creature beneath advancing.

"You didn't expect your *mamm* to fall into that pit, did you?"

"Shut up!"

"That's when your plan starting falling apart. You underestimated the love a child has for his mother. You underestimated Ike and Samuel and the loyalty they felt toward their *mamm* and *datt.* Those boys saw through your phony love and empty prom-

428

ises. And they turned on you."

"Mose did it! He did all of it! Not me!"

"You told him you were being raped every night. *Every night.* That drove him crazy, didn't it? You manipulated him. Used him."

"I didn't. Mose did it. He killed them."

"When you could no longer control your little brothers, you pushed them into the manure pit, too, didn't you? You promised them you'd come back. You had no intention of saving them, did you? You were going to let them die."

"No!"

"It was Mose who tossed the ball into the pit. He knew you were going to try to kill them and he couldn't handle it."

"He couldn't handle anything! He was stupid and weak —"

"Stop this right now!" Thornsberry shouts at Tomasetti. "She's badgering this juvenile!" He turns his attention back to Salome, trying to drag her from the room. "Miss Slabaugh, let's go."

Salome shakes him off. "I would have pulled my brothers out of that pit if you hadn't shown up! You bitch, this is your fault! *Yours!*"

"Earlier, you said you didn't even know they were in the pit," I say. "Which is it?"

The attorney grabs her arm. "Let's go."

The girl spins and strikes him on the shoulder with her fist. "Get off me!" Her eyes never leave mine. "Mose panicked when he saw you! He dragged me to the shed and forced me into the car. He might have killed me, too!"

"He's not here to defend himself, is he?" I say.

"Mose did all of it. *All of it!* I'm innocent."

"You never loved him. He was a means to an end."

"I did. I loved him. I would have married him!"

But I see the lie and push harder. "Did you think you and Mose were going to just ride into the sunset? After murdering three people?"

"We were going to live here . . . and take care of our brothers —"

"Your brothers hate you, Salome."

"No, they don't!" she screams.

"In fact, they chose me over you. *Me.* A stranger. And now they're going to testify against you. You're going to spend the rest of your life in prison —"

"You fucking *bitch! I wish I'd killed you, too!*"

The next thing I know, she's across the table, coming at me with claws and teeth. An instant too late, I push back, but she's

430

already got me. Her nails sear down my face. Her left hand fists in my hair. As if in slow motion, I see Tomasetti rounding the table, rushing at us. Adam Slabaugh makes a wild grab for his niece as she goes over the tabletop. Thornsberry reels back, his mouth opening and closing like that of a beached catfish.

And then I'm falling backward in my chair, with Salome on top of me, like a cougar intent on mauling its prey.

CHAPTER 21

My chair goes over backward and I slam into the floor so hard, my head bounces off the tile. Stars fly before my eyes. I try to kick away the chair and get my legs under me, but my feet are tangled in the rungs. Before I can move, Salome is on top of me, hair flying, nails slashing at my face.

"You *bitch!*" She lands a blow to my left cheekbone, sending another scatter of stars to my eyes. "You ruined everything!"

When I look into her eyes, I see a total disconnect from reality. Animalistic screeches tear from her throat. "Why couldn't you just go away! I wish you were dead! *Dead!*"

Vaguely, I'm aware of movement all around me — chairs scudding across the floor, the shuffle of feet. In my peripheral vision, I catch sight of Tomasetti kicking aside the chair. "Get off her!"

I hear the attorney's ineffective "Hey!"

Salome's fingernails rake across my left temple, dangerously close to my eye. "I hate you! *I fucking hate you!*"

I raise my hands to shove her away, but she's too close. I can't get any leverage. My training kicks in. I bring my elbow up hard, striking her beneath the chin. I hear her teeth click together. Her head snaps back. Stiff-armed, I jam the heel of my hand against her chest as hard as I can. A strangled scream tears from her throat as she reels back. I hear her head strike the table. Twisting, I wriggle out from beneath her, roll, bring up my feet to mule-kick her away.

Before I can, Tomasetti yanks her back. She twists and goes after him like a wild animal. He curses. Her attorney's shouting in a tinny, alarmed voice. All of it is punctuated by Salome's strangled screams. "She's lying! I hate her! She killed Mose!" Her eyes are wild when they find mine. *"Murderer!"*

As abruptly as the ruckus began, the room goes silent and still. I use the fallen chair to get to my feet. I'm aware of the blood roaring in my ears, the drumbeat thud of my heart, the burn of a cut on my face. A few feet away, Tomasetti has Salome bent over, face against the table, while he cuffs her hands behind her back. A visibly shaken

Adam Slabaugh stands to my right, shaking, breathing as if he just ran the Boston Marathon.

Tomasetti pulls Salome back from the table by the scruff of her neck and looks at me. "Are you all right?"

"I'm fine," I say automatically.

"You're bleeding." Slabaugh pulls a couple of tissues from the box on the table and hands them to me.

"Thanks." I blot at the burning sensation at my left temple, and the tissue comes away red.

"She's obviously going to need psychiatric evaluation."

All heads turn toward Colin Thornsberry, Salome's attorney. He looks like he just survived a tornado — barely — and I wonder if this is his first brush with a violent offender. He's looking at Salome as if he doesn't want to get too close.

The door swings open and I see Glock standing there at the ready. His eyes sweep the room, lingering on me a moment and then going to Salome and Tomasetti. "Everything okay in here?" he asks.

"It is now," I say, and start toward the door.

There's a universal truth in law enforcement. It's one I've struggled with for years and probably will for more years to come. Some cases turn out badly no matter how good the police work. Even though you make the arrest, get the bad guy off the street, and make the world a safer place, there is no justice done. The end result can be as sad and troubling as the crime itself.

In the case of the Slabaugh family, two Amish parents are still dead, along with an uncle who was trying to help. Two little boys will grow up without their mother and father and siblings. A seventeen-year-old boy is dead. And a fifteen-year-old Amish girl is probably going to prison, where an innocent baby will be born into a system that is far from perfect.

Justice took a pass on this one. I have no choice but to move on to the next, and hope for a better outcome. At least I have my hope. If that ever wanes, then I know it's time for me to hang up my law-enforcement hat.

McNarie's Bar is the last place I should be on a night like this, when I'm disheartened and thinking about things like a lack of justice and the end of hope. It's not exactly the kind of mind-set that's conducive to responsible drinking. I haven't forgotten about Tomasetti's warning to be careful with the booze. He doesn't broach a subject like that without serious forethought. Maybe I'll heed his advice, maybe not.

I'm into my second tonic and lime when movement at the door catches my attention. I look up and see Tomasetti and Rasmussen enter. The men saunter to the booth. Tomasetti slides in next to me. Rasmussen takes the seat across from us. I know they just came from the police station; there's a certain kind of energy that comes with the end of a big case, especially one like this. They've gotten Salome handed off to the appropriate juvenile authorities and the immediate paperwork taken care of. For the first time in the course of my career, I'm glad I wasn't there.

"I think I owe you an apology," Rasmussen says without preamble.

I make eye contact with him. He's talking about our exchange at the station. "You mean for telling me I was too emotionally involved in the case and that I was wrong about Salome?"

"That would be it." He offers a white-flag smile, and I can actually see him swallowing his pride. "I was wrong about the girl, and I came down on you pretty hard. I was out of line."

The words quash my earlier ire, leaving me feeling strangely deflated, and I reluctantly decide I like him again. "I wasn't one hundred percent certain myself," I admit.

Rasmussen's eyes sharpen. "Are you saying the two boys didn't confide and tell you they overheard Salome and Mose discussing the murders?"

"They told me Salome had put them in the pit and promised to come back for them." I sigh, wondering if I'm going to have to defend my actions. "The rest was guesswork."

"You didn't have Mose's prints on the ball," Tomasetti says.

I shake my head.

"Big risk."

"Calculated risk," I reply. "But one I had to take because I felt she was a danger to the two boys."

Rasmussen whistles. "Damn, Chief, that's good."

Tomasetti isn't so easily pleased. "Could have backfired if Salome had stuck to her story."

"I was counting on her losing her cool."

Tomasetti looks at the sheriff. "In case you haven't noticed, Kate's good at provoking people."

"I've noticed." But he softens the words

with a half smile and addresses me. "You'll be happy to hear we cut Coulter loose."

"How was he?" I ask.

"Relieved," Tomasetti says.

"Seems like a genuinely nice guy," Rasmussen puts in.

Tomasetti all but rolls his eyes. "Maybe he really *is* rehabilitated and we're a bunch of cynical assholes."

"Speak for yourself." Rasmussen chuckles.

I smile, too, but I'm distracted, thinking about the case, about the kids, Salome and the baby. . . . "Any idea how the rifle got into Coulter's closet?" I ask.

"Salome denied any knowledge," Rasmussen tells me.

Tomasetti grimaces. "But she and Mose knew Coulter had done some work for their father. It's common knowledge he's an excon. All those kids had to do was plant it in Coulter's house, and suddenly we have a suspect."

McNarie hustles over to the table holding a tray containing two Killian's Irish Red, two shot glasses — and a lone highball glass. A pack of Marlboro Lights peeks out of the top of his apron pocket.

I see Tomasetti eyeing the glass, wondering. "What are you drinking tonight, Chief?"

"Just tonic."

He looks up at McNarie. "I'll have the same," Tomasetti says. "I'm driving. Kate's on the wagon. And the sheriff was just leaving."

Across from me, Rasmussen arches a brow, and I know he just connected the dots, made the link between me and Tomasetti. McNarie doesn't even look surprised. His eyes skate to mine. I give him a minute nod, and he carries the tray back to the bar.

Noisily, Rasmussen clears his throat. "I just remembered I have something to do."

"You sure you won't stay for a drink?" Tomasetti asks.

"You asshole." Grinning, the sheriff slides out of the booth.

Tomasetti rises and the two men shake hands. "Agent Tomasetti, it was a pleasure meeting you. Can't thank you enough for your help."

"The pleasure was all mine," he says, and I wonder if Rasmussen knows he's referring to me.

The sheriff glances my way, and I think I see a smile in his eyes as he turns and heads toward the door.

Tomasetti settles in across from me. "You think he got the message?"

"Hmmm, I don't know. You were pretty subtle."

We grin at each other across the table. I know he's leaving tonight. And even though he's so close that I can reach out and touch him, I already feel him slipping away. Already I miss him.

"How are you?" he asks after a moment.

"I'm okay."

McNarie interrupts, setting two icy highball glasses on the table between us. When the barkeep leaves, Tomasetti says, "I've got to be back in Cleveland tomorrow morning."

"I know." My heart beats a little too fast. "I wish you could stay."

"Me, too."

We sip our tonic and listen to an old Chris Isaak song. Tomasetti breaks the silence. "If you're not okay, I won't leave. I'll find a way to stay."

Before realizing I'm going to do it, I reach across the table and set my hand over his. I meet his gaze. "I'm okay. I mean it." Sighing, I add, "This was just a really sad case."

"Salome played us all." He shrugs. "We should have seen it coming."

That makes me feel better, because he has the best instincts of anyone I know. "Sometimes the most difficult things to see are the ones right in front of us."

"Hindsight sucks, doesn't it?"

I nod, let the silence ride a moment. "How was Salome?"

He studies me, his eyes seeing more than I'm comfortable with. But I'm learning to let him see all of me — the good right along with the bad, and all the stuff in between — and I make no effort to hide the fact that, despite everything, I still care.

"We put her in a cell for her own safety while we did the paperwork and got a rep from the detention center en route. She calmed down after a few minutes. Started working Rasmussen and me." He shakes his head. "I swear, if I hadn't seen her go after you, I never would have believed she was capable of that kind of violence."

"It's ironic," I say. "Of all the people who were hurt or killed in the course of this case, the one who is most guilty is the one I can't stop thinking about. Not Mose. Not the parents or the uncle. But Salome."

"You were a young Amish girl once, Kate."

"I think that blinded me to the things I should have seen."

"You're nothing like her," he says after a moment.

I look away, take a sip of tonic. "Where did they take her?"

"Lucas County."

I nod. I'm familiar with the juvenile facility. "It's a good one. She'll get help and won't get lost in the system."

His gaze cuts to mine. "Bullshit aside, if she's dangerous, they'll find a way to keep her."

"What do you think will happen to her baby?"

"It'll go through the courts. If she's tried as an adult, I suspect the child will go to foster parents and eventually be adopted permanently."

"Probably the best thing."

"If you hadn't done what you did, she would have gotten away with murdering her entire family." He frowns at me. "Think about that while you're beating yourself up tonight."

"I'm not planning on beating myself up." I smile. "Promise."

"How long until you're reinstated?"

"A few days. Maybe a week."

He nods. Chris Isaak fades into an old Goo Goo Dolls song that makes me think about how small our lives are in the scope of things.

"What time do you have to be at the office tomorrow?" I ask.

"I've got a deposition at seven." He glances at his watch, sighs.

"You'd better get going if you want to get

any sleep."

"I should." But he makes no move to get up.

Instead, he stares at me so long, I have to resist the urge to squirm. "I don't know what you're thinking," I say.

"I was just thinking sleep's way over-rated." Sliding out of the booth, he takes my hand, pulls me out, and we head toward the door.

ABOUT THE AUTHOR

Linda Castillo is the *New York Times* bestselling author of the Kate Burkholder novels, including *Sworn to Silence, Pray for Silence* and *Breaking Silence*, crime thrillers set in Amish country. She is the recipient of awards including the Daphne du Maurier Award of Excellence, the Holt Medallion and a nomination for the RITA. Besides writing, Castillo's other passion is horses, particularly her Appaloosa, George. She lives in Texas with her husband.